GROUNDS FOR DIVORCE

GROUNDS FOR DIVORCE

Remy Maisel

The Book Guild Ltd

First published in Great Britain in 2021 by
The Book Guild Ltd
9 Priory Business Park
Wistow Road, Kibworth
Leicestershire, LE8 0RX
Freephone: 0800 999 2982
www.bookguild.co.uk
Email: info@bookguild.co.uk
Twitter: @bookguild

Typeset in 12pt Minion Pro

Printed and bound by CPI Group (UK) Ltd, Croydon, CR0 4YY

ISBN 978 1913913 380

British Library Cataloguing in Publication Data.
A catalogue record for this book is available from the British Library.

For my family
Thanks/I'm sorry (delete as appropriate)

"I can't think of a better choice to go to the Mideast than a bankruptcy lawyer, except maybe a divorce lawyer."

— Senator Lindsey Graham at the confirmation hearing
of David Friedman, February 16, 2017

PROLOGUE

This is how our parents told us they were getting a divorce: they said, "Girls, your mother and I have decided to separate."

Well, Dad said it. But Mom was sitting next to him and nodding to make it seem like a 'we' thing.

It was not a 'we' thing.

PART I

ONE

Today is the day I open my mail.

I repeat this as I climb each step to my third-floor walk-up. Jessica said that she will wallpaper my room with them soon, and I don't think she was joking. I informed her that it's a federal crime to tamper with someone's mail. She said, "Emily, the way you handle your problems is a federal crime. And please don't just walk into the bathroom to talk to me when it's not an emergency," and pulled the shower curtain shut.

The pile is somewhat larger than I thought. It will probably still be there if I make myself some coffee first. And some tortellini. And one glass of wine. And I'm right: when I turn around, the pile is still there, only it has grown – like the bills are tribbles. I decide to tackle it before it undergoes another binary fission.

"Hey," Jessica says, kicking the door shut.

"Hi," I say, waving a yellow envelope marked 'URGENT' at her. "Look. I'm opening bills."

"Of course, ideally you'll also pay them," Jess said. She

let out a little snort afterward, like she was hilarious.

"It's not my fault that my job is unpaid. I'm just lucky to have an office to go to every day."

"Is that what Dunning & Kruger told you?"

"I heard it on NPR. And besides – they give me a stipend."

"You're a paralegal, Em. A trained professional. An advertising agency large enough to have an in-house legal team can afford to pay you."

"They give us free Coke."

"Do you drink Coke?"

"I could."

Jess hauls her bags into her room and closes the door behind her but doesn't latch it. She's not shutting me out – just giving us each some space. Our nonverbal conversations are what I like most about our friendship. I know that she thinks I need a better job, and she doesn't hold her opinions back from me, but she doesn't berate me all the time, either.

I sort bills by envelope size and colour. I'm about to open one when the lightbulb starts flickering. This is a problem I need to solve right away, because how can I be expected to pay my bills in the dark, anyway? I'm climbing onto the table when Jessica suddenly shouts, "Emily!" and I catch myself on the back of my chair.

"What?" She's in sock feet, which maybe explains how she snuck up on me.

"Let's start by opening one," she cajoles. "Take care of one, and then you get a glass of wine."

I am trying to keep my eyes from leading hers to my

used wine glass by the sink. "That sounds more than fair."

Jess selects the single brown envelope from between the red stack and the white stack. "Emily, why are you getting mail from the State Department?"

The letter opener and I have a brief disagreement, and then I win and tear the letter open.

Thomas M. Newhouse
Operations and Administrative Officer
Bureau of Near Eastern Affairs
Washington, D.C. 20520

Ms. Emily A. Price
22 W 123rd St
Apt 301b
New York, N.Y. 10027

Dear Ms. Price,

The United States Department of State Bureau of Near Eastern Affairs has reviewed your qualifications and would like to invite you to interview for an important role within our organization. We are aware that you have not applied for this position—as you will know, the Department's business is often highly sensitive, and as a result we were unable to advertise the opening to potential applicants such as yourself.

The details of the interview are enclosed, along with the information regarding your hotel reservation in Washington, D.C. and the number for your driver, who will meet you at Ronald Reagan Washington National Airport.

Please call (202) 555-1630 and provide Personal Identification Number 3QFN78 upon request to confirm your attendance.

Sincerely,

Thom Newhouse

Thomas Newhouse

"Come on, let me see," Jess interjects.

"I think… they want me for a job interview."

"You?" Jess laughs, and then looks stricken when she sees my expression. "Sorry. I mean, did they say why?"

I turn my palms upward in a gesture of helplessness and let her snatch the paper.

"Well, you have to go," she says. She flips through the papers, and then her mouth opens slightly in surprise, and she frowns. "Em, the interview is tomorrow! And this is postmarked from last month. You'd better call this number right now." She tosses me her phone. "Quick. Maybe they'll still answer, or you can leave a message."

"Wait – it doesn't say anything about what the job is. How do I know if I want it?"

"You always do this – find a reason not to give it a shot. If you don't interview, you can't be rejected, right? Not this time. You cannot spend another day as an underemployed, underachieving millennial. It's getting old."

I sniff. "I have a very prestigious unpaid internship at one of the top three hundred advertising agencies in the city."

Jess takes out my phone and slides my purse across the table. "I'll dial for you." She unlocks the screen but waits to enter the number.

I know what she's waiting for. I take out my little pill case. The cache of pink beta-blocker tablets inside looks kind of like the salmon roe I brought my boss for lunch earlier. My stomach turns. I swallow hard and blink at them until they look like plain old pills, and then I look back at Jess imploringly. "Can't you just call for me? Please?"

"This isn't like ordering Chinese. It's the State Department. What if they have voice recognition or something?"

"Please."

Jess sighs, clears her throat and dials. I take a pill anyway, while she puts the phone to her ear. Seconds later, she presses speakerphone and sets it on the table between us. "Yes, hello, my name is Emily Price, and I received a letter—"

"Do you have your Personal Identification Number?" a cool, British woman's voice says in a low, clear tone.

"Yes, here it is: 3QFN78," Jess reads.

"And you are confirming your attendance?"

"Yes, but I was wondering if you could give me any more information—"

"In due course." The line clicks.

We stare at each other, and I take the letter back and re-fold it into thirds. I can feel a surge of adrenaline dissipate harmlessly as the propranolol intercepts it. "No way, Jess."

Disappointed, Jess pushes her chair back and gets up. She goes to the sink, washes my wine glass and puts it away, then goes to her room and shuts the door all the way.

TWO

Jess is crazy, I tell myself as I buy a $5.75 double-shot latte from the independent café near the subway station on my way to work. There is no way I'm going to that job interview. I already have a job, first of all. Second of all, DC is a terrible place to live.

I descend into the subway station, balancing my laptop bag and my laptop in one hand while I try to fish my MetroCard out of my purse with the other. I wish I didn't have to bring my own laptop to work, but interns don't get laptops at Dunning & Kruger. Someone jostles me and I spill about $0.90 worth of coffee on my jacket. Oh well – the jacket is coffee-coloured anyway.

It takes about an hour to get to the office, and I'm usually one of the first people in at 8:30. I get a seat on the D train, so I open my notebook. I passive-aggressively elbow the manspreader next to me a little more than strictly necessary in the process.

Janine said that I could pitch some ideas for the new client, a jeweller called Intelligent Design, when I told her my mom used to own a jewellery store when I was younger – but only if I didn't take up any time from my internship tasks to work on the pitch, so I only work on it on the way to work, before she gets in or after she leaves. The store is also family-owned, and they make intricate silver designs that are based on things you see in nature, like leaves and fish. I'm thinking about getting Jess a daisy pendant for her birthday, but only if we win the contract, because then hopefully there will be some kind of discount.

The business owners know that they've been super successful for such a small company with no real marketing strategy, and if they want to get to the next level, they're going to need a coherent plan, and to revamp their website and everything. The wife, Meg, is all in. But the husband, Jeremy, is a harder sell. He likes the garage-band vibe and doesn't mind a little chaos and a non-mobile-optimised website. I think I can get them both on board with a minimalist design that really lets the jewellery speak for itself, and I have some draft copy that Janine might actually like.

When the train screeches into 42nd Street, I stick my notebook back in my bag. If Janine is in a good mood today, I think I'll show her what I've got. Jess is wrong about going to DC, but maybe she's right that I should push myself. I feel in my pocket for my pill case – it's there. I'll wait until before I talk to Janine so the medication doesn't wear off.

I swipe my security badge and take the elevator to the thirty-third floor. When I get to our office, I say good morning to Julie, the receptionist. I take a couple of chocolates from the bowl on her desk. She points at her headset and rolls her eyes. I like Julie. She's wearing a peacock feather in her bun today and a truly insane shade of lipstick. When I raise an eyebrow and tilt my head towards Janine's office, she shakes her head firmly. It's a bad sign. I mouth 'thank you' at her and slink off to the kitchen for a few minutes before I face Janine.

Jonah, the graphic design intern, is in the kitchen with a bag of bagels from Russ & Daughters in his hand and a poppy seed bagel in his mouth. "Good morning," he starts to say, but before he can finish, Janine bursts through the door in a cloud of Chanel No. 5 and superiority.

"You're not going to finish that, are you?" Janine is asking Jonah as the door swings shut behind her.

Jonah takes the bagel out of his mouth. There's a small bite missing. "Do you want one?" he asks.

"No. I want you not to want one," Janine says, looking him up and down disdainfully.

"Good morning," I say.

"Oh, you're here," Janine says.

"Would you like a bagel?" Jonah offers me the bagel that was in his mouth.

I sit uncomfortably on a metal stool with no arms. I do want a bagel. "No, thank you," I say.

"I was going to do this later, but since you're here now, you both may as well come to my office," Janine says, looking annoyed. She tosses a portfolio she was flicking through carelessly at the counter, and a little succulent tumbles down and pops out of its pink pot. It looks rattled, but alive. I leave it and run after her.

There are two chairs across from Janine's desk, and

Jonah immediately sits down in one of them, but I wait to be asked. Chairs are for clients. Janine isn't even looking at us, though – she's behind her desk, looking at her laptop through her Warby Parker glasses and frowning. I cough politely and she looks up. "Sit," she says in the same voice she uses with her Malamute.

I sit.

"You've both been here for over two years. Legal informs me that there have been class-action lawsuits from unpaid interns that have been settled for back pay, so I'm going to have to let you go," Janine says.

"Are you sure it's been two years?" I ask.

"But we really don't mind working for free," Jonah says.

I'm not sure I agree, but it's probably not the right time to ask for a raise. "What if we sign something promising not to sue?" I ask.

"Sorry," Janine says. "It's out of my hands."

"But you said you'd look at my pitch for Intelligent Design," I say.

"Did I?" Janine asks, absently. "Well, you can submit unsolicited pitches through the portal on the website."

I stare at her. Unsolicited? I stand up and tug on Jonah's sleeve. He looks paralysed. "Let's go," I whisper, but Janine doesn't seem to even hear us.

Jonah follows me into the kitchen like a puppy. I pop the succulent back in the pink pot, and take it and the bag of bagels with me. Once we're in the lobby, I give Jonah one of the fresh poppy seed bagels. "What are you going to do now?" I ask him as I try to juggle everything while I take a fistful of candy from Julie's desk and leave my security badge with her. She looks at me questioningly, headset still on, but I just shake my head.

"I have no idea," he says, and he just stands in the lobby, watching the revolving doors.

"Okay, well… bye," I say, and I squeeze my way out, leaving a little trail of dirt from the plant.

I buy a sandwich, and walk to Central Park and eat it. I visit the carousel and some of my other favourite spots. I pet a police horse, and I sit on a bench and watch some Netflix on my phone for a few hours. Finally, when it's starting to get a little dark, I decide to go home. As I get to the landing, I can hear that Jess is inside.

I put my key in the lock and it sticks, so I jiggle it. That usually works, but this time it's really stuck. I put all my stuff down and grab the doorknob hard. It comes off in my hand. "Jess!" I shout, pounding the door. "It happened again."

I hear her padding down the angular hallway. "Oh no," she says. "I'll call the super."

"Can you open the door from inside?" I ask.

She jiggles it. "Now the inside doorknob came off!" she says.

I get down and look through the keyhole. She's looking back at me. "How was your day?" she asks.

"I kind of got fired," I say.

"What? Why?"

"It's hard to explain," I sigh, and sit down against the wall.

"I'm calling the super now," Jess says. I can see that

she is wearing her bathrobe and her hair is in a towel. We
wait while the phone rings. The super answers, and Jess
apologises for waking him up. I glance at my phone.

"It's seven-thirty!" I whisper-shout.

"Yes, the whole doorknob," she says into the phone.
"Okay. Thanks." She hangs up. "It's going to be about twenty
minutes."

"Okay, Jess," I say, leaning back against the peeling
wallpaper. "You win."

THREE

While I wait to go through security at LaGuardia, I stare at a sign posted on the ceiling column behind the agent in my line that says 'NO JOKES' and remember the time Gabby almost caused a scene here by muttering what sounded like 'bomb, bomb, bomb'. She'd gone wide-eyed and insisted she was saying 'lip balm' when Dad grabbed her arm and hissed at her to knock it off, but none of us believed her.

Suddenly, I hear my full name, and when I turn around to see where it came from, there's a TSA agent with a clipboard behind me. "Come with me, please," he says.

The passengers around me mutter as I duck underneath the line divider. "This is about the perfume, isn't it?" I ask under my breath, trying to suppress a surge of anxiety. I read somewhere that if you look nervous, that alone is enough to make the TSA pull you aside for further screening. It makes them think you're smuggling drugs or bombs or something. "The bottle is three point one ounces. Point. One. And I really need it. I'm going on a very important—"

"Follow me."

I am expecting to be whisked off to some dark room and patted down by a scary lady agent, but he just brings me to the front of the line and says something into the ear of the agent at the desk. She holds out a latex-gloved hand, through which I can see long acrylic fingernails with purple flowers painted on them, and I cough up my boarding pass and licence. She looks at my escort's clipboard and waves me through.

"That's it?" I ask.

"That's it," she says.

"Are you sure?"

"You want me to strip search you?" she asks, holding up a plastic-gloved hand.

"Maybe later," I say.

I am guiltily reading my second chapter of a crime novel inside the tiny Hudson News when someone behind me clears her throat and says, "Excuse me."

"I'm going to buy the book," I say, wary of her, but unable to think of anything else she could reprimand me for.

"What?" The woman's wearing a Delta uniform. Her nametag says 'Mona'.

"Never mind," I say. "What's the bad news? Flight delayed? Cancelled? Has Delta decided to re-route it through Colorado or something?"

"Why would we do that?"

"Ours is not to reason why."

"Are you Emily Price?"

"Look, Mona. Just give it to me straight. I won't be mad."

Mona frowns her beautifully pencilled eyebrows. "It

sounds like you've had some unfortunate experiences with Delta. Would you be willing to fill out a customer satisfaction survey?"

"What is going on?"

"I'm here to show you to the SkyPriority lounge. You've been upgraded. And I can take your carry-on for you. It'll be above your seat when you board."

"At my seat? On the plane?"

"Yes."

"The same plane that I will be boarding?"

"Of course."

"No thanks. I'll keep ahold of it."

"Probably wise," Mona says, arching one of her perfect brows. And it would be funny if Delta hadn't lost my carry-on with my favourite illustrated copy of *Black Beauty* in it when they made me gate-check it on a flight to California a decade ago, and then refused to admit fault or pay to replace the book. By the end of the conversation with the customer service agent, they were denying there ever was a flight to California.

"I rarely make the same mistake twice," I tell her.

The hour-long flight to Reagan Airport turns out to be just the right amount of time to take full advantage of the free peanut situation without hitting peanut overload. I emerge into daylight near baggage claim, and I'm amazed to find that there is a uniformed driver wearing sunglasses holding a sign with my name on it.

"Identification, please, Ma'am," he says.

I show him my driver's licence.

"And your PIN?"

"It's 3QFN78," I read from my letter, and hold it out for him to see.

"I'm Agent Wilcox," he says.

I swallow.

He takes me to a black Lincoln sedan with tinted windows and opens the door for me. I feel very underprepared for this job interview. I don't even know what the job is. So how can I know which of my skills I need to discuss? Do they want someone organised and competent? Do they want an out-of-the-box thinker? Someone with advanced Microsoft Word skills? Should I share an anecdote that reveals how well I play with others, or one that shows I'm a strong leader, like the time I was interning for Viacom and led the campaign to eradicate decaffeinated coffee from the staff lounge? What version of me should I be?

Wilcox pulls up next to a low building constructed from corrugated metal. I lean forward, looking around. It's not a car parking lot – it's a lot for airplanes. "We're here," he says.

"Where?"

"Where you're going."

"I'm going in there?"

"I'll get your bag."

"Okay," I say, feeling doubtful. I climb out of the car, squinting in the harsh sunlight. I can see the heat radiating from the asphalt, making the air shimmer. There's already the prickle of sweat forming in my underarms and on my palms, even though the sun's warmth hasn't even had time to thaw my air-conditioned hands yet, and I hope that the black crepe fabric of my blouse and my three point one ounces of perfume will be up to their task. I smooth down my blazer and pick a peanut crumb out from my blouse. "Agent Wilcox, I'm not ready. I was under the impression that I'd be able to go to the hotel first."

Wilcox pushes his sunglasses up his nose and sets my bag down next to me, with the handle pulled out for me to grab. "Hotel?"

"There's a reservation for me, at a hotel downtown? I have the details here. I figured the interview would be at the Truman Building." I ungracefully remove the folder from my purse and hold it out to him.

He doesn't take it. "Don't know anything about that, Ma'am," he says.

It turns out to be an airplane hangar. There is a small airplane inside – I assume it's a private jet, although I've never seen one before. There is also a makeshift office set up in the far corner, complete with a blue rug, a large oak desk and chairs.

"I'll leave you here," Wilcox says, and when he's gone, I take a deep breath and remove a beta-blocker from the little silver pill case in my purse. I don't have any water, so I just tolerate the bitter trail the pill leaves down the back of my tongue as I struggle to swallow it.

I'm making my way across the hanger when a tall, reedy, WASPy kid with a clipboard and a pen tucked behind his ear intercepts me.

"Hi – I'm Thom? Newhouse?" he says.

"Are you?" I ask him back.

"Yeah, and you're, um – Emily, right? I mean, Ms Price?"

"Yeah," I said. "Why are we in an airplane hangar?"

"It's just efficient."

"Efficient for what?"

"I can't say. It's over there," Thom says.

"You sent me the letter, right?" I ask, following him to the desk at the corner. "So maybe you can tell me why I'm here."

Thom pulls out a chair. "Do you want any coffee?"

"No. Yes. But Thom – why am I here?"

"I can't really talk about it, but Ms Harris is going to be here soon, and she'll—"

"Come on. Give me a hint."

"Well, your Middle East policy expertise is exactly—"

"My what?" I start to ask, but before I can finish getting it out, the door to the tiny plane next to us swings wide open with a thwack. A statuesque woman with dark skin and short hair wrangled into neat little twists about three inches long is standing at the top of the steps in what I recognise as a navy power suit and pointed stilettos. She is fabulous. She is terrifying. Her eyebrows are perfect. I am desperately hoping she is not the person who is going to interview me.

Thom rushes over to the stairs and takes the woman's briefcase. She strides over and sticks out her hand. I drop my portfolio. Thom scrambles for it.

The woman's handshake is as impressive as she is. "I'm Alisha Harris," she says, "and it is truly an honour to meet you." Alisha looks at me so hard that her crinkly eyes are narrowing a little, but it looks like she means it. She runs a smoothing hand over her hair, which bounces back up in the wake of the motion, and flashes me her best smile.

She is also looking somewhat familiar. 'Alisha Harris' is sounding somewhat familiar. "You look somewhat familiar," I begin, playing for time. I don't want to insult her by not knowing who she is, if I should know who she is.

"Maybe you've seen me on TV," Alisha Harris says, turning a photograph on her desk around so I can see it. She's standing behind a man I do recognise, who is shaking hands with the president. "I work with the Secretary of State," Harris continues, smiling, and she perches on the desk in front of me instead of sitting behind it. She's not as tall and angular as she appears in the photo, without the benefit of a handful of dumpy men around her. But her pantsuit is even nicer. "I'm Deputy Assistant Secretary Harris. Listen, I'm sorry about this, but I'm going to have to ask you to sign an NDA before we continue."

Thom hands me his clipboard and pen, and I see what looks like a standard nondisclosure agreement with a yellow Post-it note and an X for my signature. I notice that his plastic pen has bite marks at the top. "What's this for, Deputy Assistant Secretary Harris?" I ask, taking the pen between my thumb and index finger to avoid touching Thom's saliva.

"'Alisha', please. As I'm sure you know, given your legal knowledge, this is boilerplate. It's department policy – something our lawyers insist on. We just don't want the

details of this job position to get out. We'd have thousands
of applications on our hands. And we don't have the time
to deal with that. I'm sure you understand."

"Of course." I sign the form with a flourish I hope looks
more confident than I feel.

I surrender the clipboard back to Thom. As he takes it
from me, I notice that his nails are bitten too, like his pen.
I'm glad I put on some nail polish to stop me from biting
my own nails on the way here, and I look away to spare
him the embarrassment of my scrutiny. "Now can you tell
me what this is about?" I ask Alisha.

"We're waiting for one more person to join us," she says.
"Oh – here she is now," she says, looking behind me to the
doors I came through.

Another impressive power suit comes striding towards
me, this one encasing a tall woman with naturally greyed
blonde hair. She nods to Alisha and sits down behind the
desk.

"I'm Emily Price," I volunteer when she doesn't
introduce herself.

The woman smiles back at me. Something about her,
too, is very familiar. "Yes, I know," she says, and even her
voice is familiar. She has a crisp English accent. She sounds
like the woman Jessica spoke to.

She doesn't volunteer her own name. "And your name
is—?"

"It's need-to-know," Alisha says apologetically.

"Your name is need-to-know?" I ask, looking between
the two women. Alisha nods, but the woman just maintains
a cool smile. And it hits me – she looks like Helen Mirren.

"Has anyone ever told you that you look a lot like that British actress, Helen Mirren?"

"Yes," the woman says.

"Well, I guess I'll just call you 'Helen Mirren', then."

Helen Mirren's face remains impassive. I stare at my fingernails again.

Alisha takes the seat next to mine and scoots close enough to me to put a hand on my arm. "Emily. You have a chance to make history."

I can feel my beta-blocker wearing off, even though it's way too soon. I clear my throat and try for eye contact, but my eyes land on her nose. It's close enough. She may not even notice. "It sounds like this is a good opportunity."

"You, Emily," says Helen Mirren, sliding a black binder stamped with '[CONFIDENTIAL]' in gold lettering across the desk, "are being hired for the biggest divorce case of the millennium. You are going to divorce Israel and Palestine."

FOUR

"I'm afraid you're already committed," says Helen.

"What are you talking about?" I ask, and Alisha hands me back the NDA I just signed, and taps her pen next to Item 4, subsection B. *Once you have been briefed, you will remain in government custody for the duration of Project Kramer.* "Ugh, really? We're going with 'Project Kramer'? And you're kidnapping me?"

"'Kidnapping' is a strong word," says Alisha.

"We really prefer 'custody,'" Helen agrees.

"I like the name," Thom chimes in. He has a couple of suitcases with him. They look a lot like the luggage I took from Dad's house a few years ago. They're a little beat-up, like mine. They have the same luggage tags I have on mine – custom black plastic with a beige horse on them. And they have my initials.

I think my beta-blocker is starting to wear off.

"If you have my luggage," I ask Thom, "whose did I take off the plane?"

Thom looks uncomfortable. "That's your luggage, too," he says. "This is... the rest of it."

"What is he talking about?" I demand, looking at Alisha.

"We couldn't tell you where you'd be going in advance, so we took the liberty of sending in an aide to pack for you."

Well, they couldn't have done that, because Jess would have told me if some mysterious government officials had started going through my closet, wouldn't she? Oh no – is my cell phone still in airplane mode? I pick up my purse and rifle through it.

"We also took your phone," Alisha says.

"Please give it back."

"We'll give you a phone and computer to use in Jerusalem."

"I can't go to Jerusalem! I don't have my passport."

Thom holds up a small leather rectangle apologetically.

"I'm supposed to think that's my passport, right? Well, joke's on you, because I lost my passport years ago. In France."

"I'm a Deputy Assistant Secretary of State," Alisha points out.

'Deputy' and 'Assistant' don't sound all that powerful to me, but what do I know? "Well, I still can't go. Because of my dog. My very sick dog. I have to take him to the vet. Tomorrow."

"We know you don't have a dog," Alisha says.

I can feel myself flushing a little. I wish I hadn't lied about the dog, because now there's no way they'll believe me about a horse – but I really do need to be there for Poco. I can feel myself start to panic, but I stifle a grimace and soldier on. "Look. I'm flattered. I mean, I'm confused about why on earth you'd ask me to be a part of this, but I'm taking it as a compliment. But I'm saying no, no thanks. Okay? I don't know what you're looking for here, but it isn't me. You don't understand – my dad is right about me. I wore a pyjama top to work yesterday because I haven't done laundry in three weeks. I have eaten microwaveable macaroni and cheese for three years. And in three decades, I have never once filed my own taxes. This is a test I will fail. So, I promise I won't say anything to anybody, but this is too much to ask of me. I have to go." I stand, smooth my blazer, wipe my sweaty palms and pick up my purse.

Helen eyes me levelly for a moment or two. "If that's how you feel," she says, "we'll take you back home."

"Really?" I ask, and I think this was too easy, but maybe Jess was right after all that being honest and saying how you feel instead of acting all weird and making up crazy excuses is the way to go.

"No. Not really. Get on the plane," Helen says.

And that sounds about right to me.

I'm wearing my sunglasses and headphones when Thom comes over and sits down.

"Ms Price?" he says. I stare straight ahead, arms crossed. "I know you can hear me," he says. He tugs at my headphones until the jack dangles in his chomped fingertips.

I keep my sunglasses on. "May I use the restroom?" I ask, trying to slide my pill case up into my sleeve without him noticing, like how I would hide a tampon on the journey from the classroom to the girls' bathroom back in high school. I need more beta-blockers, but I've already taken two, so I need to cut one in half, and I'd rather do it in private.

"You don't need to ask." Thom is embarrassed. The blush on his cheeks is cartoonish; small and perfectly round, as if he had pressed a makeup brush once to each cheek.

"I haven't read what Emily Post has to say about hostage etiquette," I say.

"You're not a hostage."

"I'll decide if I'm a hostage or not!"

"Okay," Thom says, leaning away from me. "I just thought I'd show you opposing counsel's CV and give you a chance to look over your brief." He holds up a large file.

I flip through the pages with the hand that's not discreetly holding the pill case, scanning for some more clues about where I'll be staying and for how long, but there's nothing. "Where am I staying?" I ask Thom.

"Um, a hotel in… Kiryat Moshe," he says, only he pronounces the name of the Jerusalem neighbourhood as goyishly as he looks.

"Is that near the Hebrew University?"

"I think it is. Everything in Israel is close to everything else. It's not a big place."

I snap the folder shut and remove my sunglasses, because now I have an idea.

"Wait," he says. "I mean, no, go ahead. It's just, I wanted to say, it's an honour for me to meet you, and I know a renowned Middle East scholar probably doesn't need a research assistant, but if you ever need someone to—"

"I'm going to the bathroom now," I interrupt. And then
I freeze, midway through scooting across Thom's lap, and
I turn to him. "Wait a minute. Who's a renowned Middle
East scholar?"

FIVE

This is my way out. I open my mouth to call out for Helen or Alisha, who are taking power naps – or they're powerful people taking regular naps – to tell them.

Thom presses on my shoulder until I plop back into my seat and clamps a hand over my mouth. "No, no, no, oh God, please don't say anything," he begs.

"Listen, Thomas Newhouse. I don't think you understand. I. Am. Not. An. Expert. On anything. I'm nothing. I live in a shitty apartment in a shitty neighbourhood. I'm single, I think. My job is unpaid, and most of the time I'm not sure what I'm even supposed to be doing there. Yesterday, they sent me on a coffee run and told me to take as long as I wanted, maybe go for a walk, enjoy the sunshine. And just to get through that, I require thirty milligrams of propranolol a day. If you look up 'wasted potential' in the dictionary, there's a photo of me. So yeah, I think this is a pretty big fuck-up, on your part, and I'm going to have to say something."

"Wait – I can figure this out. Please don't say anything yet."

"I have to," I explain, "because I really, really can't do this job." I unbuckle my seatbelt and try to stand.

"You can! I know you can," Thom says, inadvertently knocking me back into my chair with a hand that flew out instinctively to stop me. Having grazed my boob, it has frozen in mid-air, now in front of my face.

I look at his hand. It's the colour of wood furniture from IKEA and covered in fine, black hair that spreads across the back of it like a colonising army. I reach out and push the hand aside. "I'm not even a lawyer."

"But you're a legal professional," Thom tries, finally letting his inert hand drop. "And you're Jewish. You must know all about the conflict and stuff."

Thom is more right than he knows. I was a Religious Studies minor, and I had a 4.0 GPA. I've even been to Israel. My only quibble with him is really over the term 'legal professional' – my paralegal certificate may or may not have been an accredited course. Rather, it was accredited – but not by the American Bar Association. I chose a programme based on the cheapest price, quoted my dad the cost of the most expensive course and pocketed the difference. I always have been good at sinking to my dad's expectations.

What Jess said bothered me enough to keep me awake last night, arguing with her in my head about whether I avoid taking risks because I'm afraid that I'm a failure. But I don't think I am a failure. My parents do. But I know that the reason I am where I am in life has nothing to do with me or my choices. I've been unlucky, that's all, and didn't happen to have the opportunities I needed to succeed.

Is this what they mean when they say that when opportunity knocks, open the door? There's no saying for what happens when opportunity kidnaps you and takes you to the Middle East – and doesn't even pack your favourite espadrilles – but I have to assume it's the same general idea. And there's another thing, something I'll have to be careful never to admit to anyone else, especially Jess: since this is all classified, if I fail, nobody will know.

"What are the other Emily Price's credentials, exactly?" I ask.

"Well," Thom says, looking hopeful, "she graduated summa cum laude from Harvard Law, where she wrote a paper for a conflict resolution course that got a lot of attention, because it was about Israel-Palestine. She said that it was possible to 'divorce the emotional and religious elements from the main points of conflict in order to pursue a mutually agreeable result'. That's what gave us this idea. I mean, gave Secretary Harris the idea," he corrects, as if she might hear him trying to share the credit.

I feel a pang, hearing about this parallel-universe Emily A. Price, who became what Dad wanted me to be. "If I do this," I say, "I'm going to need some assurances."

"Anything," Thom says.

"If Alisha or Helen find out—"

"I'll take the blame."

"And if I need some help getting up to speed on what each side wants—"

"I will write you the best, simplest, clearest cheat sheets in the world."

Thom gives me an expression of such naked hope that I

am repulsed. I open the file again. If they're going to get me on the Israeli side, who did they get to represent Palestine? Fahrid, the friendly shawarma guy from near my office in Midtown? But no, it's some British guy I've never heard of, with a forgettable, fake-sounding name. But I've already decided that I'm going to do this. I'm hardly going to make things any worse, even if I am outmatched.

"Okay," I say simply.

"Okay?" Thom parrots.

"Okay," I confirm. "There's one more thing I'm going to need your help with."

The last time I spoke to Mike was about a month ago, before he left for Jerusalem to start his teaching job at the Archaeological Institute at the Hebrew University. Thing is, it didn't go great. We had dinner at this little Italian restaurant on the Upper East Side we both liked to celebrate his new job, and then Mike asked me to go with him.

"I can't. It's fine for you," I explained. "You're half-Indian. You don't sunburn, and your hair is never frizzy."

"I don't think you understand what I'm asking you," Mike said. "I'm not just saying I want you to come on a six-month trip with me. I mean, I want you in my life. For good."

That was when he started fishing around in his pocket and kneeling. I panicked. And I ran. Mike started calling me immediately, of course. But – and I'm not super proud of this – I threw my phone in the East River. Mike came to the apartment later that night, but I hid in the shower.

"But what happened?" Jess asked, bewildered. "What did he do?"

"The worst possible thing," I said, and Jess made a knowing face and got the wine sorbet from the freezer.

"Fuck him," Jess said loyally, and I knew she assumed he had cheated on me. I let her. That way, she wouldn't say anything when I told her I'd dropped out of law school and re-enrolled as a paralegal.

When Thom said he could for sure get Mike to come stay with me at the hotel, and tell anyone who asked that he was a consultant for the case, I wasn't all that confident. But then again – Mike has always given me another chance. And I think our plan is good. Mike won't know that this has anything to do with me. Thom will pull up next to him in a black sedan, ask him to get in and do the NDA thing he pulled on me, and hey presto – he's hired. Poor, trusting Mike will never see it coming. And then I'll have backup.

"When will you do it?" I ask Thom.

"As soon as we get there."

"Maybe you could also write up a few ideas for what I'm going to say to him," I say.

"I'll have them to you before we land."

I feel so incredibly much better about this now. "I'd like a chicken pesto panini, too."

"As soon as our wheels touch down," he says.

"Now," I say.

Thom looks at me, wide-eyed, and retreats to the small galley at the back. I saw an empty delivery box labelled 'SKY PANINIS' on my way aboard. I let him have his moment of relief when he opens the little fridge and sees them. I let him think that the paninis are a gift from God. And when he brings me my panini, I will let him think that I'm impressed.

I want him to feel confident when he goes to fetch Mike for me. Because I really don't think there's any way I'm going to make it through this without someone on my side.

I don't know what I was expecting, but the King Solomon Hotel is not it. Far from being a standard modern chain hotel, it has an air of faded boutique luxury. It appears that it has been diligently cleaned, tidied and patched up for the last five decades, but never once updated.

The textured walls at the foot of the steep stairs to the reception desk are scuffed, and the ceiling plaster is cracked and chipping in the corners. Little alcoves are set into the walls, and they are filled with tchotchkes of indeterminate, vaguely setting-appropriate origin. A brass menorah here, a palm tree there. I don't mind, because I'm already sure that I'll spend a few sleepless nights pacing around the hotel wondering if I've officially lost my mind. Some reminders that I really have been kidnapped by my own government and dragged to Israel won't go amiss.

We are trailing behind Alisha and Helen, who are both talking on the phone, as they have been since we got off the plane. Thom, laden with all my luggage, pauses halfway up the stairs to catch his breath.

Reflexively, I reach for my phone while I stand there waiting. I miss it. I keep reaching for it – to text Jess, to check in to Jerusalem on Facebook with the caption 'You won't believe what I'm doing here' – but of course I can't do any of that. I'm completely cut off, and despite what regular sermons from Rabbi Gold led me to expect over the years, I do not feel like I'm home.

I am starting to feel a mild panic, as if each breath of warm, golden air that I take in comes loaded with one more bit of responsibility. Each one settles on my chest, and I am finding it difficult to breathe. I scrounge in the depths of my brain's language centre and try to remember the Hebrew for the phrase 'I'm thirsty', but it comes to me in a garbled, guttural mix of Hebrew and French. *Yesh li soif.* French structure and hybrid vocabulary – Hebrech? Frew? – and I think I can feel my brain throbbing from trying to remember. My brain hurts and my chest is heavy, and my tongue is too big for my mouth and—

"What's wrong?" Thom asks. "What are you thinking about? You're not changing your mind about our deal, are you?"

"No."

"Well, it looked like you were."

"I wasn't. I was thinking about French vocabulary."

"French vocabulary?"

"Yes. It's a mess. For example, I was thinking that if the French are going to refer to potatoes as 'ground apples', they should at least be consistent and call bananas 'sky carrots'. Although, to be fair, I'm not sure why we call pineapples 'pineapples'. Is an apple the default fruit? Why isn't everything else named like whatever variation it is on an apple?"

Thom looks concerned. "Are you all right? Maybe I should get you some water."

"If it would make you feel better. I'll be over there." I point at a chair in the corner of the small, furniture-crowded lobby that has one of those indoor palm trees and an air-conditioning unit beside it.

I sit in the overstuffed chair and put my sunglasses back on. It's too bright here, even inside, with antique mirrors infinitely reflecting and refracting the bright sun that forces its way through a cracked door that leads to a tiny balcony. The sunlight seems magnified by the yellow stone buildings, too, and rises from the pavement in the form of shimmery waves. I wonder if I'm going to start having migraines now, like Aunt Martha used to say I was giving her. I close my eyes and lean my head back. At least it's quiet, I think to myself, and the word 'quiet' blooms like an inkblot into a memory of my old Israeli Hebrew teacher from the third grade, Mrs Waterman, shouting at the class to be quiet. *Sheket!* she yelled. *Achshav!* Now!

"Emily?" Thom says, and I startle. I take the cup of water Thom is handing me. The *cos mayim*, I immediately rename it in my head, surprising myself with the speed at which the correct vocabulary had come to me, and I sit up straight.

"Alisha says we can call it a day," Thom says, shifting his weight and taking a key out of his back pocket.

I stifle a yawn. "What time is it?"

"Midday, but the flight was almost twelve hours, and you didn't sleep. And it's seven hours ahead here. You're due for a rest."

"I don't need to sleep." I do, but I know I won't really be able to. "Did you figure everything out with Dr Patel?"

"Not yet," Thom says, looking at his feet. "But if you go upstairs and have a rest and a shower, by the time you're up and ready again, I'll have him here."

"Okay," I say, too tired to argue. I'll have to trust that he can pull this off. He may have gotten the wrong Emily A. Price to Jerusalem, but he must have some ability. He can't have gotten the job through nepotism alone.

I'm following Thom through a narrow hallway to an ancient elevator, past Alisha and Helen, who are still standing around back to back, talking into their headsets and gesturing at the wall animatedly. It could be the same conversation they were having before, or they could have made a thousand phone calls. Hours could have passed, or only seconds, since we landed near Tel Aviv. Time is stretching out before me and then rolling back in on itself. I have a sleepy thought that maybe the problem with Israel is that it is all too aware of where it is in the world but confused about when. A place with no history, because six hundred years ago is all too present for everyone here. Maybe once you've claimed this place as yours, you find that time is a string after all, and that while you're riding the bus to your office job in Jerusalem, you can look out the window and see the Bar Kochba revolt unfolding outside your window. And maybe when a Palestinian boy in a refugee camp watches a centuries-old olive tree get bulldozed by the Israeli army, he sees his great-great-great-grandfather tumble down with it, and his sack of harvested olives spill like blood on the dusty ground.

Thom is talking, and I grab hold of the present moment by putting a hand on the wall and try to listen. "...so, he's staying on the same floor as you, but all the way at the other end of the hotel," he says. "The PLO Chairman, and the Israeli PM, they were both very concerned that nobody ends up staying on a higher floor than the other," he is explaining, misreading my slack face.

"Well," I say, getting the gist of it. "At least you've gotten the venue right. If there's anywhere in the world that we would be able to split this baby in half without killing it, it would be here, at the King Solomon Hotel."

SIX

I'm swirling around in a whirlpool of worry, eyes closed but at most half-asleep, until the sound of a familiar voice saying my name jolts me out of it. I open one eye to see who it is, and there's Mike, standing on the threadbare carpet by the door with some luggage at his feet and his arms crossed. "Emily," he says again, and I open my other eye warily. "What am I doing here?"

I met Mike during my freshman year at college. He was the teaching assistant for my introductory Old Testament course. I could tell he was several years older than me. His dark brown eyes were big and wet. Camel eyes, my grandmother used to call them. But they had the look of someone who'd seen some shit. Like mine.

One day, I stopped by Dr Metcalfe's office to talk about an essay on the *Gilgamesh Epic* and the story of Noah and the flood, but he wasn't there. Mike was, instead, grading papers.

"Oh," I said, when I opened the door and saw him. "I was looking for Dr Metcalfe."

"He doesn't really do office hours," Mike said.

"The syllabus said these were his office hours."

"They are. But I do them for him. Here, come have a seat."

I sat down and looked at the stuff on the desk in front of him. Mike had stuck a label on the nameplate on the desk below Dr Metcalfe's name, and written 'and TA Mike' on it.

"I just need a book recommendation for the essay."

"No problem. Sorry, the campus internet is really slow today, like every day," Mike said. "So, while we wait for the syllabus to load – you're Emily, right? Where are you from?"

"I'm from New York."

"The city?"

"Right outside the city. Where are you from?"

"Philly."

"The city?"

"Right outside the city," Mike said, and he laughed. "You know, a statistically impossible number of people at this college come from 'right outside' Philly."

"New York, too," I said. "Anyway, I don't think that was what you were really asking."

"Oh no?" Mike smiled. "What was I really asking?"

"You were asking what kind of minority I am," I said. "It's okay. I'm a Sephardic Jew. That's—"

"Oh, cool," Mike said. "Yeah, I know what that is. I'm the TA for Religious Studies, remember?"

"Right," I said, and blushed a little.

"Go on, you can ask me, now."

"Okay. What kind of brown are you?"

"The suntanned kind."

"Oh."

"I'm fucking with you. I think I'm half-Indian. Like, from India. Not indigenous American. Oh, here, it's loaded – I know just the book. Yep, the library has it. It's *The Gilgamesh Epic and Old Testament Parallels*, by Alexander Heidel, 1946. Want me to reserve it for you?"

"Sure. Here's my student number," I said, passing my ID across the desk to him. "What do you mean you 'think' you're half-Indian?"

"I'm adopted," Mike said. "My parents adopted me from India, and it was a closed adoption, but my birth mother was worried about my sense of identity, so she stipulated that I could only go to a home with at least one Indian parent. My adoptive dad – he's Indian-American, third generation. She also enclosed a letter. It said my surname is Patel. Which is my adoptive dad's name, too. My parents thought it was fate."

"Come on."

"No shit. And when they saw me, they figured I was half-white, which was another coincidence – my adoptive mom is white, too. They said it was like I was tailor-made for them. But I'm rambling. Here you go," he finished, handing me a confirmation that the book was reserved from the printer.

I considered what he'd said. Weirdly, it wasn't as boring as this kind of stuff often was. But I still wished I was hearing it with a drink in my hand. "Usually people buy me a drink before they make me listen to stuff that boring and personal," I answered, folding the paper and tucking it into my jeans pocket.

"Okay," Mike answered. "How about Thursday?"

We went for a drink on Thursday.

When the administration sent out internal memos to the whole faculty – including graduate teaching assistants – reiterating that the official policy forbids dating undergraduates, Mike started to worry.

When he showed me the email, I immediately dumped him. He argued, but he needed his job. I'd found out, after several glasses of wine one night, that he'd put himself through undergrad by joining the ROTC, and had ended up doing a tour of duty in Afghanistan. He said that was what made him decide to get a joint degree in Religious Studies, alongside Archaeology – every day that passed there, he said, he saw the evidence that America was dealing with a religious culture and history we did not sufficiently understand.

Mike's parents didn't have any money. He was never going to be able to join the military again because of his political views, and religious studies graduate students weren't exactly in high demand. And besides, Dr Metcalfe was one of the world's leading experts on ancient coins, and fluent in German, Hebrew and Latin. And he could read Aramaic, and some Greek. He was a fount of knowledge on all things Ancient Near East. He also had connections at the Hebrew University and could write Mike a stellar recommendation for a faculty position there, if he kept his nose clean.

I did the noble thing and broke up with him.

A year later, we were both in New York. But we all know how that ended.

I sit up in my bed, yawn and rub my eyes to buy some time. Despite not having really fallen asleep over the last couple of hours, I didn't make any progress on my plans for what I would say to get Mike to help me, either. I decide to improvise.

"Hi!" I say cheerfully. "So you've been press-ganged into service to the US government, too, huh? What a coincidence."

Mike presses two fingers of each hand to his temples and closes his eyes, like he always does when he's upset.

SEVEN

Downstairs, Alisha and Helen are waiting for us, with Thom standing a few steps behind them like a personal valet from a BBC period drama.

"Are we going to talk, or not?" Mike demands as we walk across the lobby, me struggling to keep up with him. It feels like I'm moving through water.

"Later, I promise," I lie. "For now, I really need you to be cool."

"Good morning, Emily," Alisha says, not looking up from her tablet. It isn't as big as Helen's tablet.

Helen looks at Mike and raises her eyebrows. "Who's this?"

"Expert witness!" interjects Thom, stumbling forward. "He's an expert witness."

"Are there normally expert witnesses in disunions?" Helen asks acerbically.

"Definitely," I say. "They help a lot during discovery."

There is an uncomfortable pause, in which I stifle a yawn, and Helen looks sceptical.

"I'm Dr Mike Patel," Mike offers, just to break the silence.

Alisha holds up an imperious finger as she continues to look at her tablet. We all wait, holding our collective breath, until she looks up. I see her scan Mike's light-wash jeans and endearingly rumpled button-down shirt, and I hold my breath, but she smiles with genuine warmth and reaches out a hand. "Dr Patel," she says, "Good of you to come. My deputy says that you'll be an absolutely invaluable asset to Ms Price."

"If she lets me, sure," Mike says, letting her hand shake his.

"Do you know her?" Helen asks.

"No! No," Thom interjects again. "They've just met."

Mike glances at me sideways, but I will him not to say anything. I can see that little brow crease that he gets when he's really interested. It looks a little like he's angry, but I know better. The more confusing things get, the more Mike likes it. I think it's what made him such a good student, and I'm sure it makes him a good teacher, too. I don't know if the impact of this particular trait on his soldiering was positive or negative.

While we wait for someone to give in and speak, I stifle a yawn.

"I suppose it doesn't matter," Helen says. "Thomas, give Ms Price her itinerary."

Thom hands me and Mike clipboards with a colour-coded chart on each one. We briefly make eye contact as he does, and he looks desperate and frightened. I think I can almost taste his fear – it's tangy and sickly-sweet, like fast-food barbecue sauce. I loathe him a little in that instant, and I can feel some of the goodwill he earned by fetching Mike for me slipping away. I glance over the itinerary and see that it has several 'site visits', which seem a lot like sightseeing trips. Maybe that's Thom patronising me, but I don't mind. I didn't see many sights on that volunteering trip with Mom years ago, and I never did go on Birthright. I meant to, but not after Jess came back from a Birthright trip and said the whole thing was like a summer at Camp B'nai Yisrael, but with even more sex and drugs, and bankrolled by Sheldon Adelson.

There's just one thing that seems to be missing. "Will I be visiting, um, Palestine?" I ask.

Alisha sighs. "The official policy is that we strongly warn against it."

"Put that into context for me."

"That's the same thing we say about North Korea."

"Oh."

"And we forbid our own employees from going to a lot of places in the West Bank, and especially from using public transport to do it," Alisha adds.

"What do you guys think?" I ask Helen.

"We strongly advise against it, officially. Of course, the legal representative of Palestine, a Mr Browning, is a British citizen – but he can hardly avoid visiting if he is to work with Mr Barghouti."

"But I don't get to go?"

"We'll see," says Alisha, and it sounds like it did when Mom said it – like that's that.

Mike opens his mouth like he is going to say something

but thinks better of it. He shakes his head slightly, one small, quick jerk, like a horse twitching its shoulder to dislodge a fly.

"Helen and I have to be going. But we'll be leaving you in Thom's very capable hands. And he can reach my direct line anytime, day or night," Alisha says. "We will need to sit you all down with the mediator very soon, to discuss the process, but otherwise, take today to get used to the time change."

"And the weather," Helen adds without smiling, but I think I'm starting to get her, and I'm at least eighty per cent sure that was one of those self-deprecating British jokes you hear so much about. Humour, with a 'u'.

"Do you have any questions?" Alisha asks, clasping her hands in front of her and looking at me.

"Mike and I are hungry," I say.

"I think this hotel is haunted," I complain to Mike over breakfast, when neither of us has said anything for five whole minutes.

"What makes you say that?" he asks, pushing his breakfast salad away from him and setting down his fork.

"You know," I stage whisper so he can hear me without me getting close enough for him to smell my coffee breath. "The bombing."

Mike lays his hand on top of mine. "That was the King David hotel," he says. "And it's not haunted, either."

"How do you know?"

"Emily," he sighs. "Don't start."

I pull my hand back and start to pull the petals off the

cyclamen in the tiny jug on the table. I bring my pollen-coated fingers to my nose to smell them. It makes me sneeze. I wonder if it's blasphemous to wipe my hand on one of the King Solomon's paper napkins, which are white with giant blue Jewish stars on them, like the Israeli flag. I do it anyway.

Mike has opened his mouth to say something when a very tall, very thin and very white man pulls up a chair next to us.

"Good morning," the man says pleasantly.

"You see?" I tell Mike, inclining my head at the man. "Ghosts."

The man frowns. "Er, I'm Browning. James Browning."

I appraise him suspiciously. "You're British."

The ghost gives up on me and turns to Mike, extending a hand. "I understand you're with the project, too. I'm the appointed counsel for the other side. I'll be representing Mr Barghouti."

"It's probably best if you don't sit with us, then."

"Oh, surely we're free to socialise, so long as we put up a Chinese wall regarding the work," Browning says, sitting down anyway.

"Racist," I mutter.

"What?" James says.

"So you're really doing this? You? Taking on the most acrimonious divorce of all time?" Mike cuts in.

"I'm not sure it's even the most acrimonious case I've ever worked on," I bluff, for both Mike's benefit and James's. I don't want either of them to think this is particularly scary for me. "And that's why we can't socialise," I continue, turning to James and feeling my heart beat out a quick series of staccato notes. I take a surreptitious, calming breath. "I'm going to destroy you, and if I get to know you, I might feel bad about it. Which might stop me from doing the best possible job for my client, which I would never—"

"Hang on," James says. "We all want the same thing here, don't we? Peace. A solution that works for everyone. An end to this dreadful war. We're not enemies—"

"Oh, for God's sake," I interrupt.

"Why don't we talk about something else?" Mike suggests helpfully. "Anything else."

James folds his napkin primly and stands. "Just like you people, to be thinking about this in terms of winning," I hear him say under his breath as he pushes his chair back in.

"Would 'you people' be Jews, Israelis or Americans?" I ask loudly, to shout over the sound of my own pulse in my ears. People say it sounds like the ocean, but to me it has always sounded more like cars rushing above you on an overpass.

In any case, heads turn in our direction, and James looks displeased. "I'll see you at our first meeting tomorrow, at sixteen-hundred," he says. "Good morning."

Mike flinches at this, and I hate it.

I rise quickly, my chair falling over behind me. "I'll see you at the meeting," I shout after him, and for good measure, I add, "At four!"

He lifts one hand in an infuriating little wave but doesn't turn back.

Mike looks at me with concern, which makes me feel

even more stressed out, but also annoyed. Annoyed wins out, so when the receptionist – who is apparently also the breakfast waiter – rushes over to help with my chair, I wave away his assistance and ask for another coffee instead.

Mike is just sitting there. Sitting there, looking at me. It's making me feel kind of like I did the time Poco bucked while I was in the process of mounting him and I landed hard and flat on my back and couldn't inhale. "Mike, your staring is really starting to bug me," I say.

"I'm waiting," he says.

"Waiting for what?"

"For you to be ready."

"Ready for what?"

"Ready to explain. What Helen Mirren is doing here. What I'm doing here. Why I should stay – and teach my classes over Skype, with supervision, like that beanpole idiot said I'd be doing."

"I thought Thom would have told you," I say. "You're here to help me. You know," I lean forward and whisper, "with Project Kramer."

"I know that," Mike says drily. "I'm waiting for you to answer the real question, which is why you suddenly want to see me again."

"It's for the case."

"Just for the case? There was nobody else you thought could help? And, speaking of which, no offence, but are you really the person for the job? I mean, Emily – you're not even a lawyer."

I look down at my hands, which have shredded the Star

of David napkin. I knew he'd heard that I dropped out after we broke up, but I never answered his calls, so I never had to hear what he had to say about it. "It's complicated."

"It always is with you," Mike says, and he laughs a short, bitter laugh, but he reaches out and takes the shredded napkin out of my hand gently and keeps his rested on mine.

"I did miss you, you know," I say, not able to look up from our hands in my lap.

"I missed you too."

He looks at me and waits for me to say something else. I can't, because I still can't breathe, so he sighs a very small sigh and rubs the back of my hand with his thumb. I start to relax a little, but part of me also wants to resist the feeling. I don't know why.

"I guess I can teach a few classes on Skype," Mike says.

He stands up and tugs on my hand. I grab a croissant off the table and stick it in my mouth, then follow him back to the rickety elevator and watch as he presses the button for my floor. He leads me to the room next to mine, and inside. I can see that his laptop is on the small desk, and that his corduroy jacket is tossed on the double bed, but he folded it in half before he threw it. Mike walks to the back of the room and unlocks the nondescript wooden door against the wall separating our rooms. "This'll be open," he says. "If you need me. And if you need some space, you can leave yours closed. Okay?"

I wrestle with the pit in my stomach that could either be that second croissant or the feeling of impending doom, and I nod and walk into my room. There's a stack of books sitting on my desk, next to a laptop with a Post-it note in Thom's handwriting stuck to the screen. It says:

Username: C.S. Lewis

Password: The Great Divorce (case-sensitive)

Prime Minister Liora Reznik (née Reznikoff) was born in 1957 and spent her early years living on a kibbutz with her Labor Zionist parents, who had fled from Russia to Israel in the 1920s and were active in the attempt to free Jewish war refugees in the days of the British White Paper policy in Palestine. Liora attended secondary school in Jerusalem, and after her brief military service in a non-combat, field instructing unit, she attended university in Boston. Liora got a bachelor's degree in education and worked for a few years as a teacher in the United States. When her mother became ill, she decided to return to Israel. She continued to work as a teacher while helping care for her mother, but rejoined the Israel Defense Forces during the First Intifada. She hasn't spoken about this time in her life at all, especially not about her mother's death from her illness during the uprising, but biographers have suggested that it was during this time that she became disillusioned with Labor Zionism. After Reznik left the army again she joined the Likud party and was elected to the Knesset, working under the foreign minister. Her rise in the ranks was swift, and she held several prominent positions until becoming Prime Minister in 2014. According to Wikipedia.

Encouragingly, throughout the years, PM Reznik always expressed a desire for a 'peaceful, viable, two-state solution'. And yet, of course, that's what everyone claims to want, but there never seems to be any real progress. What keeps getting in the way? Okay, maybe it isn't easy to resolve, but it's not like it's complicated either, is it? Everyone understands what needs to happen. It's just a matter of dividing the assets of two parties who can't have a civilised interaction, isn't it? I wouldn't know anything about doing that – but I'm not sure anyone does, and I do know about a thousand ways not to do it, which at least narrows it down.

I think about the house Dad bought right after he moved out – the one across the street from Mom's. At the time, it was a decision I didn't understand at all. Then when he started using his proximity to Mom's to spy on my sisters, or to put lawn signs out to communicate with Mom after she'd blocked his messages, I thought it was about asserting his dominance. It was only several years later, when a therapist suggested an alternative interpretation, that I considered that maybe even Dad didn't want to leave what had been the epicentre of our family life. I left that therapy session in a daze, reeling from the implications of this more charitable interpretation of Dad's intentions. How many other things rippled out from this initial decision – to move so close to Mom – and how our initial impression of his motives could have coloured every single one of those decisions, too. His visits to the store, his invitations to dinner – if these things weren't an extension of his invasion of our life with Mom, if they were at least partly something else – how much could have been different.

It was my biggest mistake, I know now. Allowing the first interpretation – one that probably wasn't even mine, and wasn't necessarily right – to explain everything that came after. It was the bomb that set off the nuclear chain reaction that blew up my entire family, leaving us scattered and broken, strewn across the country.

I feel anxiety blossoming in my abdomen, and it feels like I've sprung a leak internally and something hot is spilling into the space around my guts. If I can avoid repeating that mistake now, it doesn't seem likely that I will make the situation in the Middle East any worse than it already is. I look back at the computer screen, which has gone black in the time I've gotten distracted. My reflection is myself, but at age seventeen – dark circles under my eyes, and a suggestion of puffiness. I wonder whether Thom packed my concealer so I can look less like the hot mess my therapist once told me I was when I meet the Prime Minister of the State of Israel.

The thought makes me laugh.

EIGHT

The thing about this crappy hotel is that when we arrived, it must have been Friday night – Shabbat. I didn't notice at the time, but I'm noticing now. Because it's late on Saturday night, the sun has gone all the way down, and what was a very quiet fourth-floor room is now set to a soundtrack of jazz music from a bar next door, at ground level. The occasional brassy sounds drifting upward wouldn't even register to someone who's a good sleeper, but I'm a bad sleeper. I think about going down to the reception desk to complain, but the guy there seems to resent having to turn his attention away from whatever he watches on his smartphone.

And it's not like I think I can ask him to go close the bar next door on my account.

When a quick consultation of the digital clock on the nightstand tells me I've been staring at the ceiling for forty-five minutes, I throw the duvet off and stand, unsure what to do with myself. The only book I have with me is the one I brought for what I thought was an hour-long flight to a job interview – a battered, paperback copy of *Anne of Green Gables* that I read when I'm stressed out. Only it wasn't working, not even when I thought it was just an interview. It's too familiar, so there's not enough to focus on to distract me from my worry. And I tried to buy a crime novel in the airport, but I was thwarted by the Delta employee with the fantastic eyebrows when she came to upgrade me.

I should have known that I'd pay for that in some way or another. Airlines don't give away anything for free.

I walk over to my desk, looking for something to occupy myself with, but all that's there is the dreaded binder full of documents stamped 'TOP SECRET'. My stomach clenches a little at the thought of them.

A light knock on the door between our rooms tells me Mike is sleeping, and I decide I don't know what I'd say to him anyway, so instead I slip on the nearest shoes, which are unfortunately the heels I was wearing earlier – I would never have packed them myself, of course, because I know that they're excruciating, and I only keep them around like some kind of aspirational symbol. Thinking one day I might have a job that requires me to wear these shoes, or the Armani suit my dad gave me for graduation, 'for law school interviews'. But then Thom doesn't know that. Even Jess believes I sold the whole outfit to an upmarket second-hand shop in the East Village a couple of years ago.

I need to at least take a nap, but I know that if I don't get at least something done, I won't be able to. Wondering who they found to be the mediator – and picturing John

Kerry, or some blond guy named Sven, from Oslo – I flip through the papers. There's a CV, and the name on top says Sven Møkkalasset.

From Oslo.

Of course.

There's no photo, and I can't make sense of the words – too many Nordic characters – so I make a note to get Thom to give me a bio, and set it aside. I'm trying to fill out a comparison chart for the Israeli side and the Palestinian side when I name a column 'stance on occupation' and it occurs to me that I can't think of that word as a neutral choice. I cross out and rewrite three different synonyms for 'occupation' in my notes before I realise that everyone involved in this mediation is going to have to agree on some terminology before anything else can get done. It's all too easy for people who aren't emotionally involved in conflicts like these to dismiss word choice as a question of semantics, but everyone knows that if you're not clear on whether you are 'broken up' or 'on a break', the consequences could be as dire.

I make a list of the main points I think we will need to settle on. The first thing that comes to mind is what we will call my client's counterparties. I already know that they, and many people, would consider themselves Palestinians. But I suspect that among those who don't believe there's any such place as Palestine, the term 'Palestinians' is essentially a synonym for 'Martians' – entirely hypothetical, because as far as we know, nobody lives on Mars. Non-Jews who live in Israel are often referred to as 'Arab-Israelis', but although I haven't actually heard anyone say this, I feel certain that

Palestinians don't like that one, either – especially if they don't think Israel is a legitimate political entity.

But since the people who don't live within the widely recognised boundaries of the State of Israel cannot be included under any term that includes the suffix '-Israelis', it seems like opting for 'Palestinians' is the most reasonable course of action here. I don't think Liora Reznik is going to object to this, because that would be extremely petty and a terrible way to start this process – but, just in case, I jot down a justification that frames this term as the compromise choice, rather than a win for the Palestinians. After all, in British Mandate Palestine, everyone in the territory was a Palestinian, be they Jewish, Muslim or Christian. So, in a way, Palestinians were created by the same forces that created the State of Israel – and surely the Israeli prime minister would not want to find herself in the position of calling question to the validity of that? And if this point gives me a chance to get a dig in at James, well, it was certainly not my intention, but it would be wasteful not to take it.

Which leads me to the next bone of contention in this T-Rex skeleton's worth of them – what to call the creation of Israel. Again, I know what the Israelis want to go with here – Yom Ha'atzmaut, or Independence Day. While I don't know off the top of my head what exact term the Palestinians prefer here, I do recall that the British do not celebrate the Fourth of July, so I can imagine that they do not want to call it Independence Day. I scroll briefly through pro-Boycott, Divest and Sanction blogs, and discover that the preferred term is al-Nakba, which translates to 'Day of the Catastrophe'. I'm tempted to search for the term on Twitter, but Thom – or someone more competent – has blocked all the social media I can think of, and my old tricks to get around the firewalls in high school, like typing 'https' rather than 'http' before the URL, just yield exasperated-sounding error messages, like the laptop itself is disappointed in me. I could ask Mike to help, but then I'd really be procrastinating.

Day of the Catastrophe won't work, anyway. Obviously.

I think hard for a few minutes, but an elegant, noncommittal phrase isn't forthcoming. I write down 'The Events of 1948' as a placeholder, and hope to revisit it later. Maybe I will bounce some ideas off Mike when he gets back from teaching. I despair at how little I have accomplished – so much time lost to thinking about the words we'll use as the basis for discussions that will themselves be so fraught. It occurs to me that the best allegory for what we've been asked to do here in Jerusalem is found not in the Old Testament, but in Greek and Roman mythology – Sisyphus, rolling a stone up a hill, again and again, only for it to roll back down each time. It will be a miracle if none of us is crushed by the giant weight that is the Israeli–Palestinian conflict as it comes crashing back down on us at the end of each day's work.

I am skimming the same page for the third time before I spot it. In all fairness to me, I've been distracted, and who the hell reads footnotes, anyway? But there it is, in small but legible print at the bottom of the page:

The agreement reached in mediation is non-binding until ratified by the government of the United States of

America. The U.S. government reserves the authority to veto any arrangement that would threaten the national security or interests of the U.S., with respect to (but not limited to) the following: border drawing, border security, travel documents, travel authorization, weapons agreements, and admissions of liability—

I am on the hotel's phone, calling Alisha, before I can finish the list.

The phone rings twice, before a reedy male voice says, "Deputy Assistant Secretary Alisha Harris's direct line."

"Thom?"

"Ms Price?"

"Why are you answering Alisha's direct line?"

"All calls to her direct line are forwarded to my cell," Thom says.

"Well then it's not her direct line, is it? It's a direct line to you. And I do not want to talk to you. I want to speak to the Deputy Assistant Secretary of State. Are you the Deputy Assistant Secretary of State?"

"N-no. Sorry."

"Is she available?"

"What is it regarding?" Thom asks, scrambling for control.

"It is regarding a footnote on page thirty-seven of—"

"Wait! This isn't a secure line."

"But it's the direct line to the DAS!" I shout.

"But your line isn't. How are you calling, anyway?"

"I'm on the hotel phone. And I don't think that's how it works."

"Well, I'm not sure," Thom admits. "Wait – I thought we told the hotel to disconnect your phone."

"They did. I plugged it back in."

"Oh." Thom pauses. "I guess I'll transfer you. Hold on."

I don't know if the hold music was Thom's choice or Alisha's, but I'm anxiously listening to Bon Jovi's 'Livin' on a Prayer' for the third time when Alisha comes on and says, "Go for the DAS."

I clear my throat. "Hi, it's Emily."

"Emily. I thought we had your phone disconnected."

"They left the cord right by the jack."

"Oh." Alisha pauses. "Go ahead."

"Listen, about this footnote on page thirty-seven—"

Alisha chuckles a little. "I admit I've been expecting to hear from Thom, on your behalf, over this."

"Oh. Well, I'm working really hard over here, and I want to know what exactly the point of all of that is. If – by some miracle – we are able to reach an agreement, the president and maybe the prime minister, depending how the president feels, can just veto the whole thing?"

"Don't worry about it. The president wanted that in there as a precaution. We won't use it."

"Well, if you won't use it, why don't you get rid of it?"

"The Secretary of State would feel better if it's included."

"Then I need to speak to him, because I would feel better if it wasn't! I want to know why I should bother if I'm going to end up looking like—"

"Ms Price. Emily. Just go with it."

The line clicks dead.

I throw on a sweater and slip my heavy, metal room key into my pocket and close the door behind me.

Once outside my room, I realise I still don't know where I'm going, so I follow signs for ice. I don't know what it is people are doing with ice in hotel rooms, or why people who never need ice for any other occasion need to keep a bowl of it in their bedrooms when they travel. Maybe I'll understand if I get some, though, and it's not like I have any other ideas. I wish I had my phone with me, so I could at least stream an NPR podcast or something. NPR is good because it's interesting enough to give me something other than my own anxiety to focus on, but not interesting enough to keep me awake if I'm tired and my eyes are closed – and once I'm asleep, the honeyed voices of the hosts never wake me.

As I turn the hallway corner, still following the ice signs, I hear a metallic sound and I jump a little. I look up from the balding geometric rug and see a bald man's head poking out of a cracked door ahead of me. When we make eye contact, he retracts his head like a turtle and the door clicks shut. I stop and stare at the closed door when I draw level with it, but I don't see or hear anything. The hair on the back of my neck is still standing, though. I shake like a wet dog, hoping the paranoia will come off me like water. It doesn't, but I keep going.

The man was probably not watching me. Thom would have told me if these were the security measures he mentioned the other day, and there's no way someone not connected to Project Kramer could have gotten past everyone. I realise that I haven't seen any other people in this hotel since I arrived, which I assume was orchestrated by Thom – or nobody else wanted to stay in this dump. There is only so much skilled photography can do to make a crappy hotel look nice on Booking.com. I decide to stop thinking about it and at that moment it occurs to me I've lapped the whole floor and I'm back near my room. I somehow missed the ice machine entirely – or even this hotel is gaslighting me, putting up signs to see how long I'll walk around and around the narrow hallways looking for something that isn't there.

To be safe, though, I press the doorknob button to lock my main door, then push open the dividing door to Mike's room and climb into bed with him. He flinches a little when I flex my cold, aching feet and brush against his leg, but he doesn't wake up. I settle with my back pressed against his and go back to staring at the clock. I doze a little, but I dream that I get up to pee and hear noises coming from the bathtub. When I pull back the shower curtain, I see a tiny John Kerry in a tiny swiftboat – which in my dream, given that I don't know what swiftboats are exactly, is a canoe – yelling at veterans in other boats in the churning water of my bathtub. I wake up for real and realise that my bladder is about to burst.

NINE

When I wake up, the first thing I do is re-read the short bio of the mediator Thom had slipped under my door. He had scrawled a note that said 'A good guy – we wanted John Kerry at first, but we were lucky to get Møkkalasset'.

Sven Møkkalasset had first been educated at some fancy private school in Oslo, which Thom had noted taught classes in both English and Norwegian. He was the son of a diplomat, though Thom didn't specify what kind. He had studied at Columbian Law School – or, that's what the bio says, but it's got to be a typo – and though his discipline had been International Law, he also had taken several internships at firms concentrating in Family Law.

I was disappointed when I found out that Møkkalasset would be the mediator, because it made this all seem a little bit like Oslo III – and if you keep doing the same thing over and over, you get the same results. But Møkkalasset's experience sounds kind of perfect. And if we know that both sides will sit down with a Norwegian, why mess with what little about this process isn't broken? I'd tried to think of other countries that could have produced someone both sides would think of as impartial, and I drew a blank. Maybe another Scandinavian country, but in that case, we might as well go for a Norwegian. I glance at the clock and catapult myself out of my chair – I want to be extra early, so I can choose a power seat.

To my disgust, when I get to the first floor, armed with coffee and some pens, I find that James is already sitting down at the head of the table. Thom is in the room, too, and has left his belongings at the seat facing the door while he talks on his phone in the corner. Well, I may have lost my chance to decide where James sits, but I can still wrong-foot Thom. I walk across the room, ignoring James's smug expression and whispered quote from Sanchez's book about never letting your opponent beat you to a meeting, and shove Thom's stuff across the worn wooden table.

The carpets and furniture in this room are all old, but clean, and there's a stack of unopened office supplies on the table. I determinedly blank James, who is now talking to nobody about what a great night he had last night, at some ridiculous nightclub in Tel Aviv. A surreptitious glance out of the corner of my eye reveals, infuriatingly, that he is none the worse for wear. Whereas I got almost five full hours of sleep – as much as I've had since this whole thing started – and can't even remember any specific nightmares. I still had trouble getting out of bed this morning. I spin the palm tree-shaped pen I got after lunch with Mike and think about my dad. Whenever he got back from medical conferences in cool places like Vienna and Tallahassee, he always used to say that he hadn't really gotten a chance to see much of the place, and hand us a generic souvenir purchased in the airport. One time, he brought back a feather boa from Phoenix, which didn't make a whole lot of sense even then, and I was seven. But now I think I understand how he could have been to so many places but seen so little. I've been in Israel for a few days now, but I could count on one hand the number of times I've gotten beyond the hotel lobby – and this is before the negotiations have even started in earnest. It's starting to feel like my whole world is this shitty business hotel, Mike, Thom and Yossi.

The fact that I'm not listening has not deterred James from talking, so I sigh theatrically and look up at him. "Do you think we could get to work now, and choose a mediator?"

Unrelenting asshole that he is, James grins and leans back so that his chair is resting on two back legs.

I hope it falls and he cracks his head open. I realise my testy attitude is something my old riding teacher would have described as 'feeling my oats' if I were a horse, and consider reining it in. But it feels good to be more annoyed than anxious again.

"Thom?" His eyes dart in my direction, and he holds up a finger to tell me to wait, though he doesn't turn to face me. "*Thom?*" I say louder, and this time, he holds his phone to his chest.

"Sorry, I'll be right with you, Ms Price," Thom says. "I'm speaking to the DAS."

"Okay," I say, throwing a smug expression of my own over my shoulder at James. "Tell Alisha hello from me."

"She says hi back," Thom says, without speaking into his phone again.

"Close, personal friends, are you?" James asks.

I blush. "Let's just get down to it," I said. "We don't really need the DAS's goon."

"Yes, well. Are we absolutely certain that this Møkkalasset is the best person for the job? I've never even heard of him."

Thom snaps to attention at this. "Deputy Assistant Secretary Harris herself selected him," Thom says. "So if you're questioning his candidacy, you're questioning the United States government." Thom holds James's eye contact, looking more confident in his defence of Alisha than I've ever seen him.

"Far be it from me," James says, after a pause. "I don't see why not him. It matters very little who the mediator is. Only an idiot would fail to recognise the injustice of the current arrangement—"

"Oh, be quiet," I say. "He's not here yet."

"I'll make the call," Thom says.

I decide to go for a run. Fuelled by my anxiety, I'm jogging before I even reach the front door of the hotel. But just as I'm about to go outside someone grabs my sleeve. I look down at my hand, which is balled into a fist, and follow the arm that's grabbing it up until I see Thom.

"What are you doing?" he whispers. "You can't just leave."

"I have to go for a run."

"You can't. Not yet. There's some stuff I have to work

out with the local authorities before you can go anywhere alone."

"James gets to go out."

"No, he doesn't."

"You can't keep me trapped in here with—"

"I won't, okay? Only for another day or two."

I want to shout at him. I want to tell him to fuck off and go through those doors and run until I get to the airport. I want to tell him that even he wasn't convincing about my ability to handle this, and he's got incentive to be. Instead, I shake my hand free, and say, "Fine. You have one day. Then I start going wherever I want, and good luck stopping me."

TEN

When I head downstairs for my big meeting, the sun is doing its thing so aggressively that I lift a hand to shield my eyes as I pass by the little hallway windows. Determined to do better than yesterday, I arrange the water glasses, coasters, notepads and pens opposite each other in the middle of the table, and then rearrange them at the head of the table and the seat to its right. I sit at the head of the table, change my mind and move over. Then, I think better of that – am I ceding too much power to my client before I even meet her? I wouldn't want her to think I'm intimidated, which I am not. The temperature inside the conference room is set to polar vortex. Still, I feel the odd bead of sweat prickle at my temples and the base of my neck, hopefully obscured by my hair.

There are fifteen minutes left until PM Reznik is supposed to arrive. I consider making some coffee but decide that caffeine is a bad idea considering my current heart rate, and the fact that I've taken another beta-blocker from my dwindling supply. Reading over my notes seems like a good idea, but I can't seem to sit still. I pull out the BlackBerry Thom has given me, which has several restrictions on it, including programming that prevents me from being able to call the US – as I'd discovered when I tried to call Jess the previous night. "What is this, 2006?" I snapped at Thom when I shook it out of the padded yellow envelope he'd given me. He shrugged and darted off down the hallway before I could say anything else. I still don't know where he sleeps at night – I suspect he's also staying in the hotel, keeping an eye on me and maybe also on James, but I never run into him.

I try to play with my cell phone fossil, just for something to do with my hands, but there never were any decent games for BlackBerry. I've run out of things to do to the conference table itself, so I pace around the perimeter and look for things to fiddle with. There is a vase of bougainvillaea on the cart with the kettle and coffee pot. I yank out one of the branches of magenta flowers, and the whole thing topples over. Instinctively, I catch it, but no water spills out. The lurid, cheery flowers are good fakes; they're made of convincing silk, but they have no scent to them. Even the water, which had appeared to fill the vase three-quarters of the way, is fake. I touch it, and it is repulsively gelatinous and sticky.

"Shalom!" says the prime minister, voice crackly like an old PA system, and throws her arms out wide. "Nu?" she says when I freeze, uncertain what to do. "Come," she commands, and I shove the branch I'd torn out of the fake bouquet back into the arrangement and step hesitantly towards her. She draws me into a strong hug, and then shoves me away and holds me at arm's length to examine me. She could be any one of my old Hebrew teachers: loud, intimidating, abrasive, but also – at least physically – soft. Over her shoulder, I see some people that I assume are her bodyguards shut the door, and I see their shadows settle into position through the crack at the bottom of the door. She lets go of me and tosses a bag of Bamba snacks on the table, and herself into the chair at the head of the table. So much for that, I think of my plan to sit there.

Ms Reznik has opened the Bamba and popped one into her mouth before I've been able to gather myself. The peanut smell infiltrates my nose and mouth, and I feel a surge of nausea, undoubtedly connected to the time Mrs Waterman went to Israel and brought back a family-sized bag for each student – I'd loved them so much I ate the whole thing and then spent the whole night vomiting. "So," she says, crunching on the disgusting food. "I read your list." She raises her eyebrows and tsks, and pops another noxious puff into her mouth.

My heart tumbles into my stomach. "Oh?" I croak, thudding into my seat and making a pained face as she holds the bag of Bamba out.

Ms Reznik shrugs and tucks it under her left arm, brushing the beige powder off onto an astonishingly similarly coloured pair of trousers, and pulling a pen out of her breast pocket. She opens her own folio, also beige – can she actually like beige; can anyone? – and I see a printout of my ideas about terms and strategy. She has put lines through every one of the items under the subheading 'Potential Concessions'. She is quiet and appears to be refreshing her memory before speaking.

"Ah," she says. "Only once, I will say this." She looks me dead in the eye. "Israel will have sovereignty over all of Jerusalem, total control of Israel's borders and the roads between the West Bank and Gaza, and retain all predominantly Jewish settlements and the homes occupied by Israelis for two or more generations, even if they may or may not have once belonged to Palestinians – this, we will also not accept or refute. And also Palestine will agree that there will be no compensation, reparations or financial transactions of any kind, and no admissions or concessions or acceptance of any guilt, blame, or fault on the part of the State of Israel—"

"But—" I object.

"I am not talking?" Ms Reznik asks, all wide-eyed indignation. I shut my mouth.

"The State of Palestine will not ever be allowed to form any alliances with neighbouring Arab countries, have a nuclear programme or maintain an active-duty military larger than ten thousand troops," Ms Reznik goes on. "Israel will not agree to any disarmament programmes, reductions in foreign aid or any other agreements that impinge on Israel's sovereignty. Any unflattering comparisons to Apartheid South Africa, Nazi Germany or any other bad guys will not be tolerated. And also," Ms Reznik says, catching her breath, "the first thing Palestine will do is apologise to Israel."

"Okay," I say, taking a deep breath of my own and launching into my prepared speech. "First, let me just say it's an honour to meet you, Prime Minister—"

PM Reznik scoffs. "Call me Liora. It will save time. And get to the point."

"Okay. Liora," I say, but it sounds completely wrong, and I shudder. "Prime Minister, I appreciate your thoughts, but I think we need to have a talk about principled negotiation. The high-road approach."

Liora Reznik leans back and tosses another Bamba into her mouth, then inclines her head imperiously. "I am listening," she says.

Back in my room, I reach into the bag of barbecue-flavoured Bissli and frown when I touch the empty bottom of it. I must have been eating it on autopilot. It would explain my slight nausea. But I still feel the urge to put something in my mouth, so I tilt my desk chair over until I can reach the minibar and reach blindly into the basket of non-perishables. I come up with a bag of mixed nuts, which feels a little sarcastic. I don't even like them, but it doesn't matter. I pop open the bag and brush the cloud of salt and peanut dust off my notes and try to refocus.

Thom has sent me an email to let me know that I'm cleared to leave the hotel – but that I should consider only going out with Mike or someone else – and ask if there's anything he could do for me. I realise that my worries about Jess and Poco had gotten buried under my paranoid conspiracy theories about a network of spies watching my every move, but his email reminds me, so I ask him to make sure Jess is getting part of my pay cheque for my share of the rent and to pay the bills for Poco on my behalf.

Thom has already taken care of it. He forwards me receipts for grain, board and extra shavings – the kind Poco prefers – and the reply from Jess saying she had received the bank deposit.

With Poco accounted for, I can turn my attention to the other thing that's bothering me – the one I don't want to talk to Thom about yet. I close the laptop, turn the page I was writing on over and start a new list. I make some columns on the lined paper and write down 'Time' and 'Location' at the top. I jot down the sightings I've had of the bald man so far, to the best of my memory, fogged as it is by lack of sleep. At the top of the page, I write 'BM', so that if Thom or Mike were to catch sight of my notes they wouldn't know what they are. BM could be anything – bowel movement, Bat Mitzvah, British Museum, Barry Manilow, baby mama.

Thinking like this makes me feel jumpy, so I put down my mixed nuts, stand up and walk around my little room while stretching my arms across my chest like how we used to warm up for gym class. Then, impulsively, I look through the little peephole in the door – and just as quickly, pull away from the lens, because the BM is there. Instantly my heart is racing and my stomach is churning, but before I can second-guess myself, I wrench open the door. The doorknob slips a little in my sweaty hand, but it opens. There's no one there.

I crane my neck in both directions to see as far down the hallway in either direction as I can without stepping across the threshold. It's irrational, like staying firmly under the covers at night as if it imbues you with some magical protection against monsters, but I can't help it, and I wonder if I'm seeing things. You can die from not sleeping enough, and even though I've been tired enough to fall asleep, I haven't been able to sleep long enough or well enough to be sure I'm not dying, or at least hallucinating. My legs are frozen, but when I hear, "Hey!", I jump.

It's only Mike.

"What are you doing?" he asks.

"Waiting for you," I say, with a little breathless laugh.

"Okay," he says.

I stay frozen.

"Are you going to let me in?" he prompts, adjusting his bag on his shoulder.

"Right. Yes." I stand aside and let him walk past me. I follow him in, closing and latching the door behind me and trying to clear away the wrappers from my desk and close my binder in one motion.

I can see that Mike is about to ask another question, so I ask one first. "Mike, what do you think of" – I think fast – "Establishment Day, as a nonpartisan term for what Israelis would call Independence Day, and Palestinians would call the Nakba?"

"It's serviceable, but inelegant," he says, ducking into his room to put his things down and giving me a light peck on the cheek before perching himself at the edge of my bed. I watch him gingerly shove aside a growing pile of stuff I had left at the foot of the bed – also unmade, because I have left the 'Do Not Disturb' placard on the door since I saw Yossi talking to the BM – but he doesn't say anything and makes a heroic attempt to hide his judgement. I love him for doing it. Love that he does it, I mean.

"Serviceable but inelegant," I repeat, smiling a little. "That should be my motto."

"Nonsense." Mike looks behind him, moves a few more things out of the way and leans back on his hands, extending his feet out in front of him and crossing them at the ankle. "I think you're very elegant. This is just an inelegant position that you're in, being asked to do the impossible."

"It's not over until it all goes up in flames. Which could happen at any moment." I feel this in a literal sense; it feels a lot like when we'd stay at Dad's house in California and get these warnings that we might have to evacuate because of encroaching wildfires. The smoke always looked like it was headed in our direction, even when it wasn't. "But anyway," I say, doing my best to shake off my unease, "how was your Skype class?"

"Mostly the usual," Mike says. "I talked at the eighty per cent of my students who show up and called on the twenty per cent whose names I remember. Some of the students did seem to forget that I could also see them on Skype, though. If only I could digitally confiscate phones. And, of course, I couldn't hold office hours, though nobody ever comes."

"I always came to office hours," I remind him.

"That was the only reason I kept them."

"That, and that smarmy dean would have personally garrotted you with his bow-tie if you hadn't."

Mike laughs. "That, too." He kicks off his shoes. "So that's the news from Lake Wobegon. Can you take a break? It's dinner-time. We could see if Thom will let us walk to the Old City, find somewhere to sit outside. Might inspire you."

"I do like that, but I don't know," I waffle. "I've barely gotten anything done at all, and I have to meet with the prime minister again as soon as possible to go over how to approach the first mediation in a few days." It takes a while to realise what the next sound I make is – but I'm laughing, and after a moment of looking taken aback, Mike is laughing, too.

Mike is the first to get ahold of himself. "Sorry. I'm not laughing at you. I'm laughing at the situation. Anyway, you should eat," he says. "And you're not going to figure it all out in one week."

"You don't have to apologise. I was laughing too." I look at the snack wrappers on the desk. "I'm not very hungry right now. And I wanted to make a little more progress on this list before I take a break. Borders, settlements, money, Jerusalem, international recognition..." I wave a hand hopelessly at my desk. "I've barely skimmed the surface."

"But you couldn't have done any of that before what you worked on today," Mike says reasonably. "You didn't waste your time. You were building the foundation. Can't build the house until you've built a strong foundation, or the whole thing will come crashing down."

"That might happen anyway," I say, leaning over my desk and resting my face in my hands. They smell like a mixture of barbecue and peanuts. It's revolting.

"Not with you on the case. If there's a solution out there, you'll find it. So, let's go downstairs and see what Yossi can rustle up for dinner."

"Thanks, Watson."

"Any time, Holmes," he says, and I follow him out the door.

ELEVEN

Over breakfast hummus, Mike asks me where I disappeared to last night. He says he woke up to pee sometime in the middle of the night and I wasn't there anymore, so he checked my room, but I wasn't there either. He tried to wait up for me, but he fell asleep and didn't hear me come back in.

The truth was that I couldn't sleep at all, and I didn't want to disturb him, so I'd sat in the lobby and tried to brush up on mediation procedure. And the reason I couldn't sleep was threefold: first, ever since the thought occurred to me that not seeing the BM around was actually more sinister than spotting him, I can't get rid of it. Second, the stupid jazz music. And third, I suspect that my client doesn't like me. And that bothers me a lot, on both a professional and personal level. I suspect this because she hasn't been taking my calls at all for two days, even though I tried to get through several times to talk to her about the mediator, Møkkalasset, which seems like an important discussion for me to have with her – not least because I imagine that she could get a better background check on him from the Mossad or something than I can from Thom or Google. And when I asked Thom about it, he said she had things going on that weren't relevant to the case and couldn't be discussed with me. "Does she not like me?" I asked Thom. "Does she think I'm underqualified?" But Thom had dodged the question and just said he couldn't discuss it with me, but that I should focus on the case.

I told Mike all this, but he said that of course the Prime Minister of Israel would be busy, and I should try not to take things so personally. Of course I didn't want to wake him up and tell him what was on my mind last night.

"Is it the her 'not liking you' thing still?" Mike asks. "I'm really sure that's not what's happening. I'm sure everything's fine."

I try to tell him again that things aren't 'fine', but like last night, he doesn't listen to me. "This is impossible," I tell him. "The BM – I mean, PM – won't listen to me at all, and now you won't even listen to me about how she won't listen to me!"

"Even if she didn't have a lot of confidence in you yet, once you've spent more time working with her, she'll see how capable and intuitive you are," Mike insists, but it only makes me angrier.

The rage, coffee and adrenaline are swirling around in my otherwise empty stomach and making me feel ill again. I take a few deep breaths in through my mouth before I answer. "I know you 'love me' or whatever," I say, glaring at him, "but stop lying. I can't even convince my client to take my calls. She hangs up on me – or worse, has her staff hang up on me – but acts like barking 'yalla bye' at me before she does it means it doesn't count as hanging up on me."

"She's difficult," Mike concedes, ignoring my barb.

"She's fine. I'm the problem."

"Of all the things that could be blamed for the lack of peace in the Middle East, Em, you aren't one of them."

I tsk at him in disgust.

"Emily, I can honestly say I don't think there's anyone out there who would be equipped to handle this. You could have done everything your father told you, and you wouldn't necessarily be any more prepared to do what you've been asked to do here."

I look at him evenly. "There's someone watching me," I say.

"I think…" Mike trails off. "You're tired," he says.

I take a beta-blocker passive-aggressively, maintaining eye contact with Mike while I swallow it. "Forget it. I'm going to head out. Thom is sending me on another useless sightseeing trip to occupy me. He's pretending it's important. Don't," I preempt Mike, who looks ready to argue with that point, too.

He doesn't. Instead, he asks if I'm sure I don't want any company, but I give him A Look and he backs off. "It isn't your fault that Reznik isn't answering the phone," he repeats.

"I know." I stuff a cardigan into my purse and zip up my short boots – the closest thing to appropriate footwear that Thom or whoever had packed.

"I really wouldn't mind coming with you," Mike tries again, watching as I put on my sunglasses.

But right now, I would mind.

When I stop for a coffee with Wilcox, who's driving me wherever I'm going, I spot a flyer with a horse on it on the bulletin board. I ask the barista to translate the poster for me, which she does. It's a major Arabian horse show, and it's not too far away – about a forty-minute drive, maybe fifty, depending on the driver, she says. I deserve to go somewhere interesting, rather than to look at some wall, after how cooped up I've been. It's even wearing on Mike, being stuck in that hotel. I snap a grainy photo of the address with my shitty BlackBerry and show it to Wilcox. I tell him the photo came from Thom, and I'm ready to babble on about why I'm going to a horse show, but he doesn't ask any questions; he just puts the new address in his phone.

I've never much liked Arabian horses – their dished faces, narrow bodies and lifted tails smack of haughtiness to me – but then, I guess that's what some people love about them. And regardless, I'm struck by the sight of some two hundred magnificent horses when I step out of the car with tinted windows, which is inevitably being driven by the very same Agent Wilcox who brought me to my interview for this job. "This is amazing," I say to him as he offers me a hand and my bag.

"It sure is," Wilcox says, and I can tell he means it because his eyes linger on the gleaming horses being led to and from show rings by casually dressed handlers, and he makes no immediate move to leave.

"I don't mind if you want to watch with me," I tell him, with only the smallest hint of guilt that I'd said the opposite thing to Mike just half an hour ago.

"I'll be nearby, but I won't get in your way." Wilcox touches the brim of his hat, and I lift a hand in a silent thank-you gesture and head off.

I take a seat on a bench under some shade along the side of one of the main show rings. My surroundings are both familiar and foreign, and it, or the intense sunshine, is giving me a headache. It's like a hand wrapping around my brain and squeezing it. I take a drink from the chilled water bottle Wilcox had handed me in the car, and look around.

Just like at any horse show I've ever been to, there are people in boots and polo shirts leading shiny Arabians back and forth between trailers, stalls and arenas. There are longe lines, whips and saddles thrown on top of or leaning against fences, like there would be anywhere else. The horses are as well-presented as any I've ever seen at a show in the United States or Europe, though I don't think I've ever seen as many Arabians – we'd just call them 'Arabs' back in New York, but I think I'd better be more specific here – in one place before. The people, however, are less well-appointed. There are altogether more faded jeans than I'd see at the Dressage at Devon, and people are cheering and clapping noisily in the stands and at tables in cordoned-off VIP sections. I can hear several languages being spoken, and while it's clear that some of the people who came are Hebrew-speaking Israelis and others are Arab-Israelis or Palestinians, people do not seem to have self-segregated by nationality. English seems to be the language of choice for the various groups to communicate with each other, and I find I'm surprised by how lightly accented the English of some of the speakers is.

Although all the horses are stunning, even to a non-breed aficionado like me, there is one who turns heads as he's led into the ring in front of me, wearing a skinny leather bridle with a silver chain under the noseband. He's a stallion, iridescent black, and though he is more or less complying with the young man leading him, I can tell he won't be for long. He holds his tail lifted away from his body, and the curve of his neck is exaggerated, his nose ghosting his chest. His nostrils are flared, and his ears pinned flat against his neck. In one graceful, violent motion, he explodes from his coil of tension into a magnificent rear, striking out with his forelegs and – for lack of a better phrase – screaming his head off.

I must have said something aloud, because the man resting one boot on the bench beside me gestures at the stallion with his own water bottle and says, "He is Dammar – it means Destructive One," and smiles at me.

"He's…" I start, but I'm at a loss for words. The young man handling the horse has stepped aside, and is waiting for him to settle without administering any punishment.

"He is very naughty," the man says, "but very beautiful. He comes from a small family breeder, near Be'er Sheva."

"Really?" I'm surprised by this. From the way people in Israel and abroad talk about it, the Palestinian community seems too – well, poor – for anyone to be breeding quality horses there.

The man reads my surprise correctly. "For Palestinians," he says, "raising horses is not the hobby of the rich and idle, like it is in Europe and the United States."

He says it casually, and seems not to intend to offend me, so I let it go. "I'm Emily."

"Ahmed." He nods at Dammar, who is back on the ground, but pawing at the dirt, making a cloud of dust, as people cheer for him. "Maybe we are not so polite here as at your horse shows," he says, "but it is a good atmosphere here. The Arabian horse has his magic. We do not care here who you are or where you come from. We care only about the pedigree."

I consider this. "But you must face some difficulties. The political situation – it has to have some impact."

Ahmed wipes his brow with a rag from his back pocket. "Sometimes," he says.

I press him, carefully. "Do you have problems bringing the horses to Israel, from Palestine?"

"A mare died once, at a checkpoint." Ahmed pauses and takes a drink from his water bottle. He looks at Dammar, who has calmed down a little and is standing still, but with his head raised like a giraffe. "It was too hot in the box, and she waited too long. The vet could not reach her in time."

"That's horrible," I say, truly feeling it. I look down at the dusty ground.

"It was a very sorry thing," Ahmed says. "But the Israeli breeders who heard were very sorry, too. They donated the stud fee for a very famous stallion in Jerusalem, so the owner could breed his other mare. The colt is that one." Ahmed points to Dammar again. "It is not a replacement. But it is something."

"It's really something," I agree. "He's something."

"He is my brother's," he adds.

"Dammar?"

"Yes. He has a farm in the south."

"You must be very proud," I say.

"I think they will take my brother's farm," he says. "The Israelis. They are going to build a road to the big settlement nearby."

"But they can't just take it," I protest.

He looks at me for a minute. Then, he looks back at the horses. "Even your government can take land to build a road."

"Eminent domain," I guess. "But they should pay for it, at least."

"Perhaps they will pay him, but my family has lived there for many generations. Our horses have lived there for many more. And he," he says, lifting his chin in Dammar's direction, "may not adjust well to a move."

"What makes you think they're going to take it?" I ask. Maybe I can help. I don't want anything bad to happen to any more horses. Especially not any more of his family's horses.

"Some men came, asked to look around. They said they wanted to buy some property. My brother told them it was not for sale, and they went away. But they came back. He found them on his land when he was checking the fences early in the morning. He told them to leave again, but the next day he woke up and some soldiers were blocking his back fields."

"Why?"

"They said for security. My brother did not argue. He is not stupid."

I don't want to offer my help, because if I can't do anything, I don't want to disappoint him. So, instead, I ask if I can come see Dammar sometime soon.

Ahmed looks at me with an assessing gaze and says, "I will tell my brother to expect an American girl."

"We have to go, ma'am," Wilcox says, reappearing.

"Now?" I ask.

"You're not supposed to be here," he says, pressing his lips together.

"I'll leave after this class finishes."

"Now," Wilcox says, and steps closer, like he's going to scoop me up if I don't come myself, so I do.

When we get to the car, Wilcox glares at me in the rearview mirror.

"What?" I ask him.

"You told me Mr Newhouse said you were permitted to come here," he answers, in a voice that says I'm Not Mad, Just Disappointed.

"Well, they couldn't give me a good reason."

"It seemed like they had one to me," Wilcox says, and he passive-aggressively turns on the radio.

I don't know why they're acting like it's such a big deal that I went to a horse show. I mean, it's not like I said anything I shouldn't have. And if they can't give me a good reason not to go, I'm going to go visit that farm, too.

I must have fallen asleep along the way, because we are stopped at a gas station and Wilcox is shaking me by the arm. "What's wrong?" I ask him.

"You were having a bad dream," Wilcox says, removing his hand. "You were yelling about dead horses."

"Remind me not to watch *The Godfather* again," I mumble, sitting up straighter and looking away from him.

Out of the corner of my eye, I see him touch his cap before he closes the door emphatically, but without slamming it, and gets back into the driver's seat. We drive on in silence for a few minutes, before Wilcox says, "Ma'am?" and catches my eye in the rearview mirror. "*The Godfather* is overrated."

TWELVE

"Well, that was nice," I say, flinging my purse on the bed. Mike chose one of his favourite, hole-in-the-wall places in Jerusalem for dinner. It was American-themed in an almost culturally insensitive way that makes you wonder about your favourite ethnic food restaurants back home. How many paw-waving golden cats are there on counters in restaurants in China, anyway? But there were forty different types of beer on tap, which seemed to excite Mike, though he mercifully said nothing else about beer all night, and the onion rings were not nearly as 'horribly disappointing' as TripAdvisor reviewer FlatbushFoodie72 had led me to expect – they were moderately disappointing, but I ate them all anyway.

We did not, however, go to the restaurant. We made it to the door, all dressed and everything, and Thom appeared out of nowhere to stop us. After I made it clear that I was either eating onion rings or quitting, Thom went and fetched us takeout – even a beer, somehow. The concierge, Yossi, let him set it all on a table for us in the breakfast room.

"I'm glad you liked it," Mike says, picking up my purse and draping it over the back of my desk chair. "You've been working hard."

"The onion rings were actually all right." I throw my jean jacket on the bed.

Mike picks up my jean jacket and drapes it over the back of the chair, too. Out of curiosity, I take off my sandals and throw them on the bed. "What are you doing?" asks Mike.

"Nothing."

Mike picks the sandals up and places them between the desk and the closet. I am down to my dress, so I have nothing else left to throw on the bed. I watch as Mike takes off his own sweater and shoes, slides his wallet out from his back pocket, and puts it on my desk, next to my binder. Then he sits down on the bed, looks at me and pats the spot next to him.

I sit down. It's uncomfortable to sit when my stomach is this full. "I thought the game was that we weren't letting anything touch the bed."

"What?" Mike is scooting closer.

"You know, like the game we played with your cousins the time we babysat them together. The bed is lava."

"What are you talking about?"

"You kept moving everything I put on the bed."

Mike laughs and leans in to kiss me.

I let him for a minute, and then I pull back. "So the bed isn't super-hot lava?"

"You're super-hot lava," he says, wrapping an arm around my waist and coming at me again.

"Gross." I wriggle out of his grasp and stand up.

"Couldn't resist," Mike says, grinning. "Sorry. But you do look amazing tonight. I like this dress." He fingers an end of the bow of my dress and tugs on it so that it begins to come free.

"What are you doing?"

"What does it look like? Taking your dress off."

I clamp a hand over the knot before it can come undone. Mike lets go. "Do you want me to stop?"

"No – yes!"

"What's wrong?" he asks, standing.

"Nothing's wrong with me!"

"I didn't say anything was wrong with you. I meant, are you okay?"

"Of course I am," I say tersely. "It's just very late. Dinner took a long time, and I have a lot of work to do. So if you don't mind" – I gather up Mike's things and dump them into his hands – "I'll see you in the morning."

"Okay," Mike says, and he looks back at me once as he goes through the door between our rooms.

I close my adjoining door but leave it unlatched. I look around my empty and plain room, and I decide it would be more stressful not to work than to at least try and work a little. I take a beta-blocker, trying hard not to count how many I have left, and open my binder.

Eventually I realise that I'm staring at my notes but not reading the words, and I close my binder in defeat.

This is exhausting, and I've barely even done anything yet. Now even being with Mike is exhausting, though it's not like I'm not happy he's here. I'm just not happy he's always so nearby he's practically on top of me, not tonight, when he's trying so hard to be on top of me.

When I collapse into bed, having transcended exhaustion, I do manage to fall asleep – without even needing to stream any public radio or take another beta-blocker. As soon as I do, I dream that I am hosting a press conference in the White House briefing room, and my mom, my dad, Maxi, Gabby and Zara are all here. They're firing questions at me that I can't answer.

"Think, hon. What year were the Oslo Accords signed?" Mom asks.

"Ninety-three?" I try.

"Wrong!" Dad yells. "Why don't you ever make a goddamn effort, after all this money I spent on your education—"

Maxi is wearing her tailored lab coat and stethoscope. "Why is your stomach hurting?" she asks accusatorily.

"I don't know!" I say.

"Then you're going to need an enema," she says, holding some tubes up menacingly. And then she lunges at me, and I wake up, rush to the bathroom, and vomit some identifiable onion rings into the toilet.

THIRTEEN

I have basically not stopped eating since I got here. I have also not stopped drinking coffee, which is what happens when you haven't started sleeping. My stomach feels like an overfilled balloon. I think I can hear the coffee and buffet croissants sloshing around in there.

I decide to change into looser clothes after breakfast.

When I get back to my room, I notice that there is a manila envelope with a handwritten note paper-clipped to it on the floor. I pick it up, and see that it's signed 'JB'.

Dear Emily,

I'm glad everything is sorted re: mediator. Please review these interrogatories from my client and be advised that we will be proceeding straightaway.

You'll note that the formatting on the docs is a bit odd; my client insisted we use the Microsoft Word font Al Tarikh even though we are conducting all communication in English. It has made the text kerning slightly strange, but I have every faith in your ability to make out the words. My client also graciously extends you the offer of submitting your responses in 'Arial Hebrew' or even 'Arial Hebrew Scholar'. It will be equally difficult for us to read.

Best,

JB (Room 802)

If you had asked me before I got this note, I would've said that I'm capable of divorcing my personal feelings from my work. Even when it comes to, well, divorces.

Well, that was before.

There is a lot of overlap between the rules for dealing with smug assholes in life and in divorce. The set of guidelines Helen and Alisha gave us all made it clear that this would not be the kind of legal proceedings I'm used to, but that we would prepare as we normally would for a formal – and binding – mediation. So I'm going to treat this like any other case I've ever handled, which is zero, and the client like any other, except way more important. I sit down and compose a reply.

Dear 'James,'

My client and I find this communication very hostile and immature. We have every intention of being forthcoming and will review and respond to your questions as soon as you present them to us in a normal, serif, Latin font.

Worst,

Ms Price

(How did you get my room number?)

I am slipping this note under James's door when it opens so fast it makes a whoosh. "Emily!" James says. He is wearing only a towel slung loosely around his hips, exposing sparse hair that is a shocking black against the white of his chest, and trails down his midline until it meets terrycloth and disappears. I can't help but notice that he is very sinewy, and his hip flexors are extraordinarily defined.

"What can I do for you?" James asks.

"Nothing," I say, shaking my head forcefully and locking my eyes on his face. "And everything I have to say is in my note. So, bye."

"Well, hang on – you can't have had time to review these questions with your client and provide complete responses."

"No, I did not. But as you'll see when you read my note, that is explained."

James starts to say something, but I add, "Do not contact my client directly. And I think we should confine all of our communication to the page, from now on. Everything must be in writing and sent to me. God help all of us if Prime Minister Reznik had seen your stupid note."

He raises his eyebrows at me and bends to pick up my note. He reads, and begins to chuckle. "You might just know what you're doing after all," James says.

For a moment, I am panicked. Does he know? But James has a satisfied smirk on his stupid pointy face that tells me he thinks he's rattled me, and that that was all he'd meant by his remark.

As far as whether I do in fact know what I'm doing, I admit I was sceptical when Thom argued that the fact that

I'm not technically a lawyer shouldn't prevent me from getting a chance to represent Prime Minister Reznik and the Israeli interests, since these are not technically legal proceedings. But James has no right to be sceptical. He has no reason to assume I'm anything other than great at my job. And who does he think he is? The Brits don't own Israel anymore. None of us have any actual power here at all, not really. If we want a real say in Israeli policy, we will have to go to America and donate to AIPAC like everyone else.

"Of course I know what I'm doing," I say, crossing my arms and staring at him coolly.

"Right. Of course. It doesn't do to underestimate one's opponent."

"It would be the last thing you ever did."

"That's the spirit," he says, pinching my cheek.

I am growing very tired of men trying to manhandle me. I reach out and yank his towel free. It pools at his feet. He looks momentarily surprised, cheeks pinking, but he recovers and crosses his arms nonchalantly, leaving the towel on the floor. I consider myself lucky that I am in fact blinded by rage. But to be safe, I raise my gaze, making my eyes slide from his slender feet to the shiny, coiffed black hair of his head quickly, like I am seeing in fast-forward, and pivot on one foot. I am halfway down the hall before I hear him call out, "Underestimating you is a mistake I won't make again, Ms Price."

The hallway fire door swings shut behind me, muffling James's laughter.

I guess the good news is that I feel very awake.

I stomp back to my room as fast as I can, fast enough that my heart thudding in my chest drowns out my brain, and I get to work before I have time to think about it. My leg bounces under my desk as I sort through the resources Thom gave me, and settle on *Fuck Me? Fuck YOU!* by John Sanchez, JD. It's a contentious divorce guide for dummies by some lawyer who says he always makes his client's ex cry at least once in court, like that's an accomplishment.

I last a few minutes, but the rage and panic are making me nauseous, and so I slam the book shut and put my head in my hands. I don't have time to learn a whole new set of skills. Horrible, shiny-haired James may be right that I don't know what I'm doing. But there are a few things I do know that might help me out here. One of those things is that direct communication between the parties is a bad idea. After a while of receiving notes from Dad, Mom would try asking him to stop, refusing to respond, throwing them straight into the lit fireplace, sending them back with me or my sisters in pieces and making threats, but that only made it worse. My dad and his attorney could see how much it rattled her, and once they knew it was working, they had no reason to stop. I know I was right to put the kibosh on James's nasty little games before they could get to my client. Me, I can handle it. It's nothing personal for me, so he can't rattle me. But I'm sure Liora would have seen that note for the condescension it was, and had it made its way directly into her hands, this whole thing would be over before it really starts.

People used to talk about staying together for the sake of the children, but of course that never worked. Keeping the divorce proceedings civil for the sake of the children never worked, either. But this case might prove that there's another option: conduct the divorce negotiations in absolute secrecy. Don't mention it at all until the ink is dry on a deal. They'll still have to live with whatever the adults decide, but at least they'll be spared first-hand knowledge of just how horrible their parents are. It's the moment they hear you arguing over who gets the oriental rug and how much child support will be paid for how long on paper that the trouble starts. That's when they start having the kids deliver maintenance checks and spying on each other. Otherwise, as any child from a dysfunctional home will tell you, Mommy and Daddy fighting is business as usual. Absolutely nobody other than the government attachés, relevant heads of state and appointed counsel can know this is going on. That means no change to the levels of tension and dysfunction that already exist. Nothing that will make the lives of the people any more difficult or cause them to act out any more than usual. No calls from concerned teachers asking why little Billy seems to have started wetting himself at naptime or why sweet Jane punched another girl in the face in the cafeteria, seemingly unprovoked. Just matter-of-fact negotiations in a closed room and a swift adjustment to a new normal that is better than before.

Look at me now. A disappointment to both Mom and Dad. Not quite a lawyer, but not quite not, in that same purgatory gefilte fish inhabits as a not-quite-edible food.

But still, thanks to them, a certifiable expert in un-amicable divorces.

And litigating the case of the millennium.

A rustling noise distracts me from my thoughts, and I follow the movement I see in my peripheral vision to the door to my room. Another note, also covered in James's spidery scrawl. I open the door and will my lungs to capacity with shouting air, but he's gone. It has gotten dark in my room, with the curtains drawn and night beginning to fall, and my pupils blow out the minute I open the door. I stand in the doorway to read it by the light of the hallway lamps.

Ms Price,

I'm so terribly sorry for my appalling behaviour earlier. If you will allow me, I would like to make amends.

I ran across your delightful friend, Mike, and he mentioned that you might forget to eat if you're working. I made a reservation for you at the restaurant next door for eight o'clock tonight. I asked them to give you your favourite drink, with my compliments.

I have exchanged words with my client, and we will be resubmitting our questions, in a legible font, but not until tomorrow morning. Enjoy yourself tonight. This city really is spectacular in the evening – Jerusalem of Gold, indeed.

Best,
James

I tear a sheet from my legal pad and start to write, "No thanks, asshole," but I change my mind. Instead, I fold up the paper, insert it into my place in the middle of 'Chapter 2: Getting a Douche to Disclose' and head into the bathroom. In the weak, too-hot shower, I decide that I will order at least five cocktails, even though neither Mike nor I could ever drink that many, because that's the fastest way to run up a bill. There's no better way to make a divorce lawyer pay for his sins than financially.

FOURTEEN

Mike has the smug look of someone who has already exercised, showered and read five major international newspapers in five languages before anyone else managed to get their eyes open. I watch him for a minute while I finish waking up, not saying anything. He's wearing chinos and a tucked-in blue shirt, with the top three buttons undone and without a tie – his teaching uniform – and organising papers into stacks on his desk. He glances over his shoulder at me, sees that I'm awake and looks back at his papers.

"When did you get to bed last night?" he asks, not looking at me.

"After I gave up looking for the ice again. Three-ish. Maybe four."

He doesn't say anything else and keeps fiddling with his papers. I know he's avoiding looking at me, because that's how I look when I'm doing the same thing. I push myself into a sitting position and yawn. It's very bright in the room, and I can feel some warmth in the sunlight coming through the windows. "What time is it?" I ask, even though the clock is right there, just to have something to say.

"Almost nine," Mike says.

"And you've already been on the treadmill and read the major newspapers?"

Mike half-turns his face to me, and one of the corners of his mouth turns up a little. "Graded papers, this morning," he says, gesturing at the stacks of paper in front of him.

"What time is your Skype class today?" I ask, thinking about breakfast.

"Not until three."

"Good, then you have time for breakfast," I say, yawning again and jumping out of bed.

"Actually," Mike says, turning around for the first time since I woke up and crossing his arms. "I was hoping you might finally be ready to talk about—"

"There's still a man watching me," I blurt out.

"What?"

"The other night, when I went to go get ice, I saw that guy watching me, and when he saw me looking at him he hid," I say in one breath. "I think we need to change rooms."

"What on earth did you need ice for?" Mike asks.

"I don't know."

Mike presses closed his eyes again. "Emily," he says, rubbing his index and middle fingers in small circles against his temples, "please stop it."

"Stop what? I'm trying to tell you that—"

"Just stop it. Stop derailing the conversation. Even I have my limits."

I take a step back and wrap my sweater around myself. "I know."

"You can't just drop me and not talk to me for months and then pick me up again on a whim," he says, and he opens his eyes and looks directly into mine. "And this – I don't know what you're doing here, or why you agreed to this, but you have to know that this is not what I meant when I said you should take more risks and push yourself a little."

"I don't—"

Mike holds up a finger and keeps talking. "I've met your parents. I know that your under-achieving has something to do with revenge, or proving your dad right."

"It's not—!"

"I'm still not done talking," Mike says, and speaking of my dad, he sounds so like him in that moment that I feel cold for a minute, like there's a breeze inside somehow. "I have never tried to change you, or control you. I've always only wanted to help you. I also know you're not telling me everything now, because I know you. I'm not here to rescue you, but I am here to help. So if you'll start talking to me like a human fucking being, and stop making up crazy stories to deflect hard conversations, that's what I'll try and do."

I am quiet for a moment. "Okay," I say. "Sorry."

"Don't say it if you don't know what you're saying it for."

"I do."

Mike nods once and starts putting his papers in his bag. "Come on," he says. "The hotel stops serving breakfast at ten."

I nod and head for my room to get presentable, and

Mike adds, "If it'll make you feel better, we can talk to that concierge about switching rooms."

"No, I do not understand," I tell Yossi.

"Okay. So, I will show you," he says, and turns the screen around, highlighting the 'additional notes' section in the spreadsheet he is showing me. It says:

> *If by chance Ms Price requests to switch rooms for any reason, please do not allow it. Many thanks.*

"Who said that?" I ask.

"I don't know her name. She looked like, eh, the British lady – *eich kor'im lach?*"

"Helen Mirren?" I guess.

Yossi narrows his eyes. "*Aht m'daberet Ivrit?*"

"A little," I concede. "*K'tzat.*"

"*Lamah k'tzat?*" Yossi asks accusatorily.

"Because the girls in Hebrew school were mean and the teachers were worse."

"Why you don't move to Israel, learn Hebrew?"

"I'm not such a huge fan of falafel."

Yossi purses his lips disapprovingly and looks back at the monitor. I notice an empty nose piercing in his right nostril. A lot of young people here, men and women alike, have pierced noses. I wonder if someone made him take his nose ring out for work, or for his military service, or if he just got tired of it.

"The English lady who told you I can't switch rooms," I tried again. "She looked like Helen Mirren?"

Yossi nods.

"I see." I do not see. "Here's the thing – she doesn't know why I need to switch rooms. I didn't want to say anything before, but there's roaches in my room. Big, flying roaches!"

"*Mah zeh*, roaches. We have not roaches in this hotel! The King Solomon is very clean."

"Okay, fine. I'll tell you the truth. It's one of your other guests. He's bothering me."

"Who? What he did?"

"James Browning, on the same floor. He put a note under my door."

Yossi looks at me as if to ask, 'so?'

"I don't want to talk to him," I say.

"So don't talk to him," Yossi counters.

"*Touché.*"

I am waiting on an overstuffed love seat in the lobby, hiding behind a newspaper, for the concierge's shift change – something I can only assume happens, even though I've only ever seen Yossi around – and that's why I don't see James until he's practically on top of me.

"Morning, Ms Price!" he says, entirely too cheerfully. I peek out from under my newspaper, which is in Hebrew, and I'm realising now I've been flipping the pages in the wrong direction. I see pointy, shiny shoes and the bottom of some tapered trousers.

"Savile Row's finest," I grouch, feeling self-conscious in my inexpensive pants, though I am grateful for how the Lycra component has accommodated my stress-eating this morning.

"Oh, you can call me James," he chirps.

"Okay, Jim. Jimmy Jams. Jimbo. Ji—"

"Or not," James says.

"What do you want?"

"I was just wondering about last night," James says.

For a second, I think he's asking about my run-in with the bald man. I lower my newspaper and look for signs that he knows something weird is going on. "It was fine," I say, and raise it back in front of my face.

"How were the piña coladas?"

I relax a little. If he hasn't noticed anything, maybe I made it up. "You'd have to ask Mike."

"Really?"

"Why, because I'm a woman, so I must have had the piña coladas and Mike must have had the Glenlivet?"

"No, because there were three of them on the tab, and ordering three seventy-shekel cocktails to spite me seems like something you would do."

Touché again. "Well, you don't know Mike."

"He seems," James pauses, and I lower my paper again so I can glare at him, "nice."

"He is nice," I confirm, still refusing to take the bait, or worse – say thank you. "I like nice. Not that that's any of your business."

"So, you had a lovely time. I'm glad to hear it." He looks at me expectantly. I raise my newspaper to block my face again, but it's too late to prevent him from seeing me blush. I hear him chuckle all the way back to the elevators.

When it dings and I hear the doors open and shut again, I put my inscrutable paper down and sneak a look at reception. Yossi is still there, and when we make eye contact over the shoulder of a bald man he is talking to, he gives me a look that suggests he would not be very impressed by further attempts to persuade him to change my room.

I can feel the pain starting in my temples again. I'm going to need another espresso *hafukh*, which means 'upside-down coffee', but is basically a cappuccino, or sometimes a latte, depending on where you go – Yossi explained this the other day, when I was trying to read the hotel coffee maker's helpfully provided but inept English translation of the user guide – so I take another beta-blocker pre-emptively. Yossi said the reason it's called an upside-down coffee is because there is more milk than coffee in it, and then launched into a confusing anecdote involving cross-dressing on Purim – Jewish Halloween – which can also be described using the term '*hafukh*'.

I am anxious to avoid another one of Yossi's anecdotes.

As I stomp off to the buffet area, I wonder if the bald man with Yossi is the one I saw the other night. But there must be a lot of bald people in Israel, too, so I resist the urge to turn around and check – but I decide that anecdotes or no anecdotes, I won't let my guard down with Yossi, either.

FIFTEEN

Mike knocks on the adjoining door on his way out for the day. "Dinner tonight?" he asks. "Thom said we could go out now, right? With pre-approval?"

I glance up from my work to acknowledge him, but then I get back to it. "Yeah, he said we just need an escort now. But I can't, sorry. Maybe a late dinner, but I might be tired. We're meeting Møkkalasset today. Me and James." I still haven't been able to get in touch with Liora to talk about him, and Mike still doesn't agree with me that this is a big deal. I don't want to argue about that again, so I don't say anything about it. I turn a page and highlight a line of *Fuck Me? Fuck YOU!* that reads, "Always demand at least one thing you don't actually care about so they can't tell what's most important to you."

"You spend more time with James than me," Mike says.

"Don't be such a baby." I don't even glance at him this time, figuring that barely deserves a response at all, but that I'd better nip this nonsense in the bud.

It seems like Mike wants to argue with me, however, and is still standing there, pouting.

"It's work," I add.

Mike sighs. "I know," he says. "I'm just not sure why I'm here if you don't want to see me at all."

"I don't not want to see you," I say, and I frown. That came out wrong. I repeat the words in my head, and nod a little. It was clunky, but more or less what I meant to say.

"At least let me know when you might be done?"

"I'll try."

"Okay." He pauses. "Have a good meeting."

"Thanks. Have a good class."

I'm as prepared as I'm ever going to be to meet Sven Møkkalasset. There's really not much information out there about him. I've done the best I can. I've read his website over and over – the website is a slick but basic WordPress site, just a homepage and a contact page. The only associated physical address is a PO box with a New York zip code.

Google did turn up a few interesting results, however: like a *New York Post* cover story from 1998, detailing the successful settlement of a custody dispute that centred on a prominent, wealthy Manhattan couple's pair of French bulldogs. The quoted lawyer represented the husband, who brought the suit against his wife after a dispute brought mediation proceedings to a halt. The pair would split custody of the two dogs, rather than each taking one, as the wife had originally wanted and her husband had argued would constitute animal cruelty. The story was called 'Ain't Divorce a Bitch', and someone called Sven Møkkalasset was quoted in it as saying, "It's all about what's best for the dogs." The story also mentions that the lawyer argued his entire case with his pet cocker spaniel on his lap, having produced documentation of his status as an emotional support animal to the bailiff, who initially tried to prevent it from entering the courtroom.

This can't be the Møkkalasset I'm going to be working with, though – it just doesn't fit. This is not the slick Norwegian diplomat Thom described. But it's too bad. Crazy animal people are my people.

I am expecting a tall, thin, pale man. He has blond hair and wears, in my imagination, ski pants over a fitted charcoal suit.

It makes sense that the man in front of me is not wearing ski pants, but it does not make sense that he is short and round, and distinctly Danny DeVito-esque. I look at James, who is standing five feet away from me, facing the door. His eyes are narrowed, and he's folding his arms. "You're not Sven Møkkalasset," I say to the man who just came through the door, and then hesitate. "Are you?"

"I am," he says.

"But you look all wrong," I say.

"*Ja*, well, we can't all be Pål Sverre," Møkkalasset says.

His accent is interesting – I've never heard anything like it. I guess I expected him to sound kind of German. He almost does, but by way of Staten Island. I realise that Møkkalasset has said a name. "I don't know who that is."

Møkkalasset rolls his eyes. "He is a very famous Norwegian actor."

I decide to start over. "Who's this?" I ask cheerfully, brightening as I lean down to greet the small dog under Møkkalasset's arm.

"This is Prince Charles. No relation," Møkkalasset says, as he shifts the dog under his left arm so that he is free to extend his right hand. I shake it, then I reach out and shake Prince Charles's paw. Møkkalasset grins.

James shakes Møkkalasset's hand, too, but doesn't touch the dog. Instead, he does a little bow and drawls, "Your Highness," at him. Prince Charles shows his teeth and growls a little.

"He doesn't like you," I say to James. "Smart dog," I add, stroking the wet nose with one finger.

"He likes you, though," Møkkalasset says.

"I love animals," I tell him, and take a photo of Poco out of my wallet to show him. "This is my horse. I've had him since I was sixteen. He goes everywhere with me, even to college, but he's back in New York right now and I miss him lots." It occurs to me, with a surge of panic, that his special feed needs to be re-ordered, or the barn might stick him on their standard grain, and he doesn't like it. He'll only dump it on the ground and start trying to kick the door down, and when I see him next time he'll be skinny and—

I close my eyes for a second and breathe deeply through my nose. This has already been taken care of. Thom showed me proof. Everything's fine.

"It's too bad you couldn't bring him here," Møkkalasset says, admiring Poco's blue eyes and two-tone coat, which is a lot like Prince Charles's coat.

James clears his throat. "Shall we?" he asks.

Møkkalasset looks irritated that our animal talk has been cut short so rudely, and I agree with him, but he nods and hands the picture back.

"Stairs, or lift?" James asks.

"What?" says Sven, sounding even more annoyed.

"He means 'elevator.'"

Møkkalasset sets Prince Charles down and affixes a leather leash to his bright blue collar. "What room?" he asks.

"Conference room 105, on the first floor," I say, and I point across the lobby at the elevator. Yossi is watching us from behind his desk, but he doesn't look troubled, and he doesn't come over to us – so I imagine that Thom must have forewarned and fore-bribed Yossi to allow Prince Charles to stay here. Thom has already brought Møkkalasset a key and whisked his luggage off to his room, and though he'd suggested Møkkalasset could go freshen up if he wished, he had seemed insulted by the suggestion and said he preferred to get right into it. Møkkalasset also reminded Thom that his government was paying him for all his time in Israel, no matter how he spent it, and accused Thom of wasting money by encouraging him to waste it by giving himself spa treatments. It's all very austere and Scandi.

Møkkalasset and Prince Charles are legging it to the stairs, so James and I fall into step behind them. "This is absurd," James mutters at me. "He's brought a fucking dog. This is ridiculous."

"So what?" I say, barely paying attention to him. "You're just touchy because the dog is a good judge of character."

"I am not 'touchy,'" James says. "I just don't think he's an appropriate choice."

"Whatever. The Norwegians are very good at this sort of thing. They've done it so many times before," I say, nodding at Møkkalasset, but unable to resist doing a quick scan of the area for the BM. I've been relieved not to have seen him for a few days, but now I'm starting to worry that not seeing him is a bad sign. Maybe if I went for another walk around the hotel alone, I might see the BM – and with any luck, I'd find the courage to confront him. After all, enough is enough.

"Yes," says James. "Except it didn't work any of those times. So it's a bit like saying Jeremy Corbyn is great at standing for prime minister. Or, to put it in terms you can understand, it's like saying Ralph Nader is great at running for president."

I glare at James as Møkkalasset ushers me through the conference room door. James catches it before it swings shut and gestures at me to go ahead, but I refuse. He sighs and goes ahead. Møkkalasset sits down at the head of the table and lifts Prince Charles onto his lap. The dog rests his chin on the table. James sits down, leaving an empty seat between Møkkalasset and himself. Møkkalasset seems to notice but doesn't say anything. Still, I make a point of sitting right next to him and drawing my chair even closer so that I can stroke Prince Charles's head. It has a calming effect on me that's not unlike the beta-blockers' effect, which I'm not sure is real or imagined because I once read an article that said studies proved having pets lowers their owners' heart rates. Either way, I am grateful, because I am running seriously low. It's getting harder and harder not to count them when I slip one out of the pill case. I will have to start psyching myself up to ask Thom for some more, even though I'm embarrassed to be so reliant on them.

James's lips are pressed so tightly together that they have disappeared, and this makes me smile, but I turn away from him and look at Møkkalasset.

Sven Møkkalasset clears his throat. "Okay. Let me tell you guys how this is gonna go," he says, glaring at James. "Firstly. My courtroom, my rules. *Ja?*"

I guess Møkkalasset's time in New York has rubbed off on him. "*Ja*, Mr Møkkalasset," I say, at the same time as James says, "This isn't a courtroom."

"Call me Sven," Møkkalasset says. "Not you," he says to James, unnecessarily.

"Mr Møkkalasset," James says, puffing himself up with indignation and wounded pride. "I'm very concerned—"

"Browning," says Møkkalasset. "I am talking now. We will have our first meeting in three days. You will both come prepared to discuss one issue for each meeting. You will stay on topic, and you will ensure that your clients do the same. Talk amongst yourselves in your own time to decide which topic we'll tackle first, and submit your arguments, in writing, twenty-four hours in advance. Got it?"

"Got it," I say.

James sticks his tongue between his teeth and his upper lip and juts his chin, but then nods once.

"Great," says Sven. "Now, you shoo."

I shoo, feeling pleased. I hear James calling after me in the hallway, saying something about needing to have a discussion, but I pretend not to. I'm practically skipping.

Thom is preoccupied with Møkkalasset, so there's a window of opportunity. I don't want to get Wilcox in trouble again, though, so I ask Yossi to arrange a taxi for me, now that he's seen me leave the hotel. He doesn't ask any questions, but I'm prepared to explain that Wilcox has a flat tire if I need to. I know that he doesn't have a way of reaching Wilcox directly, and Thom never seems to be anywhere to be found. It was annoying at first, but now I'm relieved.

Ahmed's brother's farm is right outside Be'er Sheva, a large town in the desert that's halfway between Gaza and the West Bank. I Googled it on the way over and found that *Lonely Planet* says of it that, "The only compelling reason for travellers to visit is to transfer between the train service that comes from the north and the bus services heading south." I look out the window a bit and see nothing to challenge that assertion.

The taxi driver's GPS says something to him and he hits the brakes hard and takes a very sharp turn onto an unpaved path. There's a gate halfway down the drive, so the taxi stops. The driver turns around and looks at me balefully. "Here's fine," I tell him. He asks for 120 shekels.

"Yossi said you agreed to eighty."

"Yes, but with the traffic, and this dust…" he says, gesturing around him.

"It's a desert. There's going to be dust. And I only brought eighty," I lie.

"Okay, *b'seder*," the driver says, with a 'what can you do?' kind of hand gesture.

I climb out of the cab and pass the twenty-shekel notes through the window. The driver executes a questionable three-point turn and disappears.

I look at the gate nervously, but see it only has a chain looped around the gate and fed through a metal divot, just like the ones we use at Poco's barn. There's no padlock, and since there doesn't seem to be anyone around, I slip my hand through the bars and unwrap the chain.

"You're the American girl," I hear a man's voice say. I whip my head around and trip a little at the sound of it. I find the man sitting on a plastic mounting block to my left, smoking a cigarette and watching some horses eating hay in a bare, dusty paddock.

"Emily." I exhale, trying to calm down.

"Farooq," he answers. "You met my brother."

"Yeah, I guess. He said it would be all right if I came to see Dammar?" I say, like it's a question.

Farooq inhales cigarette smoke deep down into his lungs and stares at me, like his brother did, and lets it out in a series of dainty smoke rings.

"So... is it all right?" I ask, trying not to breathe in the smoke.

Farooq drops his cigarette in the dust and grinds it out with the heel of his boot. Then he picks it up again and tucks it into the pocket of his jeans, and adjusts the brim of his cap. "So, let's go," he says, and walks towards a ramshackle building with a tin roof.

I wonder if I should say anything, but I can't think of anything to say. Farooq makes me nervous. I can't tell if he minds that I'm here or not. And I do want to see Dammar, and see if I can find out anything about what Ahmed was referring to.

"You are a journalist?" he asks as I follow him into the barn. It's filled with familiar sounds and smells: horses chewing, sweet grain, cats leaping onto bins of supplies.

"No, not a journalist."

"NGO?"

"Uh, no."

"Why have you come?"

"Um… I'm Jewish," I say.

Farooq scoffs.

"I didn't mean it like that, I just meant it's sort of like… a pilgrimage, you know?"

Farooq stops in front of a stall and I blink as my eyes adjust to the lack of light. Eventually, the darkness inside starts to take the shape of Dammar. He is turned away from us, with his head in the corner of his stall. I can see from his uneven hips that he has one hoof cocked. He cranes his neck around to look at us, and as it gets closer to the aisle, the low light is enough to show that his ears are pinned flat against his head.

Farooq rolls his eyes at him. I grin.

"He is beautiful, but he has a bad attitude," Farooq says, slipping a slender leather halter with a nose chain off a hook.

"Well, who doesn't?" I watch Farooq, but he pauses, turns to me appraisingly and then holds out the halter. "Me?" I ask, leaning away from his outstretched hand a little.

Farooq shakes the halter at me in reply.

I take a deep breath, trying to wrangle my nerves so

that Dammar won't sense my stress and think he ought to be all worked up, too. I slide the bolt on the stall door open, and Dammar's left ear rotates in the direction of the sound. "Hello, gorgeous," I say in a low, quiet voice, reaching out a hand slowly to lay it on his flank. I take one slow step so that I'm not directly behind him, in the prime kicking zone, but then wait for him to react. He turns his head a little, but doesn't shift his weight or show his teeth, and his ears are pricked upright and alert. I take slow, small steps towards his head, trailing my hand along his ribcage as I do, and stand still so he can check me out. I pass referencing, after a few bumps of his nose in the general area of my pockets, and when he blows out a puff of air and a little snot through his nostrils, I reach my right hand under his head and slip the halter on.

Dammar resists a little when I tug on the chain, letting his neck bend to follow my hand, but not moving his feet. I tug again without looking back at him, and hear him shift his weight and take a few steps to turn around. "Where to?" I ask Farooq, who is watching with his arms crossed and the same blank expression on his face. He leads me to the small paddock we passed on the way to the barn, which is dusty and hot. I look over my shoulder, where I can see larger, empty paddocks with at least some greenery and shade stretching back into the distance behind the barn. But Farooq opens the little paddock's gate and stands aside, so I lead Dammar inside. I'm not sure what Farooq wants me to do, but I see that he's holding the gate closed behind me, so I turn Dammar to face it and slip off the halter. I step back, and he tosses his head and trots off with big, showy paces, each leg remaining suspended at the height of its trajectory for a half second, like an Olympic dressage horse executing a passage. His tail is lifted high, his neck is curved dramatically and his coat has a high-gloss sheen in the sunlight.

Farooq and I watch him prance around in silence for a few moments, admiring what is the most flamboyant beast of burden I've ever seen. I'm uncomfortable when people are quiet for too long, because I don't like what I can imagine them thinking. But Farooq's silence feels friendly enough, so I clear my throat a little. "Farooq," I start hesitantly, "Ahmed said you were worried that some people might take your farm?"

He blinks at me.

"That the Israelis might take your farm," I correct, looking him in the eye. "Do you know why?"

"Why not?" he asks.

I wait.

"But, probably for a road, for the new settlement in the West Bank, not so far from here."

I nod and watch Dammar again. He's scratching his ear on a fence post. "Do you think I could maybe have a look at the part of your land where you saw the people looking around?"

"They have put up tape. They said it is forbidden to enter. My own land!"

I hesitate. "But if you don't mind…"

"Do what you like. They will not shoot you."

"Sorry."

Farooq shrugs very much like Liora would, I think, in a universal Semitic gesture that says, 'what can you do?'

"I don't want to promise anything, I just think I have a friend that could help."

Farooq nods at the field without looking at me, so I shield my eyes from the sun and head in the direction of the enclosures. When I get to the top of the hill behind the barn, I can see the cordon that Farooq mentioned. The tape is wrapped around some palm trees, and I can't determine acreage just by looking, but it's a lot of land that's cut off. I can see big water troughs that appear to have been kicked out of the way, though of what, I can't tell. I start down the hill, shielding my eyes and staring into the distance – and then I trip and stumble.

Cursing, I look around for the rock I must have tripped on, but it's not a rock – it's a plastic device that looks like a walkie-talkie, with a long stem. I pick it up and blow off some of the dirt. It doesn't seem to be broken, but the digital screen stays blank, so it might have lost its battery. I take it with me and look around a little, but I don't see any other clues, so I call the taxi driver to come back for me and return to Farooq, who is doing something to an old truck. I slip the gadget into my bag before I call out a goodbye to him, and yell that I'll be in touch as I climb into the taxi.

SIXTEEN

"Where were you?" James asks when I return.

"Be'er Sheva."

"Why? That place is the Milton Keynes of Israel."

"I don't know what that means," I tell him, and slide past him for the stairs.

In his room, Mike is grading essays again. I know that's what he's doing because he's frowning at the papers in his hands and there's a purple pen sticking out of the corner of his mouth. Purple is his grading pen, because red is too harsh and blue is too friendly, but the combination of the two stands out from the black type just enough not to be either.

"I need to talk to Jess," I say.

He looks up and takes the pen out of his mouth. "Okay. Why?"

"I need her to come up with an environmental reason to tell Liora why she can't let her government seize that farm I told you about," I explain.

"Okay... no, I need more," Mike says.

121

"I told you, there's this horse farm, and the guy I met at that show, Ahmed, he said his brother was being given the run-around by some suits who were poking around on his land and then came back with soldiers and cordoned off a bunch of his fields."

"And?"

"And something bad happened to one of his horses once, and it was Israel's fault. The government's. The other horse people gave him another horse – well, sort of – and, Mike, he's incredible, you should have seen—"

"I'm sure he is, but so what?"

"So, I think they should leave this guy and his horses alone. They can build their road or whatever somewhere else. The thing is that I know Liora, and she won't want to lose face, so she'll need a reason that makes her look good if she's going to change her mind about something. I think Jess can help me come up with something. Oh – do you know what this is?" I show him the radio-like gadget I found at the farm.

"No."

"Neither do I. But anyway, Jess will probably know."

"Wait a minute," Mike says, "doesn't Jess work in marketing?"

"Yeah, but it's marketing for some environmental group. And she's Jess. She knows things," I tell him.

"Do you want to see if Thom will let you call her?"

I hesitate. I'm not sure what kind of reaction Thom will have to this request – or Jess, for that matter. And I honestly don't think I will be able to take it if she tells me this is my problem, or that I should walk away from the whole mess. I'm already full of doubt and half-regurgitated stomach acid.

"Or I can send her an email, say you're not able to talk but that you need her here," Mike offers. "I got through Thom's software. I'm just not sure if someone will notice, so I'm not using it much so I don't draw attention to it in case we need it for something. But I can get through to Jess."

I smile gratefully at him. "Would you?"

"Done," Mike says.

Jess will be able to help, I decide. And I would like it if she came for other reasons, too. She always seems to know if I'm being dramatic or paranoid or not.

"Good news," Mike says minutes later, interrupting my reading of a poorly translated Hebrew article about Israeli government land seizures since 1967. Any interruption of that is automatically good news, but I feel a blade of hope poke its way through the concrete lining around my heart.

"Jess was thrilled to hear from me," Mike elaborates. "Well, not at first – what did you tell her when we broke up?"

"Um, nothing, why?" I ask.

"Well, anyway – she was glad to hear from me, or from you, really. And she'd love to come here. She says she had the best time on Birthright and always meant to come back."

"Typical Jess."

"She thinks she might be able to help, too, of course."

"When's she coming?"

"Apparently, she hasn't taken a vacation in over a year,

so her boss at the Sierra Club said she could go right away and take as much time as she needs. So, she'll be on a plane tomorrow."

"Wow, great!"

"She'll text updates to my email, through iCloud. I wasn't sure if she would be able to stay here – so I said she could stay at my apartment. I'll have her meet my office mate at work so he can give her a key. I'll text you where to meet her."

"Thank you, Mike," I say earnestly. "I'm going to go downstairs, get coffee, call Farooq and let him know I'll be coming by again soon, with Jess."

I skip down the stairs, feeling like I'm finally making progress on something.

And then I stop dead in my tracks because through the frosted window of the door to another meeting room, I see the fuzzy but familiar outline of a bald white head, and Thom over its shoulders. Thom looks out the window and through a horizontal stripe of clear glass, we lock eyes, and he frowns.

Thom has an explanation. Of course he does. He makes me feel very silly when he explains it all, in fact. "You didn't think I was the only person here to look out for you, after all, did you?" he asks.

"Of course not." That's exactly what I'd thought.

"And you can understand why I might not have wanted to burden you with the knowledge of how many people it takes to run Project Kramer, right?"

"You could have introduced us," I say, biting back my

anger, because I don't want him to know how much stress this caused me, and being angry would be a dead giveaway.

His mouth stops short of saying 'Silly girl', but his face doesn't.

"Excuse me if my life experience tells me that men sneakily following me around aren't usually doing it for my health."

"I can introduce you now," he offers.

"No. I don't like him. Get someone else to protect me."

"But Anderson is our best guy."

"I'll settle for second-best."

Thom sighs. "I'll have to clear it with the DAS," he says, and waits, as if I might rethink my decision because of all the trouble I'm causing him.

I don't. He has caused all this trouble for himself.

"Fine," he says, when it's clear to us both that I'm not going to say anything else. "But this is completely irrational—"

"Don't gaslight me!" I snap. "Do not. I am having a perfectly reasonable reaction to being followed around by a strange man." I know this to be true. I had no reason to think that Thom would hide it from me if he had other staff watching me – watching out for me – in the hotel. What was I supposed to think? I'm not overreacting, I'm just reacting. And if Thom had deigned to tell me what was going on, or Mike hadn't dismissed what I was seeing entirely, maybe it would have occurred to me that the BM – Anderson – was with us.

"Thom," I continue, in a calmer voice, because I need him to know that I am serious, "you need to tell me right now if there's anything else going on that I don't know about." I'm thinking about the cancellations, and the difficulty getting ahold of Liora, but I don't give it away in case there's anything else.

"Like what?" Thom asks, putting on an innocent face.

"Anything at all," I say, determined.

"There's really nothing else," Thom says.

"Then I can expect to see my client when?"

"Tomorrow."

"Tomorrow?"

"Yes."

"I can't even get ahold of her on the phone for days and days, and now just like that she'll be here tomorrow?"

"It's not just like that. I was going to tell you. That's what I was discussing with Anderson, in fact. Giving him a heads up, you know, as security personnel."

I look him up and down contemptuously, and walk away.

SEVENTEEN

So we finally meet for our first official round of negotiations. Liora and I had breakfast together in the morning, along with two of her silent bodyguards, and went over our strategy again, but she was solid: we're staying on the high road. No being combative, no yelling and no threats.

And she made sure that I was clear on which issues were absolute deal breakers for her, and what was negotiable. I just have to remember that after hearing me out, she decided she still wants everything she wants.

Otherwise, she's prepared to compromise.

And she would have me know that if it were actually important to discuss who the mediator was, she would have taken my calls. But it isn't, because any idiot can see that she's going to win on the merits of her argument.

Two men in suits – probably Barghouti's – are standing on either side of the door already, and they too exchange blank looks with Liora's two as they shuffle around to let us pass. I take a beta-blocker on the way into the room.

We sit down around the little wooden table in the room

on the first floor again. Sven Møkkalasset is already seated at the head of the table – with Prince Charles on his lap – and Thom is standing behind him wearing a Bluetooth headset and holding a clipboard. James and Mahmoud Barghouti are sitting, too, but James half-rises and nods at us when Liora and I walk in. It's crowded with all of us in here, and not for the first time, I find myself wondering why a hotel like this even has meeting rooms.

"Remember," I whisper to Liora one last time as I close the door behind her. "Non-combative."

"Here, take a seat," Thom says, pulling out a chair for Liora.

"Why not? She's taken everything else in my country," Barghouti says to James under his breath.

Thankfully, Liora doesn't seem to have heard, but she has sensed that whatever he said wasn't a friendly overture. She prepares to say something, and I decide I'd better beat her to it. "Excuse me, what was that?" I ask in the politest tone I can muster. "Didn't quite catch it."

Sven clears his throat. "Let's just start," he says. "Who wants to go first?"

"I will start," Liora says. "We will be keeping Jerusalem. All of it."

"Liora!" I admonish. "What did we just agree?"

"What? I'm not being combative," she says. "I'm being straightforward."

"That's the same thing and you know it."

"You will keep Jerusalem over my stinking corpse!" says Barghouti, leaping to his feet so quickly his chair falls over behind him.

"That can be swiftly arranged," says Liora, over-enunciating menacingly.

"Control your client," James snaps at me.

"Me control my client?" I say, outraged.

Bang! Bang! Bang! We all jump and look for the source of the noise.

Sven is banging a gavel on the table in a very non-Nordic display of emotion. "Shut up! Shut up!" he's yelling.

"Where did you get a gavel?" I ask him. "You're not a judge."

"I ordered it on Amazon," Sven says, looking extremely self-satisfied. "And I said, everyone shut the hell up!" He bangs the gavel three more times, sending drops of coffee flying out of his mug.

"Easy, Sven," I say. "You'll strain something."

"You are hearing this?" Barghouti asks James, incredulous.

"Sit down, Mr Barghouti," James says. He turns to me. "I don't think it's appropriate for you to be speaking to the mediator in such a familiar manner."

"I do not think it's appropriate for you to be such a condescending—" Liora starts.

"Liora!" I say. "But she's right. Don't be such an asshole."

James shoots Sven an aggrieved expression. "Your Honour—" he starts.

"Oh my God," I say. "He's not a judge."

"Order! Order! Be quiet!" Møkkalasset shouts, accentuating his words with bangs of his gavel. "Go on," he tells James.

"Your Honour," he says again, giving me a smug look.

"My client and I have some concerns about your ability to act as an impartial mediator given your... friendliness... towards opposing counsel."

I suppress a smile. I was worried about James having had an opportunity to strategise with his client about Sven, when I hadn't had the same chance. But if James thought calling Sven 'Your Honour' would generate enough goodwill for a comment like that, well, maybe not.

Obligingly, Sven inflates like a threatened porcupine. "You sayin' I can't be impartial?" he says, and his accent goes very strange – almost sounding like he's from the outer boroughs.

"No, no, nothing of the sort!" James says, holding his hands up and shaking his head, as Barghouti vigorously nods his head 'yes, that is what we're saying' next to him.

I scoff.

"We do not think at all that you have a problem being impartial," Liora says, laying a reassuring hand on Sven's arm.

"*Ja*, thanks," Sven says, straightening his tie with his free hand, then resting it on his dog's head.

"I'd take anything she says with a grain of Kosher salt," James mutters, looking at me. I narrow my eyes at him, but he holds my gaze.

Barghouti reminds us of his presence by announcing, "We are leaving!" He taps James's shoulder with the back of his hand. "This is a farce, and we will no longer participate."

"My client is absolutely right," James says, rising and slotting his papers back into his leather folio. "We will be raising our concerns with Helen." Barghouti tosses his keffiyeh over his shoulder as if it were long hair and glides out of the room. James follows, giving me a meaningful look as he closes the door behind him.

There is stunned silence for a few seconds after he leaves. Thom decides to break it. "Wow," he says, laughing constipatedly. "That escalated fast!"

I shake my head and turn to Liora. "Look, don't worry. I wouldn't put too much stock in any declarations made by a guy who wears open-toed sandals. Or his goon."

"*Mah zeh*, 'goon'?" asks Liora.

"If you look it up in an English dictionary, there will be a photo of James next to the word," I explain, stuffing my pile of papers back into my purse.

Liora turns her hard, evaluating stare on me for a moment, then shrugs. "*B'seder*," she says. Then she wheels around abruptly and points at Sven. "You will fix this," she tells him in her usual no-nonsense Israeli tone.

"Nothing to fix," Møkkalasset says, leaning back in his chair and slurping his coffee. "I will summon you back to the table when you are all ready to be reasonable."

"See? There's no problem," I say. "Anyway, they're bluffing. And James going along with Barghouti like that is just him handling his client. He knows there's no way they're getting their hands on Jerusalem, and they have nothing to negotiate with."

We leave Sven in the somewhat capable hands of Thom, to whom he is dictating a long and complicated dinner order. "We dodged a bullet there," I tell Liora as we squeeze into the tiny elevator. "There's no way Thom is going to get that right, and something tells me Møkkalasset gets very irritable when he's hungry."

"Only when he is hungry?" Liora asks.

"Look at you," I say. "You're getting irony! Let's try that in the next meeting, instead of the direct approach."

I decide to find Wilcox and go for a walk after I put Liora in her car. It's still light out, and though I'm tired, I'm buzzing with nervous energy. It doesn't feel great, but it feels better than being paralysed with nerves. Mike doesn't answer his phone, so I leave him a message saying that I'm going to be in the Old City and that he should meet me there.

On my way out of my room, I see movement out of the corner of my eye. I feel a little chill run up my spine. I tell myself I'm being crazy again, but ever since Thom told me that the BM was undercover security, I've been looking twice at everyone I see, and feeling eyes on me. It doesn't help that Mike was even more dismissive of my anger, when I recounted my conversation with Thom to him, than he was of my fears in the first place. I take a deep breath and walk to the corner of the hall.

Sven is pacing at the end of the hallway, talking into a cell phone. I try to walk by him quickly, since he doesn't have Prince Charles with him, and because he's on the phone. As I get closer, he stops talking and gives me a little smile – but the moment the door to the stairwell swings shut, he starts up again. He sounds different than usual – I think I hear him say something like, "Tell Ma I'll be home in a couple of weeks." I guess 'Ma' is what they call moms in Norway. Still, I want to ask Liora again if she can have her people do a little digging. It could be my paranoia, but something feels off.

Fortunately for me, Wilcox is in the lobby, but Yossi isn't. I still don't trust him, because at the very least, he was helping Thom and everyone else hide things from me. I signal to Wilcox to follow me, which he does – but he keeps at a discreet distance, probably because he's still mad at me for getting him yelled at by Thom.

The further I get from the hotel, the better I feel, and when I get close to the Old City I start to feel the awe I feel every time I come here. I'm ignoring my tall, male shadow and perusing some oriental rugs in a narrow shop in one of the charming cobblestone alleys when my BlackBerry rings. I check the caller ID, fully intending to screen the call if it's Liora, but it's Mike. "Hold on a sec," I say, putting in my headphones. I drop the phone back into my purse so my hands are free to feel up the rugs. "Okay. What's up?"

"Where are you?" Mike asks.

"I told you. Don't you check your messages?"

"'Somewhere in the Old City' is not really enough information for me to find you."

"Oh." I poke my head around a huge pile of carpets. "Where am I?" I ask the shopkeeper, who is sitting on a stool in the corner and playing on his iPhone.

He looks at me for a moment. "You are in my shop," he tells me. I give him a thumbs-up, then pop back behind the pile in case this is one of those countries where the thumbs-up is an obscene gesture.

"I am in a nice gentleman's rug shop in the Old City," I tell Mike.

"What's the name of the shop?"

I pop back out and hold the microphone away from my mouth. "What's the name of your shop?"

"Old City Rugs," says the shopkeeper.

"Thanks," I tell him. "It's called Old City Rugs," I say into my microphone. "Anyway, the Old City is not that big."

"Which quarter are you in?"

"The Muslim Quarter, I think. I was in the Western Wall Plaza and then I went into a tunnel and I popped up on this little street with souvenir shops." I glance at the shopkeeper for confirmation. He gives me a thumbs-up. Wilcox does, too, behind a tall, rolled-up rug, but I ignore this.

"You made me nervous," Mike says. "After all that talk of how you still think people are following you around. I thought I saw someone at your door today, so I checked with Thom, and he swore to me, too, that he doesn't have anyone else monitoring you."

"So now you believe me?" And I left a message about where I was, I want to add, but this is more important. My own feelings, I can dismiss – but Mike is rarely wrong.

"Just stay where you are. I'll come find you."

"Wait – have you heard from Jess?"

"Not yet," Mike says. "See you in a bit."

"Well," I tell the shopkeeper, wrapping my headphones around my phone and putting it away again. "I think I'm going to be here a while. You might as well try and talk me into buying a rug."

The shopkeeper, Faisal, pats a short pile of rugs near his stool, and I sit. He weaves me a tale about magical flying carpets, a hundred per cent authentic, sold only at his shop, while I wait for Mike. And for half an hour, I delay feeling worse that Mike is no longer dismissing my worry that I'm being watched – and if not by anyone Thom knows, then who?

EIGHTEEN

I am shocked when I spend another three days trying to get in touch with my client. Rather, I'm shocked that I am still shocked. And it cements my suspicion that I still don't know the whole story.

When there's still nothing from Liora or Thom or Jess or anyone else by the morning of what is to be our second mediation session, I call Alisha to check if he's heard from any of the clients whether they plan to attend this week's scheduled mediation. I have a sinking feeling before the phone stops ringing, but I'm relieved when Alisha answers.

"Didn't Thom tell you?" she asks.

"Tell me what?"

"There's something the PM needs to attend to – top secret, classified – and she has been called away for several days. She called me personally to explain, since it's above your clearance level. Someone was supposed to let you know. They've arranged to reschedule one of your site visits."

"Oh. Okay." It isn't okay. I feel as powerless now as I did dealing with my own parents. I have nominally more authority now than I did as a child, but I don't seem to have any real power in practice. I'm frustrated that after our first, disastrous meeting, several more days have gone by with not only no progress, but no contact with my client. I'm frustrated that Thom is still either hiding things from me or neglecting to tell me things. I'm even frustrated with myself, for still being anxious about being watched even after Thom promised it is just the one guy, and he's protecting me, anyway.

It's like every time I manage to take one difficult step forward, everyone forces me to take three steps back. In fact, it's almost like I'm being sabotaged. "Actually, no. There's always something classified happening whenever I need to reach someone. Nobody picks up the phone or shows up to things. Do you not want us to succeed here? Because I can't think of any other reason for you all to obstruct me at every opportunity."

"This happens all the time when you're dealing with heads of state," Alisha says, reassuring me. "Everything is Priority One with them."

"I know," I say, but before I can change the subject and ask her some of the questions that have been forming in my mind about Møkkalasset, she interrupts to tell me that the meeting has been rescheduled for three days from now, and that everyone will be there.

I wonder if James has spoken to his client, but I don't ask, in case the answer is yes. Alisha reads something into my silence and offers me Wilcox to borrow for the afternoon. "Take him for a walk or something if you want," she says.

And there's that nagging worry again – is she trying to

get me away from the hotel for some reason? "No, thanks –
I'll just do the site visit. But another time, I'd love to."

"All righty, then," Alisha says.

Thom answers my call on the first ring. "Sorry, sorry, sorry,"
he chants. "I'm sorry. I was going to call you but I got stuck
on the phone with the DAS."

"Stop showing off," I tell him. "And lying. I just spoke
to her."

"Sorry," he says again. "Anyway, yeah – you'll be doing
Site Visit 3; if you check your documents the itinerary is in
there. It's all the same, we've just moved it up since the PM
has been called away."

I exhale loudly, to steady myself, and make sure he can
hear it. "I don't have my schedule in front of me. Tell me
where I'm going."

"The Dead Sea. We'll send you a car again, so you don't
have to worry about anything. It'll be there at ten-thirty."

"Why do I have to go look at a salty fucking lake?"

"You'll travel through the West Bank, but on Israeli-
controlled roads. And it's on the border with Jordan. So
it should be safe, but interesting. And the Israel–Jordan
water deal—"

"Fine. I'll go. But I'm bringing Mike." I hang up on him
in case he would have argued with me, though I don't think
he still has the necessary life force for that.

And I'm out of beta-blockers.

When I ask Mike if he wants to come along to the Dead
Sea, he jumps up like a dog who's heard the word 'walk'.

He doesn't ask me a single question, just rushes to gather his things like he's worried if he takes too long, I'll change my mind. This makes me feel terrible. I tell him he doesn't have to rush, because we still have an hour before the car arrives, but Mike says we can have a nice, relaxed breakfast in the hotel restaurant, then. I toss some things into one of Mike's backpacks. There's nothing but a light coating of pink dust inside my pill case. But today is really a mini-vacation, so I'm unlikely to need them anyway. I'll have to tell Thom to get me some more when we get back.

Still, I throw a few bags of Bissli and nuts into the pack. Just in case.

The itinerary Thom went on about doesn't really have anything on it – no meetings or anything like that – so it seems like I'm a glorified tourist, again. I know that people swim and slather mud on themselves at the Dead Sea, so I figure I need to bring basic beach things with me. When I unpacked the suitcase Thom brought for me and found a bathing suit, I was curious. But I guess he'd made a packing list based on my itinerary, and honestly, he didn't do a terrible job packing for me. No worse than I'd have done, anyway.

It's not the bathing suit I'd have chosen, though. It was a gift Jess brought back for me from St Thomas, and its bright orange colour is a little garish for me.

Mike is bouncing on the balls of his feet by the door when I look up to tell him I think I'm ready. "Let's go!" he says.

We both have shakshuka and coffees for breakfast. Yossi gives me a disapproving look as he sets mine in front of me, and I give him my best New Yorker's patented The Fuck You Lookin' At? face – chin jutted, brow furrowed, hard eyes. I'm uncomfortably full again when we get into the black car with tinted windows that pulls up. It's Wilcox again, and his driving and choice of radio station – quiet, classical – combined with my full stomach and comfortable position leaning against Mike puts me to sleep. It's a surprise when, about an hour later, Mike wakes me up by stroking my arm.

"We're here," he says.

"Dammit," I grumble. "I was supposed to be looking around or something."

"You can look on the way back," he says, holding out a hand to help me climb out of the car.

"Are you going to sunbathe with us, Wilcox?" I ask, squinting at him in the sunlight that seems to be refracting off the water. I can't imagine him in anything but his black suit, white shirt and black tie.

"No thanks, ma'am," he says. "I'll be in the visitor centre if you need me." He gestures at a building behind a parking lot full of tour buses.

I wave at him, and Mike and I head down to the start of the beach, looking around. There's nobody paying any attention to me here. Everyone is sunbathing, floating in the water, or slathering themselves or their companions with mud. I will myself to relax, but the hair on my forearms is raised despite the heat. "Have you been here before?" I ask Mike, to distract myself as much as anything else.

"Actually, no," he says.

The water is a teal blue beneath a cobalt blue sky. The

sand around it is the colour of a camel. There's a faint smell of sulphur. A sign tells me that we're in Ein Gedi, and it's a public beach. There are some uninspiring facilities, including the visitor centre and a spa, as well as public bathrooms. "Let's change and meet back here," I say. "I want to go cover you in mud."

I pretend I'm not doing it, but I change as fast as I can so I can get straight back to Mike. I don't want to be alone for a second longer than necessary, and I walk back out to the edge of the parking lot as fast as I can without running.

When I find Mike, he's waiting with two dingy chairs and an umbrella that he's rented. It reminds me of a public beach back home that Mom hates – Jones Beach – which was nice enough, but Mom hates it because of the 'public' element. But as we head closer to the water, and put the dingy bathrooms behind us, I take in a deep breath and start to relax a little. On my chair, I close my eyes to focus on the earthy mineral smell of the salt water – and startle when something cold touches my nose. Mike is dabbing zinc oxide on my nose. "Stop it," I tell him, batting his hand away.

"Just trying to protect you," he says, in a light tone, but with wounded spaniel eyes.

"Let's go in the water first. Hope you don't have any cuts or scrapes."

"Okay, I'll just run to the restroom first," Mike says, but I'm already throwing my cover-up onto the chair and jogging into the water.

I stop with just my toes getting wet and look out over the water. I don't see anybody floating with a newspaper, like in the pictures I saw of people in the Dead Sea. It's mostly couples and families, the former slathering each other with mud, and the latter trying to keep children from floating too far away. I wonder if it's even possible to drown in this buoyant water, but then I remember hearing once that little kids can drown in an inch of liquid.

Turning around, I scan the crowd to see if Mike is coming to join me yet. He's still messing around with his sunscreen, even though I've never known him to get a sunburn, so I decide to wade in a little more. But as I turn back to the water, a couple catches my eye. I feel a small surge of adrenaline as I wonder if the reason I noticed them is because they're some of the people I've seen around the hotel, who might be watching me. I take a steadying breath and squint to try to see better.

A man is carrying a small woman into the water. The man has a stripe of zinc oxide on his nose, and the woman is wearing bug-like oversized sunglasses, and both are covered in mineral-rich mud. I wrinkle my nose in distaste at their public display but find that I can't look away. Something about them, I think, is familiar – but I don't have the feeling that they're any of the suspicious-seeming people from the King Solomon. As they splash into the water, I see that the man has a bald spot on the back of his head, obscured a little by overlong hair.

Unconsciously, I take a few steps closer to them as I stare intently. And then I am breaking into a jog, and calling out to them, which becomes a shouted, *"Hey!"* They turn and face me, and it can't be, but it is, so now I'm screaming and running at them, so blind with rage that I don't see the

Israeli soldiers who were moments ago milling around and looking bored until a small but fierce female soldier has tackled me to the ground.

"Get *off!*" I yell at her, but she's an immovable object.

"What are you doing?" her partner, a very young man, asks me.

"Nothing, just get off!"

"We are going to have to ask you some questions," the woman says, still pinning my shoulders with her knees. "Do you have any weapons?" she asks, starting to pat me down.

"I don't have any – where would I have weapons? Why are you patting me down? I'm wearing a bikini!"

"Why have you travelled here today?" the young man asks.

"I have to go talk to that couple!" I scream. The soldiers look at each other and hesitate. "Look," I say, trying to modulate my tone. I take advantage of their momentary weakness to wriggle one arm free and hold up the Star of David pendant on my necklace. "I'm not a terrorist. I just need to speak to those people, urgently. Over there." I drop the pendant and point at the water.

The woman leaps off me, cat-like even laden with some pretty big guns, and offers a hand to help me up. I'm a little concerned that holding my Jewish star up like a sort of badge worked that well, but there's no time to discuss it. People are staring at us, though they've kept their distance, and this includes the couple I saw before.

I brush myself off, lift my chin high, and walk calmly towards Mom and Dad.

NINETEEN

"No!" I scream pre-emptively when Dad opens his mouth.

Mom tries next. "E—" she says.

"*No!*" I scream again. "Me first!"

They bob quietly in the salt water and look at me. I stamp my foot, which is surprisingly hard to do with the resistance of the water. It splashes me in the eye, which stings and makes my eyes tear. "Ugh!" I yell. "I am *not* crying. The stupid water is just burning me."

Dad opens his mouth briefly but appears to think better of it. Mom does the same thing, but twice, so she looks like that horrible wall-mounted plastic fish Dad had (has?) in his den at the new house in Rockland County. I imagine that Candace would have prevented him from bringing it to LA when they moved, or at least 'lost' or broken it in the move. And that thought at least gives me somewhere to start. "Where is Candace?" I ask, looking back and forth between Mom and Dad.

"In LA," Dad says, paddling with one hand to stay

facing me as he continues to bob in the water. And it is then that I realise that Mom and Dad are still holding hands. Which, for some reason, makes me think of Mike – so I turn around to look for him. He is standing by the water several yards to my right, looking out over the crowd in the water with his hand over his eyes, trying to spot me. I feel a little surge of affection for him, thinking that he was so focused on his superfluous application of sunscreen in the bathroom that he missed my little scuffle with the soldiers.

But I think I need back-up, so I shout his name once and wave at him. He breaks into a confused smile when he sees where the noise is coming from and jogs over.

"What are you doing over here?" he asks.

"I am interrogating my parents," I reply, gesturing at them.

"Your—"

"Correct."

"Why?"

"Why am I interrogating them?"

"Why are they here?" Mike corrects, and there's a flinty look about him. It's like I can see everything I ever told him about them flashing before his eyes. But his sense of decorum wins the day, and he takes a hesitant step into the water, reaches down and extends a hand to shake – first to my mom, who gives an infuriating little frog kick to be able to reach him before she takes it.

"Who are you?" she asks Mike, as he lets go and reaches for Dad.

"Emily's…"

"Boyfriend," I fill in for him, and he smiles at me.

"Not Mike?" Dad asks, shaking his hand limply.

"Yes Mike," I say, frowning at him. "Why not Mike?"

"Maxi said—"

"No, no. No," I interrupt, remembering what's happening here. "You need to tell me right now, and in the fewest words possible, what the actual hell you are doing here, and I mean hell literally."

Dad makes that pursed lips face again, a selfie pout gone awry, and stands up. Mom moves to follow him, and they let go of each other's hands but stay standing very close to each other.

We all stand around and I wait to hear an answer, but the temperature of my blood is rising, and by the time they spit it out I'm afraid I won't be able to hear it over the sound of the steam whistling through my ears.

"It was Rabbi Gold's idea," Mom begins.

"To have the wedding here," Dad finishes for her.

I bolt.

"Drive," I say as I open the door of Wilcox's car and fling myself onto the seats. The leather is warm against my bare, sticky skin in my bathing suit. "Just go right now, Wilcox," I say, lying down flat against the seats, pressing one hand over my eyes and the other over my mouth and breathing through my nose.

When there's no immediate movement, I move my hand off one eye and open it a crack. "Wilcox?"

"Not Wilcox," says a deep voice back, and I open both eyes wide.

And push myself upright and back against the passenger-side door.

The Bald Man clears his throat.

"You," I say. "Where's Wilcox?"

"Something came up," the BM says.

This is setting off all sorts of alarm bells in my head, but there's nothing I can do about it now, because Mike will be running after me, with Mom and Dad close behind.

"Please just drive," I tell him.

He does, and we pull out of the parking lot and turn down the main approach road in silence. Once we get back on the highway, he asks, "Where to?"

"Home," I say, thinking about my little shoebox apartment and Jess and our quasi-pet Subway Rat at 125th Street. "Just... back to the hotel, please," I clarify.

The BM doesn't say anything, doesn't nod, doesn't glance at me in the rearview mirror. I try to decide whether I am going to cry, and if so, whether I should ask the BM to turn on the radio so he won't hear me. Instead, I surprise myself by asking to use his phone.

"Where's yours?" the BM asks, without seeming too interested.

"I left it back there. I was in a hurry."

"Who do you need to call?"

"It's an emergency."

"What kind of emergency?"

"A woman emergency. My uterus feels like—"

"Nice try," says the BM, and he surprises me by laughing. "I have four daughters."

"I'm one of four," I say. "I need to reach one of the other three."

"That's really who you're going to call?"

"Really," I say.

The BM is quiet for a few minutes, and when he glances in the mirror and changes lanes, keeping both hands on the steering wheel, I think he's going to ignore me. But then he surprises me by reaching into his jacket and handing a phone over his shoulder. "Thom says to let you call someone on your friends and family list if you get really upset, but I'll have to listen in, and you can't tell them where you are."

"Fine. It's going to be international," I say, equal parts apologetic and challenging, taking the phone quickly so he doesn't withdraw it.

"I surmised," he says.

"Okay, then."

It crosses my mind fleetingly to wonder what time it is in Boston, but only after I have dialled Maxi's number. And before I can do the math, she's picked up, which surprises me. "Dr Price-Adams," she says.

"Oh!" I say. "You answered."

"Emily? What's wrong?" Maxi asks.

"Did you know?" I ask.

"Know what? Emily, is this an emergency? I'm very busy with patients—"

"Just tell me, right now, if you knew."

Maxi sighs. "I may have spoken to Dad last week, and he may have let something slip."

"You knew. You bitch! You knew Mom and Dad are together."

"What?" Maxi says, after a pause so pregnant it must be twins.

"Wait, what?"

"Dad said he left Candace," Maxi says. "What did he tell you?"

"Tell me? Nothing. But he and Mom are together. I saw them."

Maxi is quiet again. "But maybe—"

"I saw them, and I spoke to them, and they're getting married. And they're in Israel."

"But," Maxi says.

"They're together, and they're getting married. Again."

"But where are you? Are you in Israel?" she asks.

"I'm—" I begin, but that's as far as I get, because the BM reaches behind his seat and plucks the phone out of my hand. I hear Maxi saying, "Emily? Emily?" before he ends the call without looking at the screen.

I stare at his ear while he keeps driving, as if nothing untoward has just happened. I count out the passing seconds of silence in my head, because they are stretching on in a way that is unnatural. After three minutes have passed, I clear my throat. "Excuse me," I say.

"Yes?"

"Why did you do that?"

"Oh, because you were about to confirm your location," the BM says, then starts tapping his fingers on the steering wheel and humming nonchalantly. "How about some music?" He hits the CD button on the car radio, and within seconds, I've identified the band as Fall Out Boy. This makes me feel a little better, because anyone who listens to Fall Out Boy is a kindred spirit, and worse, because it instantly makes me seventeen again to hear them. I reluctantly hum along to the rest of '20 Dollar Nose Bleed', even though the lyrics about jet lag feel a little pointed.

I'm ready to try talking to the BM about the phone call again when the next song that starts is Paramore's 'Misery Business'. "Okay," I say instead. "Just what the fuck is going on?"

"I thought it would make you feel better," the BM says, only he sounds like I've somehow offended him.

"Did you hack my iTunes account?" I ask.

"'Hack' is a strong word," he says.

"I'm getting really tired of all this," I mutter to myself, and when the BM asks what I said, having failed to hear me over Hayley Williams's sing-shouting, "I said," I repeat, louder, "I'm getting really tired of all this!"

The BM turns down the music as he pulls over on the highway and turns around to look at me. I feel like he's Dad, having turned around to yell at me and my sisters for bickering in the backseat and threatened to turn this car around right now, young ladies. I have the same urge to fling myself out of the car and bolt, because it would serve him right. I go as far as moving my hand to rest on the door, but the BM sighs. "You sound upset," he says. "We're just trying to help without compromising the project."

"Who are you?" I demand.

"My name's Johnson."

I scoff. I remember that Thom told me his name, and I'm glad he did – because now I know the BM is a liar.

"Fine, it's Anderson."

I turn away from him and look out the window,

watching the passing cars, almost universally dusty but still gleaming because of the sheer will of the sun.

"It really is Anderson," the BM says.

"Are you working with Thom?"

"More or less."

"Look. Do you even understand what I'm dealing with here?"

"Yes," says Anderson. "I do."

"I need…" And I trail off, because I'm not sure what. "I don't know. To talk to someone, probably."

"I couldn't let—"

"I know," I say, a note of frustration creeping in, "but I didn't really need to talk to Maxi, anyway. She doesn't feel the same way I do about things."

"Who does?" Anderson asks.

I think about this for a minute. "Do you think," I start hesitantly, wondering if I should let myself cry now for maximum effect but deciding against it, "I could make just one more phone call?"

Anderson accepts my promise not to say anything about where I am in exchange for his phone, and I dial Jess's number as he continues to drive. "Hi, Jess, it's me. You're not going to believe this."

PART II

PART II

TWENTY

Mom had left me a note asking me to pick up Gabby and Zara from school. "Maxi, do you want to come with me?" I asked as she swept past me to open the fridge.

"To get Gabby and Zara?" she asked. "Are you allowed to have three people in the car with a junior licence?"

"Yes, if they're all related to you," I said, "and besides, the elementary school is just a few blocks away."

Maxi deliberated. "Why does Mom want you to get them?" she asked.

"I don't know," I said. The house was quiet. Nobody was home.

She closed the fridge. "There's nothing to eat here anyway," she said. "Can we go to Starbucks first?"

"If we leave right now," I said, glancing at the oven clock.

Maxi slipped her feet into her Ugg boots and put on a North Face jacket. "Ready," she said.

Just then, as we were stepping out the front door and walking down the path to where I'd parked my new car, it sounded like the garage door was opening – but I couldn't see it from there. It could be Mom, but if she was home, why would she ask me to pick up Gabby and Zara?

"Come on!" Maxi called out from the passenger seat of my Mazda. It was raining a little, so I trotted around to the driver's seat. I took my time making sure all my mirrors and the seat were adjusted correctly, even though nobody else drove my car, and put on my headlights and wipers. Maxi sighed.

I pulled around the circle in the middle of the driveway slowly, and, peeking around the rhododendron in the middle on the way out, I could just see the garage door closing. So Mom was home. But it didn't matter. Nothing was going to come between Maxi and her java chip Frappuccino now, anyway. I signalled and turned out of our street carefully and headed to Starbucks. Maxi looked out the window at the wet green trees on the side of the road. There was nobody out walking – there never was in Rockland. She didn't remember as well as I did, but it was one of the things we'd tried to keep doing when we'd moved up here from Manhattan – walking. People thought our car broke down and kept trying to offer us rides home. Eventually, we stopped.

At Starbucks, I pulled into a space and let Maxi hop out. "Get me a mocha," I told her, and handed her my debit card. I kept the car running and the windshield wipers wiping, and listened to someone on NPR quietly droning beneath the sound of the rain on the sunroof.

"Jess was in there," Maxi said as she catapulted back into the car with a drinks holder in one hand containing both coffees – or rather, my coffee and her milkshake.

"Oh, well – I'll talk to her later," I said, and reversed carefully around a giant Escalade with one blonde lady in it.

Maxi chattered to me for the rest of the short drive to the elementary school, the caffeine – or, at least, the sugar – perking her up considerably. She was explaining how her gym class team had won the volleyball tournament on a technicality when we got there.

"Are you ready for this?" I asked. Elementary school pickup was a war game, conducted on the battlefield of the parking lot with walkie-talkies and military precision. I could see the crossing guard already gearing up to yell, "*Move up... and stop!*"

Maxi nodded and put one hand on the buckle of her seat belt and one on the door handle, ready to launch herself out of the car when she saw Gabby and Zara and scoop them into the car.

As we inched along the sidewalk in front of the school entrance, we kept our eyes peeled for them – and then, we saw them. Gabby was standing next to Zara, who was holding a bird-cage with our pet African grey parrot, Barbra Streisand, in it. Gabby – whose too-cool-for-school tutu, leggings and Converse outfit was slightly rumpled and getting wet in the rain that was blowing under the roof – looked mortified. Zara was grinning broadly, though struggling with the big cage.

"Was it show-and-tell day today?" Maxi asked.

"Yes – but I could swear Mom told her she was not allowed to take Barbra out of the house," I said, frowning. The crossing guard put up her hand in a gesture to stop, right in front of my face. "Okay – *go!*" I said to Maxi.

Maxi shot out of the car like a cannonball, and before I knew it, she, Gabby, Zara and Babs were in the car again.

"How was school?" Maxi ventured.

Gabby rolled her eyes.

"Great!" said Zara. "I brought Barbra Streisand."

Babs shrieked at the sound of her name.

"I can see that," I said. "Does Mom know you did that?"

In the rearview mirror, I saw Zara shrug.

"Definitely not," Gabby said petulantly.

"Squawk, squawk, divorce, divorce," said Babs.

"Shut the hell up," muttered Gabby.

We pulled into the driveway and I noticed that Dad's car was parked behind the garage, which was weird.

"Everyone out," Maxi said. She opened the back door closest to the path and stood aside. She took the cage from Zara, who was struggling to stand up under Babs's weight as she shook and preened.

I thought about telling her to take her garbage, too, but I decided to take it myself this time. I grabbed the empty java chip cup, napkins and straw wrappers, and followed the flock inside. And then I saw it: Mom, Dad and a Samsonite suitcase in the foyer.

When Dad walked out of our house, with his briefcase and his garment bag and one huge Samsonite suitcase, Gabby, Maxine, Zara and I stood together by the bay window in the kitchen and watched him go.

Oh my God, I thought. What will happen to my horse?

Mom was sitting in their bedroom – her bedroom – and she was crying.

"Mom?" I hesitated in the doorway.

"We'll be okay, Emily," she said, opening her arms for a hug.

"What will happen to Poco?" I asked.

Mom's arms and face fell.

"Well, Shelby McNamara's dad split, and she had to sell Zeus."

"Get out."

In the living room, Maxi, Gabby and Zara were still standing around. Maxi was rolling her soccer ball back and forth between her feet. Gabby was chewing on the ends of her long hair. Zara was crying.

"Maxi Pad, stop playing with the ball in the house. Gabby, don't eat your hair; I don't want you hacking up a hairball on me. Zara, shut up. Why are you even crying? You don't even know what's going on."

"Don't tell me what to do, bitch," said Gabby, spitting out her hair. "And don't call Maxine 'Maxi Pad'. And don't tell Zara to shut up!"

"Yeah!" said Maxi. She picked up the ball and threw it at my face, but I hurled it back at her even harder. Zara stopped crying.

"What should we do now?" Maxi pushed her glasses back up her nose.

"I don't think Mom is going to make dinner, so we should probably do it," Gabby said.

Maxi snorted. "I'm not hungry."

"I am," Zara said.

"Then you can make dinner," I told her.

"I'm not allowed to use the stove until I'm ten."

"Then ask Gabby to help you!"

"I already said I would!" Gabby yelled.

"Then go do it!" I yelled louder.

We all looked at the hallway, waiting to hear Mom's footsteps and see her come bursting through and yell at us for yelling. Gabby sighed and took Zara's hand. They disappeared into the kitchen. Maxi and I listened to the cabinets and the fridge opening and closing.

"What do you think those two will make?" Maxi asked, grinning.

"Hot dogs with mac and cheese," I said. "Sorry I hit you."

"No, you're not."

"I'm not," I agreed.

Maxi sank to the floor, cross-legged. "Do you think Dad has a girlfriend?"

I sighed and walked over to the bird-cage. Babs studied my face, her head tilted at a quizzical angle. Then she stretched out her claw and mauled my hand. "Fuck you, too," I said, shoving her away and closing the door.

"Emily," Maxi said. "Does Dad have one?"

"Of course he does. Why else would he leave?"

Maxi sighed, and her eyes welled up a little.

I sat down next to Maxi. We watched Babs preen, shake her feathers out and then stand there, yelling. "Don't worry," I said. "We'll think of a way to fix this."

"Maybe we can get a dog now that Dad's gone," Maxi said.

"That's the spirit," I said, although that wasn't what I'd meant.

We stayed on the floor until we could smell the hot dogs and mac and cheese and the microwave stopped dinging. Then I stood up, tried to shake off the bird debris and pulled Maxi to her feet.

We were done eating before Mom came out of her bedroom but were still sitting at the kitchen table. Zara was playing on the computer, and Maxi, Gabby and I were doing homework.

"Hi, Mom," Maxi said carefully.

"Do you want some mac and cheese?" Zara asked her. "We made it ourselves."

Gabby punched Zara in the arm. "She doesn't want mac and cheese, stupid," she said.

I leaned across the table and punched Gabby even harder. "Don't punch your sister."

Mom started to cry. Gabby sprang to her feet and put her arm around Mom. Maxi and I exchanged a look. *Suck-up*, Maxi mouthed at me. I giggled.

Zara took a deep breath, getting ready to ask a question. I slapped a hand over her mouth. "Not now," I whispered.

"But—" she began.

"No!" I hissed.

"I just wanted to ask Mom when Dad is coming back!" Zara shouted.

This just was not how things were supposed to be. Mom sat me down a few days after Dad left, once she'd stopped crying, and said that things would start to get better soon.

But they couldn't get better, not if Dad wasn't coming back. Parents are supposed to be together and kids are supposed to have one house.

"Are you buying this?" I asked Maxi, Gabby and Zara once Mom had started crying again and left the room.

Gabby and Zara blinked at me, and Maxi said maybe we should have this discussion without them.

"Fine," I said. "Gabby, Zara, go to the playroom and play *Rock Band*."

"I don't like *Rock Band*," Gabby said, chewing her hair.

"I don't care."

Gabby huffed at me but stood and took Zara's hand and led her upstairs.

I looked at the door to the library, which Mom had shut behind her, and Maxi and I listened to the loud classical music emanating from the room.

"Diiiiiii*vorce!*" screeched our parrot.

"Can you just put her to sleep or something?" I said.

Maxi got up and put a sheet over the cage.

"I meant permanently," I said, "but whatever. We need to get started on our plan."

"What plan?" Maxi asked.

"To force Mom and Dad to get back together," I said, loudly and slowly, so that Maxi would know I thought she was very stupid.

"I don't see how we could do anything about it," Maxi said.

Maxi was always pragmatic, even as a baby. She'd learned just enough words to communicate her basic needs, and used them sparingly. She'd made piles of Cheerios on the tray of her high chair and eaten them in stages throughout repeat viewings of *Beauty and the Beast,* so that she didn't run out before it ended. Each Hanukkah, she'd request one large gift and seven smaller ones, so she'd be nearly guaranteed to get everything she asked for. And now, she was telling me that we had no say in whether our parents were together or not.

"That's why I'll be in charge. I just need to know whether or not you'll have my back."

"Of course I will," Maxi said. "I want them to get back together, too."

"Okay, then," I said.

An informal poll of my classmates whose parents had split revealed a few things: first, that almost all of them went through a phase of almost getting back together all on their own, but then something inevitably came up that ruined it. Second, that most of the parents would still band together if one of the kids got in trouble. And third, that the parents mostly did feel guilty about ruining their kids' lives, so you could get away with a lot.

"But if they have a girlfriend or something already, you're pretty much screwed," Mark told me between AP Gov and Chorus.

"And if one of them moves anywhere more than a twenty-minute drive away, you'll basically never see them again," Priya added bitterly.

"Best to nip any of that in the bud as fast as possible," Mark agreed.

"Sorry about your dad, Priya," I said, squeezing her hand.

Priya shrugged. "He has to sit in the LA traffic for three hours every day, so I guess the joke's on him. Fucking sunburned, cancerous suburb growing on the good parts of California."

"Yeah, but at least you can get in-state tuition at UC Berkeley now," Mark pointed out.

Then Mr Lombardo came in, so we all shut up, except to sing 'Con Te Partirò'.

In between the lines of sheet music, I scribbled down what they said:

1. Do nothing and stay out of way
2. Break up boyfriends/girlfriends
3. Don't let them move away
4. Get into trouble

TWENTY-ONE

None of us noticed that the house across the street had a 'For Sale' sign on it until we saw the lady from the ShopRite cart ads taking it down.

Maxine and I were doing our homework on the porch, and Gabby and Zara were playing their hula-hoop game.

"Who do you think is buying that ugly house?" Maxi asked.

I looked at the house, with its grand stone façade and cheap vinyl siding and one-foot strip of grass on all sides. "Only one way to find out," I said. I rolled Gabby's soccer ball across the road. "Gabby! Your ball is escaping," I called to her.

"Be careful," Maxi added.

Gabby bounded across the street after it. Shopping Cart Lady stopped it with a stiletto. I angled my head at the house and raised my eyebrows. Maxi shrugged, and we followed Gabby.

"Do you girls all live across the street?" Shopping Cart Lady was asking Gabby.

"Yeah," Gabby said. "We're sisters."

"How nice! The gentleman who bought this house has daughters, too. Four, I think. It will be so nice for you to be able to play together."

"We don't really *play*," Maxi said. "We're not babies."

I elbowed her. "Of course we play," I said to Shopping Cart Lady, and I extended my hand. "Hi, I'm Emily. Where did you say the guy who bought this house was from?"

"I didn't," Shopping Cart Lady said, taking my hand in a soft, clammy grip. "Um, he's a doctor, local guy – in fact, there he is now," she said, withdrawing her hand and waving.

Maxi, Gabby, and I turned around. A yellow Porsche 911 we had never seen before was pulling into the driveway, but there was something familiar about the way the headlights were flashing hello.

"It can't be," I said.

"Is that—?" Maxi started.

"Dad?" Gabby finished.

Across the street, Zara set down her hula-hoop. A boat shoe emerged from the Porsche.

"Girls, meet your new neighbour," Shopping Cart Lady said. "This is Dr—"

"Price," I finished.

"Hi, girls," said Dad. "Hello, Nina; thanks for getting this taken care of so quickly."

Nina flashed Dad a confused version of her bleached smile, and at us. "Are these…?" She trailed off.

"Yep!"

I wished I could still feel how Nina looked. "How…" –

she searched for the right word – "nice," she managed, but her $149.99 smile faltered.

"Girls, there are some groceries in the back seat. You can each grab a bag and I'll show you the new house."

"What back seat?" I muttered as Maxi, Gabby and Zara started trotting towards the car. "Wait!" I said, and flung my arm out to stop Maxi. Gabby hesitated, but I told her to go ahead. I crossed my arms, and Maxi put a hand on her hip. We stared at Dad, and he stared back. "What?" he asked.

"Who gets to tell Mom?" I said.

"Okay. Please help your sisters and go inside, and I will speak to you when I'm finished talking to Nina."

Nina handed me a set of keys on a smiley face chain.

Nobody had been in this house for a long time. It smelled of apple cinnamon candles. Maxi's sneakers squeaked on marble flooring as we took a few cautious steps into the foyer, and the sound bounced all the way up two stories to a gigantic chandelier. A pool was visible behind a stone wall at the back of the driveway.

"Wow," said Maxi.

"It looks like the kind of house Akon's manager would live in, or something. It was probably a million dollars."

"No way it cost a million dollars."

"Want to bet?"

"No."

"That's because you know I'm right. It cost at least a million dollars."

"You're not right, I just don't want to bet."

"I'll prove it right now. I'll Google it and we'll see," I said. "Nina looks like she has a website. Anyway, are Porsches German? If they are, we're going to have to find a way to make him get rid of it, before Mom sees."

Maxi looked like she was about to ask me a question, but then Gabby and Zara came through the doors with the shopping bags.

"Cool!" Zara said, looking around.

"Dibs on choosing my room!" Gabby shouted, dropping the bags and tearing up the stairs. Maxi and I charged up behind her. "This one's mine!" we heard Gabby shout from the end of the hallway. We followed her in. This was the only room we'd noticed that had any furniture in it. A white fur rug lay at the foot of a large metal bed with a black leather headboard and silky charcoal bedding.

"This is the master bedroom." I found the bathroom through the door in the far corner. It had the same marble floor as the foyer, a glass shower, his-and-hers sinks and a large white Jacuzzi set underneath large, textured-glass windows. Chrome gleamed everywhere.

"So?" Gabby asked, flopping onto the bed.

"So it's Dad's," Maxi said. "Where's Zara?"

Zara, it turned out, was on the walkway, clutching the banister and hyperventilating. Dad was coming up the stairs behind her. "What's the matter?" he asked Zara, frowning.

"You know she's afraid of heights, Dad," Maxi chided.

"And you've managed to buy a house with a bridge in it," I added.

"And a car we won't even fit into," Gabby said. The situation was becoming clear to all of us. Zara's eyes were wet and sad.

Dad sighed. "She isn't really afraid of heights. It never occurred to her until your mother put it into her head. She never used to have to take those ridiculous pills to drive across the Tappan Zee bridge before."

"It isn't Mom's fault!" Maxi said.

"She's been afraid of heights since she was four," Gabby said.

"Hon, you can have one of the downstairs bedrooms," Dad said to Zara, prying her off the railing. Zara nodded, and a fat tear escaped.

"How many bedrooms are there?" I asked.

"Four," Dad said.

"You mean four plus the master bedroom, right?"

"I mean four."

"So there aren't enough seats in that new car, and there aren't enough bedrooms in this new house. Are you trying to tell us something?"

"I'm not made of money," Dad said. "Why don't we order some takeout?"

Dad, Maxi, Gabby and I were looking for a table in the Simcha Room when Zara reappeared from wherever the bored kids disappear to. She was looking a little the worse for wear.

"Have you ever noticed that at every synagogue in the world, there are always two trips on the itinerary – to Israel, and to Auschwitz?" I asked nobody in particular, picking up the plastic stand with the synagogue's announcements from next to the silver platter of bagels.

"Hi, hon," Dad said to Zara, ignoring me.

"Daddy, I'm tired," Zara said. "And the grape juice is rotten." She promptly lay down on the floor and curled up in a ball.

I plucked the Kiddush cup out of her hand and smelled it.

"Man, oh Manischewitz," I said. "This was wine."

"Oh my God," Gabby muttered, and Maxi crouched, awkward in her long skirt, to check on Zara – who seemed to be sleeping.

Dad laughed.

"This never happens when Mom brings us to temple," Maxi observed.

Dad stopped laughing.

"She'll live," I said. "Manischewitz doesn't actually kill you. You just wish it would."

Dad's jaw muscles were jumping under his skin. "I'll take her to the car," he said.

"Be sure to crack a window," I called after him.

"How are you girls doing?" Rabbi Gold said, his tall figure appearing behind us, and placing a large hand on one of Gabby's shoulders and one of mine. His dishevelled sandy-brown hair, poking every which way except where it was pinned down by his kippah, was backlit by one of the Simcha Room's skylights, making him seem godly.

"Great," Gabby lied.

"Particularly Zara," I said.

"Oh?" asked Rabbi Gold. His eyes were lit up, already

sparkling a bit, primed to cry tears of joy. Tears were only ever seconds away with Rabbi Gold. Such joy, such nachas, he would say, crying happily at some good news – quiet tears streaming down the neat lines of his face. His blue eyes would well up in sympathy when one of the old-timers cornered him by the bagels to tell him they enjoyed his sermon, or when he read the synagogue's announcements after the Mourner's Kaddish and one of them was a reminder that someone was sitting shiva and needed a minyan. So I felt a little ashamed when I saw the telltale sparkle, ready to cry in celebration of Zara's happiness.

Maxi, as usual, stared daggers at me, while Gabby blushed. "Oh, she just really liked the children's service today," I lied to the rabbi.

"Did she?" Rabbi Gold was scanning the room for her now. "I would love to ask her if she understood Morah Schwartz's demonstration of the Torah reading. I wasn't sure if interpretive dance was the clearest way to explain the chaos before creation, but dancing makes her so happy," he said, and he teared up again.

"We all love it when Mrs Schwartz dances," Maxi brown-nosed.

"Zara's taking a rest in the car," Gabby blurted.

"Well, say hello to her for me," Rabbi Gold said, "and say hello to your mother. We miss her energy."

"Don't we all," I said.

Dad was quiet as he drove us back on the parkway. Gabby and Maxi were mashed together in the backseat, with Zara lying across their laps, snoring. When he pulled into the driveway, he shut off the engine and sat still.

"Can you let us out?" Gabby asked, looking pointedly down at Zara. "I can't breathe."

"In a moment," Dad said, and he tried to twist around to look at all of us. "We need to have an important discussion."

"Can we have it in the thirty million square feet of house in front of us?" I asked.

"Let him talk," Maxi said.

Dad took a deep breath. "You girls know that some dads, when the parents separate, move across the country and have nothing to do with their kids anymore, right?"

"Yeah..." said Maxi.

"You're not moving away, are you?" Gabby blurted.

"No! No," Dad said.

"He just bought this house," I pointed out. "Across the street."

"He could sell it," Gabby said.

"In this economy?" I said.

"Actually—" Dad said.

"Where are you going with this?" I asked.

"Well, the fact is, this house was pretty expensive—"

"So?" asked Gabby.

"So we are all going to have to make some adjustments."

"I wonder what that would be like," I said. "To have to change our lives from the way they've always been."

"You're being disrespectful," Dad said. "I'm just telling you that I can't maintain two households financially by myself, so we're going to have to make a few changes."

"If you sell Poco, I'll show you disrespectful!" I shouted.

"I didn't say anything about selling the fucking horse."

"*My* fucking horse," I corrected.

Dad's jaw muscles started jumping around again. Before he could say anything, Maxi interrupted. "Are we having money problems?"

"Dad, you don't have to worry about money!" Gabby cut in, grinning. "It's all going to be fine. Mom said she's tired of taking money from Shylock, whoever that is, because she's running out of pounds of flesh. So she bought the jewellery store in town."

One grey Thursday, inside Mom's empty new store, I sat at the counter polishing a new bangle I had made. The safety goggles I had stolen from the school lab perched on my nose, though I'd turned off the torch. A jingle from the bells on the door startled me, and I dropped the bangle.

"Mom fancies herself a silversmith now, does she?" Dad grinned at me.

I blinked back at him. "I'm the silversmith. I smithed all that silver over there," I said, standing and pointing to the bowl of randomly sized hammered silver rings and the bracelet bar of silver bangles.

"Where's Mom?"

"I don't know. A meeting."

"A meeting, for a jewellery store?"

I shrugged.

"She left you alone?" he tried again.

"I'm sixteen."

"Were you using a blow torch by yourself?"

"It's really a solo instrument," I said. Dad frowned, but there was a gleam in his eye, one that was familiar and one I did not like. "Is there something I can help you with?" I asked, in my Customer Service Voice.

"I just came to say hi," Dad said.

I put my hands on my hips and shifted my stance wider. "Can I help you pick out a gift for... Candace, is it?" I asked sweetly. "I think I saw on LinkedIn that her fourteenth birthday is next week."

Dad pressed his lips into a thin line. "Nancy from temple said she saw you girls working here," he said. "I was just coming to see the place where my daughters are spending so much of their time."

"Where did you park?"

"Behind the store, why?"

"You know, Gabby warned me you might do something like this." I sat back down behind the glass partition. Dad started to follow me, but I said, "Employees only," and he stopped in the entrance.

"I'm not doing anything," Dad said. "I'm just concerned about you."

"You're right. There is something you can do to help. I need twenty dollars," I said, and held out my hand.

"Mom doesn't pay you?" Dad asked, hopeful, but I kept my hand outstretched by way of reply. He rolled his eyes skyward and sighed, but slipped his wallet out and forked over two crisp bills.

"Thanks," I said, tucking them into my bra because I knew this made him uncomfortable. I could see him mentally listing dirt and grime and trace amounts of cocaine and everything else on the bills. "You can go now," I said. "As you can see, I'm wearing eye protection, and I get regular breaks. Mom tried to get me and Gabby to work

Saturday, but we threatened to unionise and she backed off. Also, Mom puts half of our pay cheques in our college funds." This was true, but I also withdrew it each time.

"Sounds very by the book," Dad said thoughtfully.

"What's that supposed to mean?" I asked.

"Never mind," Dad said, and he put his sports sunglasses back on. "I'll see you this weekend."

I made a face at Dad's retreating back, but it made me feel better anyway. I took my phone out of the scrap silver drawer on the counter and texted Mom.

> Heads up - Dad came to the store. Asked questions about us working for you.

> K.

I hoped it was 'K'.

But I was worried about what he might do. If things went too far, he would make my and Maxi's job even harder.

TWENTY-TWO

"Maxi, we need to talk," I said, walking into the living room and throwing my bag down on the couch. Maxi looked up from her computer. "I know," she said, pointing at the hearth.

There was a bicycle by the fireplace. It was wrapped in Hanukkah wrapping paper like everything else, but it was still very much bicycle-shaped. The bicycle was Gabby-sized. It also had a label on it that said, "To Gabby, Love Mom." This was a problem, because if Mom didn't get the bicycle from Target or something, she got it from LoHud Bikes, and this was a problem because the new guy who'd started working there was twenty-five and tattooed.

Also: his name was Jared.

But the moms called him Hot Jared.

And Mom had told us that a friend called Jared would be coming over for dinner.

"What did you want to talk about?" Maxi asked me, after a few moments.

"I was just going to say that I'm getting sick of this

already, and we need to figure out something to speed things along."

"Like what?" Maxi asked.

I sat down next to her and slid down into the cushions. "I think it's time to involve Gabby in the plan."

Maxi thought about it. "Has Gabby even seen *The Parent Trap*?"

"It doesn't matter. This isn't anything like that."

"I just think it might help."

I rolled my eyes. "Fine. We can watch it after dinner."

"Why don't you want me to be happy?" Mom said, slamming her wine glass down when she asked us all if it would be okay and Gabby blurted out a no before any of the rest of us had a chance to. But we all agreed with her.

"Your father has Candace over for dinner all the time."

"We don't like her, either," I said.

"Maybe it would be all right," Maxi said. "Just don't act like he's your boyfriend in front of us."

"I won't be told what to do by my own children," Mom said. "I deserve to be happy, too."

"I want a new saddle for Hanukkah," I said.

When I'd had dinner at Jessica's house the week before, I told her family about Thanksgiving at Dad's. I'd told them about how Candace came, and she brought a Shih Tzu wearing a pink collar, and how Dad kept sneezing all over the turkey but insisted he was fine. The Shih Tzu, Candy, had its own seat at the table. Maxi, Gabby and Zara were stuck at a 'kids' table' in the living room. Candace's parents came, too.

"You forgot to tell them that when Candace's father shook your dad's hand, he said, 'I've never met a Jewish before,' to him," Jess reminded me.

I nodded sombrely. Jessica's mom and dad looked aghast. "You know you always have a bed at our house, and a spot at our dining table, right?" her mom said.

"Any time," her dad repeated.

"Thank you," I'd said, and Jessica's mom put another big scoop of eerily green mint chocolate chip ice cream in my bowl and patted my cheek.

I couldn't find any decent luggage in our attic, so I went across the street to Dad's house and let myself in the garage. "*Dad?*" I screamed as I came through into the mud room. I listened for a few seconds. A pair of Candace's shoes was lying on the tiled floor. They were probably upstairs or something, and I didn't have any time to talk to them. I had to get packing.

I crossed through the second living room to the stairs to the semi-finished basement, and I noticed a fluffy lime green blanket and a chew toy on the floor. I could feel the time slipping away, but something was up. I dragged a couple of Dad's black Samsonites up the stairs and through the living room.

Candace's stuff was never here on a weekday. She was only supposed to come up every other weekend, when we were all the way across the street. I called for Dad again, and when I still heard no answer, I marched up the stairs to the master bedroom. "Dad?" I said, more quietly, stepping inside. I didn't have to go far before I understood. Candace had moved in. There wasn't one pair of tennis whites and a pink robe hanging in Dad's massive walk-through closet anymore. There were five. Half of the many shelves and cubbies were now exploding with things that were fluffy, and pink, and sparkled. The 'hers' of the 'his-and-hers' sink was crowded with gleaming bottles. I ran my hands along them, feeling residual sliminess from recent use. It was Friday. She had been using this stuff, in Dad's house, this morning, while we got ready for school across the street.

I rolled my luggage back across the street to Mom's.

In my room, I started packing the essentials for a couple of weeks at Jess's.

> I'm moving in. Will explain tonight.

> Mom and I will pick you up in 20 on the way home from the place you like. What kind of pizza would you like?

> Plain. Thanks.

> We love you.

"Are you okay?" Jess asked, sliding open the door of her mom's minivan before it came to a complete stop in our driveway.

"Yeah," said my mouth, but my head shook itself no, and Jess hopped out of the car to hug me while her mom took my bags and put them in the trunk.

Jess and I sat quietly in the back seat, texting each other so that her mom wouldn't hear us.

So - what happened?

Candace moved in.

Oh shit

Yeah.

What are you going to do now?

I don't know yet. But I'm not going back to either of their houses until Dad moves back in.

Jess looked at me and bit her lip. I pressed mine together and looked out the window.

"It'll be all right," her mom said as we drove down the road to their house, warm pizzas on Jess's and my laps.

"When?" I asked.

Jessica's mom thought about it for a minute, and then she said, "You'll be going off to college before you know it."

TWENTY-THREE

"Do you want to get a bagel with me?" I asked Gabby over the phone.

"From where?" Gabby asked.

"Goldman's," I said.

"Can we go to the one by the JCC instead of the one on Main Street? I don't want to run into my friends," Gabby said.

"Whatever. Be ready at eleven."

"I can drive you," Jess offered, looking up from her math textbook.

"You don't have to. My mom will be at temple. You can just drop me at her house and I'll get my car. Unless you want a bagel, too."

"Bread makes you fluffy," Jess said.

"I don't think that's correct."

"Do you want me to come?"

I shrugged.

"Then I'll take you to get your car. Where's Gabby?"

I thought about it for a second. "Almost definitely with Gabbi-with-an-i."

"Are all of you guys staying with friends?"

"Maxi and Zara are home."

"Which one?"

I gave Jess A Look.

"Right, at your mom's," Jessica answered herself.

I stood up to get dressed but frowned at my open suitcase on Jess's guest-room floor. It was January, and occasional cold raindrops were plopping down and making ostentatious splashes on Jess's windowsill. I picked up a pair of jeans. It felt weird not to be getting dressed for synagogue on a Saturday morning, but I'd told Mom and Dad that I wouldn't be back there again unless it was as a family. Maxi had had my back on that one, but reluctantly, because she really liked the pizza bagels. Gabby couldn't, because of her Bat Mitzvah, but said she would stop going afterward – if Zara would bring some pizza bagels home for her. Maxi said if Gabby would only stay home if someone brought her pizza bagels, then she would too, so Gabby had to bring some for her until the Bat Mitzvah. Zara was still small enough to pick up, so she would be going every week, but she didn't have a bag to sneak pizza bagels in.

"You can borrow something of mine if you want," Jess offered kindly, misinterpreting my hesitation over my clothes.

"It's okay," I said. "Gabby wants to go to the Goldman's that's further away. We won't run into anyone we know there, anyway. Doesn't matter what I wear."

"You can wear that coat I have that you really like."

"The navy pea coat?"

"Sure," Jess said. "But then you should take an umbrella, too."

"Thanks," I said, feeling better.

After dodging an attempt by Jess's mom to feed me a pre-breakfast, we were off to Mom's house. It felt weird to be driving down our cul-de-sac, and weirder to let myself in without yelling *Hello?!*

The keys were where I'd left them, on the hook by the door. In and out, and gone before anyone knew I was there.

Gabby climbed into the passenger seat and shook her umbrella off before closing it and the door at the same time.

"How's Gabbi-with-an-i?" I asked her.

"Okay," Gabby said.

"Are you excited for your Bat Mitzvah next week?" I asked.

Gabby shrugged. "Rabbi Gold says that where Mom and Dad sit isn't for me to worry about."

"But if we tell them you won't do your *dvar Torah* unless they sit together, I really think they would," I said. "And they won't cause a scene in front of the rabbi. Plus, you know that speech the parents give the kid after the Torah service? If they give it together, it might remind them of how things used to be, when we were a normal family."

"I just don't think there's any point," Gabby said.

"Why not?" I asked, playing dumb.

"I found out," Gabby said.

"Found out what?"

"You know what," Gabby said.

"That Mom made up the Hanukkah Goblin to scare you into eating your veggies?"

"Emilyyyyyyyyyyyy," Gabby said, already weary of me.

"Okay," I said. "How?"

"I went to Dad's house early last Wednesday to get my permission slip for the trip to the Bronx Zoo, and Candace was there. I know it was Wednesday because it was flute lesson day."

"Sorry I didn't tell you. Didn't want to upset you before your Bat Mitzvah."

"I don't want to make things worse for next Saturday. But I promise I will never, ever spend time with Candace. And I won't go in Dad's house while she's living there." Gabby drew a heart in the fog in the window and made a jagged line through it. She looked at it for a minute and then smeared it with the sleeve of her hoodie. "I'm getting a corn muffin," she added.

When Jess and I pulled into the parking lot for Gabby's Bat Mitzvah, there were hardly any cars – just Mom's minivan and a cluster of Mercedes and BMWs. "You know my mom refused to let Dad buy a BMW because she thinks they're Nazi cars?" I asked Jess as we climbed out of the car and transferred our stuff from our purses into the cases for our prayer shawls.

"My mom says the same thing," Jess said. "She says the logo is the propellers of a helicopter or something. From when they made Nazi planes."

"Yeah," I said. "But you know that one?" I pointed at a

scarlet S-class in a handicapped spot. "That one belongs to a Holocaust survivor."

"Hmmm," Jess said.

"Yeah. So I'm thinking, if it doesn't bother him – do you think it really bothered my mom, or she didn't want to let Dad have what he wanted?"

"Don't forget your notes," Jess said, handing me a highlighted photocopy of my Torah portion.

"Do you think it really bothered her that the car is German?" I repeated, stuffing it in the tallit cover, too.

"I don't know, Em. Let's just go inside."

It's important, though, I thought. It makes a difference. It does.

We hung up our coats in the cloakroom, put on our prayer shawls and walked into the sanctuary. The morning prayers hadn't even started. We liked to come around ten-thirty, right on time for the Torah service. I scanned the grand room for my family, who should have been there already.

In the diagonal rows of seats on the right side of the room – facing the altar – where the family of the Bar or Bat Mitzvah sits were Dad's parents, looking suitably grim for a funeral, and unsuitably grim for a *simcha*. There were my aunts and uncles, looking equally like they smelled something bad. I didn't see Dad, but I hadn't seen his car yet. Mom's car was outside, though – so where was Mom? I started to walk down the aisle, head turned to the right to scan the few faces in the seats.

"Em," whispered Jess.

"What?" I said, still scanning the congregation.

"They're there," she said.

I followed her gaze to the left-hand-side diagonal rows, and there, sitting on the edge of her seat with a pinched expression, was Mom. Maxi was next to her, looking uncomfortable, and Zara was on her other side.

"Jesus fucking Christ," I hissed.

"Isn't that where the rabbi's wife and sons sit?" Jess asked. "Which side do you want to sit on?"

"Let's sit in the middle," I said, trying to sound casual, and Jess followed me to the short, straight rows smack in front of the main podium. "Better chance of nailing Gabby in the face with one of those candies we get to toss at her."

Mom lifted a rigid hand in an almost wave, like the Queen of England. I held up two peace signs and hunched my back, doing my best Richard Nixon greeting in response. Mom started to smile, but then her face went slack and she looked at something behind me. Jess and I turned to see.

Dad was walking down the aisle towards us. And on his arm: Candace, in a magenta bandage dress, shoulders bare and blonde hair gleaming like the Eternal Light above the ark.

And Rabbi Gold began to sing: '*How good are your tents, O Jacob; your dwellings, O Israel!*'

TWENTY-FOUR

Maxi, Gabby, Zara and I were having a meeting at the library when Mom came to pick them up on her way home from the store. "I'm telling you," Maxi was saying. "Him bringing her to the Bat Mitzvah was really the last straw."

"So you just want to give up?" I demanded.

"Hi, girls," Mom said, appearing behind me. Gabby shot me a look.

"Mom, did Dad talk to you about this weekend?" Maxi asked, closing her notebook as Mom pulled a chair up next to her.

"I don't know," Mom said.

"What do you mean, you don't know?" I asked.

"He wouldn't stop harassing me. I called Verizon and had his number blocked. Zara, let me see your homework chart."

Zara handed over a blue folder containing a chart with stickers on it. Mom pulled out the chart and looked it over. For Math, Zara received three unicorns. It wasn't bad, but it wasn't five unicorns. "Did you do your math worksheet, hon?" she asked. Zara nodded. Mom flipped over the chart and slid it back into the folder – and then she froze. She removed a piece of loose-leaf paper with chicken-scratch handwriting we could all see was Dad's from the folder. From my seat on Maxi's other side, I could see that it was addressed to Mom, and it began, "Since you refuse to return any of my messages like an adult…"

Mom crumpled the paper into a little ball and tossed it at the recycling bin. It missed. "Okay, girls. Let's go. We'll see what we can scrounge up for dinner." She stood and pushed in her chair, and then looked at me for the first time since she got to the library. "Are you coming?"

"No thanks," I said. "Jessica's mom made a lasagne. You know – like you used to."

The following week, I took the shortcut past Mom and Dad's houses to get to the stables. I glanced to the right as I passed Mom's. Hot Jared's car was in the driveway. I slowed down a little to see if I could catch a glimpse through the kitchen windows, but they must all have been in the living room, because I couldn't see anyone at all. Checking that there was no one in the road behind me, I stopped and looked to the left at Dad's house.

A yard sign, like the kind political candidates give out, was sitting in the little strip of green yard in front of the gate. But instead of 'Ken Liebovitz for School Board', it said '72h & settlement offer disappears'. I pulled over in front of Mom's driveway, parked my car and yanked the sign out of the muddy ground. I saw Candace peering out from a little gap in the curtains. When she saw me, she let go of the heavy red fabric, and the curtain fell shut. As I tossed the yard sign into my backseat, I glanced at Mom's house again. There was a slight movement to the blinds in the mud room windows. I slammed my car door shut and floored the gas, making a satisfying screech.

Angry, I chewed on one of the unpeeled carrots I had on the passenger seat for Poco. They tasted like dirt, but the crunch was satisfying. I rolled down my window, ignoring the cold, damp wind rushing in, and threw the carrot butt out the window. When I arrived at the barn, I parked my car by Poco's turnout, where he was grazing near the fence. I slammed my car door shut and saw Poco's whole body tense and lurch forward, in an aborted bolt. "Sorry," I muttered at him, and held up a carrot. "You dumb fuck," I added affectionately when he made a big show of coming closer, but cautiously, as if my motives could not be trusted.

"How's our loco Poco today?" asked Donna, the barn manager, sneaking up on us as I tricked him into putting his nose through his halter by dangling a carrot in front of it.

"We'll see. He hasn't tried to kill me yet, but I just got here."

"Well, I have money on you staying on longer than eight minutes today, so don't disappoint me. You, either," she added, making a stern face at Poco, who made crazy eyes back at her.

"We'll do our best," I said, and I started to lead Poco to the main barn, but Donna didn't move out of the way.

"Emily," Donna started, and then she sighed, reaching out a hand and resting it on Poco's shoulder. He twitched his muscle, and she removed it. I rolled my eyes at him. Donna laid her hand on my shoulder, instead. "Your father called this morning."

I started to feel trembly, but I tried hard to hold it in for Poco's sake. "Oh?" I said, but it came out croaky.

Donna sighed again, put her hands in her pockets, and looked at the ground. "Yeah, he said that you're giving him some trouble. He asked me to keep you from seeing Poco for a while. No, don't worry," she said, seeing my expression, "I told him to go to hell. Politely. Said it's none of my business what goes on between you and him, just what goes on between you and your horse. I wasn't sure I should even mention it. But I thought you should know."

"Thanks," I said, wobbly from the sudden adrenaline surge and then the overwhelming relief. I put my hand on Poco's withers and leaned on him a little. He shifted his weight to accommodate me but didn't object.

"You know I would never have any part of that, right?"

I shrugged. "He'll try again. Or my mom will. He could stop paying. Neither of them really wants me to have him."

"Emily, I will do whatever it takes to help you. Okay? If your dad stops paying, we'll lease him from you for a lesson horse. Not actually, of course. I can't put anyone else on Poco. My insurance doesn't cover gross negligence. But we'll work something out. This isn't something you need to worry about." Donna wrapped me into a hug.

"Thank you," I whispered into her shoulder.

"No stirrups today," Donna answered.

As Poco and I walked around the ring to warm up, I thought about Donna's offer. So it was my fault when I hit the ground. I hadn't seen the deer coming, and I wasn't ready when all four of Poco's hooves left the ground at once in a hop-buck-twist movement that would have won him a title on *So You Think You Can Dance*. I pushed myself into a sitting position in the dirt and watched my horse racing around in wild circles, stirrups and reins flapping.

"*Get the fuck back on that damn horse!*" I heard Donna holler through the office window, where she'd witnessed my mistake. "Do you want four or five aspirin?" she added, coming over to the gate with the bottle, kicking the office door shut behind her.

I spat out a mouthful of blood. "I'm fine," I said. "I'm great." I gave her a beatific smile, and I got the fuck back on that damn horse.

TWENTY-FIVE

Jared spent his free time modifying bicycles for kids with special needs, according to Maxi and Gabby. We had pizza together at Mom's house while she and Jared were out, and they told me everything about him.

"He volunteers in the special needs school all the time," Maxi elaborated, sounding impressed.

"He tricked out my new bike," Gabby added.

"He fixed the TV," Zara said.

"So?" I asked.

"So he's not that bad, really," Maxi said. "You'd like him."

I raised my eyebrows at her.

"I didn't like him either, but…" Gabby started, but she trailed off.

"But nothing," I said. "It's totally inappropriate. And you won't talk to Candace. So you're being a hypocrite."

"What's a hypocrite?" Zara asked.

"It's what Emily calls people who don't agree with her," Maxi said.

"Shut the fuck up," I said, kicking her under the table.

"Ow!" Maxi snapped, and then we were quiet for a few minutes. I watched oil drip from the fold in Gabby's pizza and make a giant grease stain on her paper plate.

"So all of you idiots actually like having Hot Jared in our house?" I asked.

"I didn't mean to," Gabby said.

"He's just really hard not to like," Maxi said.

"He fixed the TV," Zara repeated.

"I thought we were in this together," I said. "You all disgust me."

Mom called me to say she missed me and ask if I wanted to come have dinner with her and Jared at home. I thought about it for a moment. I thought about seeing him cycling to Mom's house in the frigid afternoon yesterday, as Jess and I drove past him. He was wearing neon green spandex and an extra layer of environmentalist self-righteousness. "No, thank you," I answered politely. "I would rather go to Times Square on New Year's Eve than have dinner with you and Jared. I would rather drive into Manhattan when Obama is in town. I would rather—"

"Message received," Mom said.

"And by the way, I wouldn't try to get between me and my horse. Both of us bite." I hung up the phone by tossing it across Jess's room.

"She cannot be serious," Jess said, looking up from her computer screen. "Have dinner with her and Hot Jared? What is she thinking?"

"I need to go talk to an animal about this," I said.

I drove to the barn on icy roads. "Call Gabby," I

instructed my car, keeping my eyes on the road.

"Sorry, I don't see Maggie in your contact list," my car chirped.

"Never mind," I said.

On Main Street, I passed by Jared cycling. I gripped the steering wheel hard until my knuckles went white. And then I was going too fast, too close to Jared. I yanked the wheel hard and skidded away from him on some chunks of road salt. I looked in my rearview mirror, heart pounding. Jared had pulled over, and was yelling something and gesticulating at me.

I drove the rest of the way to the barn in shock at what I almost did. When I got there, I ducked into Poco's stall without stopping in the office to talk to anyone. I could see through the window fog that Donna and some of the old-timers were in there, drinking coffee with a splash of Bailey's in it and warming their cold, wet socks against the radiator. I put on my cold, stiff riding gloves – the fleece-lined ones – and exhaled on my fists to warm them. Poco snorted at me as I fumbled the buckles of his blanket in my stiff fingers. Calm down, I told myself sternly, as my horse started to pick up on my racing heartbeat and shallow breath. His eyes were bright and his nostrils flared, and when the blanket strap slipped through my gloves and my hand jerked to catch it, his head shot up into the air in alarm.

"I'm sorry," I told him. "I'm sorry."

After staying in the barn with Poco for as long as I could handle the cold, I crept into the empty office and picked up a three-year-old Dover Saddlery catalogue. The feeling was starting to come back to my numb skin, which prickled under my jeans. I felt my phone vibrating in my pocket, and I pulled it out to look at the screen.

"Maxi?" I answered.

"Emily, the police are here," Maxi said.

"Where 'here'?"

"Mom's. They're talking to Jared."

I felt a slight panic. "What about?"

"I don't know. Mom told me to wait upstairs. I'm listening through the vent in your room, but I can only hear a few words—"

"Does Jared look okay? Is Mom okay?"

"Yes, they're fine. Listen. I think it has something to do with Dad. He's watching. From his house. I can see him at the window. Wait – Mom's yelling. Be quiet."

I waited, and I could hear the faint, tinny sound of Mom's voice coming through the vent, and Maxi breathing.

"Dad called the police," Maxi said, her tone amazed. "He said that they had to remove Jared from our house because he's a paedophile and can't be around his daughters."

I froze. I knew for certain that Dad had not called the police. I knew, because it was me. I saw an episode of *Law and Order: SVU* that gave me the idea. People take this kind of thing seriously – they have to.

"But Jared is basically a saint," I said, breathing through my nose so Maxi wouldn't hear me hyperventilate through the phone. "Except that he's twenty-five, but that's not his fault. It's Mom we should be angry at, anyway."

"They're saying Jared can't go near the school he

volunteers at until there's an investigation," Maxi said. "Wait – I think Zara just got home. I'll go get her."

"Is Gabby home?"

"No, she's with Gabbi-with-an-i, luckily."

"Listen – don't tell Gabby that Dad had anything to do with this. And don't say anything to Zara."

"Yeah, of course," Maxi said. "I can't believe Dad would do this, though. Jared's really nice."

"And Dad's not really nice."

"Would you please come over?"

I hesitated. "Yeah, okay," I said.

When I got to Mom's house, there was a lady in a cheap pantsuit sitting at the table with Mom. I looked at her, and she looked back at me with a blank expression and said nothing. "Emily, meet our caseworker," Mom said drily.

I turned on my heel and marched upstairs to find my sisters.

TWENTY-SIX

I was in AP US History when the guidance counsellor buzzed the classroom over the intercom to ask me to come to her office.

"Ooooooooh," said a handful of my classmates, and my history teacher. "Emily's in trouble!"

"Grow up, Mr Levine," I said, trying to look unconcerned as I stuffed my things into my bag.

"Mr Levine, can I go with her?" Jess asked, hand in the air.

"You can join her if one of you can tell me what year Nixon was impeached," Mr Levine said.

"Trick question," I said. "He resigned. In 1974."

"Goodbye, Mr President," Mr Levine said, gesturing at the door.

"Goodbye, Mr President," Jess answered.

The noise of our footsteps ricocheted off the grimy tiles as we walked to the main building. Focused on staying calm, I said nothing.

"I'm sure it's nothing bad," Jess offered, after a few minutes.

I didn't meet her gaze.

In the guidance office, the secretary told me to have a seat. "And what can I do for you, Miss Siegel?" she asked, looking at Jess over her glasses.

"I'm here for emotional support," Jess said, and sat next to me without waiting for permission.

Mrs Martinez pursed her lips. "You'll have to wait out here when Miss Weiss calls Emily in," she said disapprovingly. "And I'm not going to be able to write you a pass for your next class."

"I have a lunch," Jess said.

Miss Weiss poked her head out of her office. "Emily, great, come in. Hi, Jess," she added. "You just here with Emily?"

"Yeah," Jess said. "It's okay, I have a lunch period next."

"That's fine, you can wait for her out here."

Jess gave me an encouraging smile as I slung my bag over my shoulder and walked slowly towards Miss Weiss's door.

I was shocked to see Maxi sitting in one of the chairs when I entered the tiny, concrete-walled office. Maxi raised her eyebrows and flattened her lips into a thin line.

"Is this about the CPS case?" I started to ask, at the same time as Maxi started to say, "Is this about the engagement?"

"Engagement?" I asked, stunned.

"Child Protective Services?" Miss Weiss asked simultaneously, also stunned.

"What?" Maxi said.

"What the fuck is going on?" I demanded.

"I called you both in here to let you know there's been an accident," Miss Weiss said. "Your mother called. She's fine, but she won't be home when you get there. Her, um, friend, Jared, was hurt. It's serious, but he's stable. She's with him in the hospital, though. What was that about a CPS case?"

"Jared's her fiancé," Maxi said. "He's hurt? What happened?"

"What do you mean, fiancé?" I said.

"He was run off the road by a car. What CPS case?"

"Our father says that Jared is a paedophile," I answered. "Mom got engaged to him?"

"Last night," Maxi said. "I was going to tell you before she said something. I was waiting to see you in person."

"Come on," I said to Maxi, picking up my stuff.

"Wait—" Miss Weiss said, looking overwhelmed, and like she wanted to stop us and ask us more questions I couldn't answer, to her or even to myself.

"We have to go," I said.

"Your mother and her fiancé are at Nyack Hospital," Miss Weiss said, deciding not to try and stop us. "Girls?" she called after us, and Maxi and I turned at the door. Miss Weiss sighed. "Here's my home phone number," she said, scribbling on a piece of paper. "And here's early dismissal passes for you both, and Jess. You can call me any time. And please come see me tomorrow morning when you get here. Or on Monday. Whenever you're back."

I reached for the piece of paper, but she didn't let it go. "Can I hug you girls?" she asked.

Maxi swallowed. "Yeah," she said.

"If you must," I said, because it would make her feel better.

Jess stood up when she saw us coming out of Miss Weiss's office. "What happened? Is everything okay?"

"We have to go," I said. "You too. Here's a pass. I'll explain in the car. Let's just go right now, please."

"Yeah, of course," Jess said. We walked quickly out the main entrance, past the security guard, who called out, "Hey—" to us and half-rose as we made for the door, but sat back down and waved us on when Jess held up the pink early dismissal pass as I held open the door for Maxi.

"It was only a matter of time before something like this happened. He was asking for it. Drive to Nyack Hospital, okay?" I told Jess, buckling my seatbelt. "Take the causeway. Maxi, explain what's going on while I call Dad, okay? I need to tell him to pick up Gabby and Zara today and take them home. And tell him I swear to God if he doesn't make sure Candace isn't there I will key his stupid car."

As I held the phone to my ear, I imagined I could actually hear that old, annoying Nick at Nite show character whining nasally, "Did I do that?"

But I didn't. I just wanted to. And it's not what you feel that counts. Only what you do.

TWENTY-SEVEN

"Are you going to tell the court all this stuff?" I asked.

"Only if you're okay with that," Dr Stein said.

"I don't believe you. You work for Dad, technically. He pays you. I'm sure he would want the judge to hear about how Mom is acting. Even though he's just as bad."

"Emily, I'm on your side here."

"Nobody's on my side. Everyone is on Mom's side or Dad's side, and it changes a lot and it can be hard to keep track of who's on what side every day, but nobody's ever on my side."

"Your family is a hot mess, but they love you."

"That's the technical term, is it?"

Dr Stein was quiet. She maintained eye contact with me, but she was scribbling on her lavender-coloured legal pad. She caught me looking and changed the cross of her legs so that it was harder for me to see the page.

I crossed my arms and glared at her.

"Why don't we talk about something different – if you were to choose one parent to live with for the year or so you have left before college, which one would it be, and why?"

"I would live in the apartment over the barn."

"The options are Mom or Dad."

"C – none of the above."

Dr Stein put down her pad and leaned forward, with her elbows on her knees and her chin in her hands. This was her Earnest Pose. Her face was too close to my face. I liked her Listening Pose better, with her hands pressed flat together and her fingertips underneath her chin, like a Paget illustration. Sherlock Holmes in *The Adventure of the Very Bad Parents*.

I sighed. "I guess Mom. No – Dad. Wait – what did Maxi, Gabby, and Zara say?"

"It's confidential. And I'm wondering where you want to live."

"I'm thinking. This is a real Sophie's Choice. I think. I've never actually seen it."

"Why don't we try talking it through?"

I go into the Thinking Pose to see if it will help. It does. "Well, I think Zara should probably live with Dad, because she's little, still, and she probably doesn't even really understand that Candace is his girlfriend, or what he did to Jared and Mom. But he'll always remember to make sure she brushes her teeth, which Mom doesn't now, because she's too busy taking care of Jared since he can't really do anything in the wheelchair yet."

Dr Stein had picked up the legal pad again while I was talking and was again scribbling furiously on it without looking. I could see that it was slanting off the lines but couldn't read it at that angle either.

"And Gabby, she should definitely live with Dad, at least until she's in high school," I said. "Because when she's with Mom, nobody tries to stop her from eating ten corn muffins every day."

"Corn muffins?" Dr Stein repeated.

"Corn muffins," I confirmed.

"Go on." Dr Stein underlined something on her page.

"It isn't neglect. Letting her eat too many corn muffins. You try and stop her."

"I didn't say it was. But you think your dad could do that? Make sure she eats well?"

"I didn't say that. I said he would try."

"Okay. Continue," she said.

"Maxi should live with Mom, though."

"Why?"

"She's sensitive. She comes off all bossy and shit. It's just that she's insecure."

"That's very perceptive," Dr Stein said, nodding her I Agree nod. "So, you think she would be better off with your mother, because she's sensitive? Why is that?"

"Well, you've met Dad."

"Okay," she said, and this time she gave me her I'm Listening and Not Judging nod. "Dad isn't warm."

"Was that a question?"

"I'm clarifying."

"Like I said. You met him."

"Okay," she said. "So," she made a big show of setting down her notebook on her side table and leaning forward again, "what about you?"

"I'll get back to you."

Jess didn't know about the psychiatrist. She knew about everything else – the CPS worker, even. All embarrassing, but somehow they didn't have anything to do with me, really; not the way talking to a therapist did. So, she knew almost everything.

Just not this.

I told her I was going to the barn. In the parking lot, I switched my flats for paddock boots and stomped around in the muddy divider between the exit and entrance lanes before getting in my car. I picked a piece of hay out of the footwell and swept it up with my hair into a low ponytail.

Do psychiatrists have to take an oath, like real doctors do? I wondered, driving back to Jess's house. Do they have to promise to do no harm? Or are they more like cops, who can lie to you about what other people have said and what they know, and who don't have to keep any promises they make? And what if the psychiatrist works for the courts, but is paid by Dad – what then?

I hadn't told Dr Stein anything I wouldn't have said to either of their faces. Nothing embarrassing, and nothing untrue they could use to catch me out if they questioned me. Even Maxi couldn't get mad if she heard what I'd said about where I should live. It was only my opinion. You're allowed to feel how you want to feel, even if someone else doesn't like it.

I pulled briefly over onto the muddy shoulder of the county road to get my tyres dirty and clicked on the radio. Leonard Lopate was hosting a debate about the aftermath of a failed attempt by the Israeli intelligence agency to assassinate someone from Hamas.

I wondered how many more rungs Mom and Dad had to go down the Intractable Conflict ladder before we got to that new low.

On Monday, in English class, we were given the assignment of writing a poem. Mrs Greenberg said it could be about anything we wanted.

On Tuesday, I got called into the school counsellor's office.

TWENTY-EIGHT

The most poetic way to die
Is the subtle knife, sliding by
The quiet poison slipping in
A changing heart, from within
And yet the prettiest death of all
Is death by gold, the wherewithal
Slinking heavily through the veins
A weighty pulse, and pretty pains
And as it cleaves to the walls
Of hearts and limbs and lungs, enthrals—
Prettily poisoning, the cost is dear
Of the pretty gold, so near
Lustrous death, and ductile pain
As the metal makes its gain
It slithers before the ruby heart—the pulse will stall
And far too prettily to appal
The harbinger's beauty does belie
First pretty pains, and then you die
The ruby flits and flutters and then it stills

And the pretty pain cries, for the precious rubies it spills
Pay dearly for beauty, beauty that kills
More pulchritudinous than arsenic or pills
Stopped the ruby, with gold
The ruby grows still and then grows cold
Still so poetic, and as such
The pain is never, never too much
Malleable meanness, ductile death
Has forever taken another's breath
And forever to another watchful eye
The very prettiest way to die

I'd written it knowing that I would get called into the guidance counsellor's office. The thing was, I was counting on them calling Mom and Dad. If they'd come, I would have gone through with it, and said I was really depressed because of their divorce, and then at the very least they'd have to work together to help me through it. And maybe that would be enough to get them to see that things weren't any better now that they were apart – they were just worse.

But they didn't come, so I had to improvise.

"*House*. It was inspired by an episode of *House*," I said.

They glared at me, nonplussed and suspicious.

"You know. *House*. The FOX channel? Sherlock Holmes with a lab coat? Witty one-liners and prescription painkiller abuse?"

More staring.

"Hugh Laurie. Half of Fry and Laurie. No? Nothing?"

"I've seen the show," Miss Weiss conceded. "I didn't realise Hugh Laurie was British. His accent is very good."

"What does this have to do with a television show?" Mrs Greenberg asked.

"There was a re-run the other day of an episode where this woman wants out of her marriage, so she poisons her husband. With gold. The assignment was to write a poem."

The three adults were staring more angrily now.

"Well, *I* thought it was poetic."

"Are you having any thoughts of harming yourself?" Miss Weiss asked.

"C'mon. I'm already having my head shrunk, on the reg," I said. I turned to Dr Stein. "Back me up here."

"I've observed no signs of suicidal thoughts in Emily," she said.

"Homicidal thoughts, on the other hand…" I said.

Everyone frowned at me.

"I'm kidding."

TWENTY-NINE

I was taping a poster of Stephen Colbert posing as Uncle Sam over the window in my shared bedroom in Dad's house when Maxi burst in, holding a notebook aloft. "Look…" – Maxi paused dramatically – "at this."

"What is it?"

Maxi held it out by way of reply. I sighed and abandoned Colbert to dangle by one scotch-taped corner.

"Dad's going to be angry that you are taping things to the walls," Maxi said, flopping on our child-sized trundle bed and bouncing her heels against the lower mattress.

"It's not the walls; it's the windows. And he didn't give us curtains. And anyway, good. This house is bullshit." I sighed, sat down on a suitcase and opened the black marble notebook. "What is this?" I asked, looking at Dad's doctorly chicken-scratch handwriting on the pages. I saw hand-drawn columns for dates, times and notes.

"It's a ledger," Maxi said. "Dad's been spying on Mom."

"Great. Our very own *American Psycho*," I said.

"He's been doing it for years."

I flicked through the ledger, words blurring a little, but not enough that I couldn't read them. Acid rose in my throat and tickled my tonsils. What would it say about me?

"This is legitimately fucking terrifying," I said. "Here: 'Zara tired at dinner, up too late?' It sounds like Dad has been using this to build a custody case against Mom."

"Oh, there's even better ones than that in there. There's one about Mom's short haircut. He wrote the word 'lesbian' with a question mark next to it," Maxi said.

"What does that even mean?" I muttered. "By the way, where did you find this?"

"I was looking for printer paper, and I found this in the drawer of the built-in desk in the library," said Maxi.

"He didn't even bother to hide it?"

"He didn't even bother to hide it," Maxi confirmed.

"Incredible," I said, though it wasn't – and continued flipping through the pages.

February 3, 2009 4:18 a.m. Mini Cooper with bicycle rack still in driveway

As I read it aloud to Maxi, an idea crossed my mind. "Do you know what I think?" I asked her. "I think this is the key to unlocking the great mystery of Dad's brain. This happened right before Dad made those accusations about Jared. I bet this is why he did it."

"What do you mean?"

"Look – the day before, he insists to Mom that he has a right to meet and approve anyone who is spending the night in the same house as his kids, and she tells him to fuck off."

"So it was – what? Revenge?"

"I don't think it was revenge. I think he was trying to force her to introduce Jared to him, prove he wasn't dangerous, whatever. Only it wasn't about actually being worried about us; it was that he didn't like how Mom refused. I bet he threatened her with this before he did it. But when she didn't give in, he had to follow through."

Maxi took the ledger back from me and flipped through it herself. "Wow," she said simply.

"But it doesn't really matter why. What matters is what we do with this new information. If there are notes—" I began.

"Do you think there are also pictures?" Maxi finished my thought.

"Exactly. A picture's worth a thousand words. And if we found them…"

"Where should we look? His computer?"

"Well, we can't now; it's already six. He could come home any minute."

"Then we look tomorrow."

"Works for me. What do you think, should we tell Gabby and Zara about this? Do we tell Mom? Should we confront Dad, or put it back where we found it?"

"I'm thinking tell Gabby, but not Zara or Mom yet. She's busy dealing with Jared right now," Maxi said, thinking as she spoke. "And we probably need to think about exactly what we want from Dad before we confront him."

"Good thinking. So we put this back where you found

it, and don't let on that we know until we're going to do something about it."

"I guess we'll just know when the time is right."

"I guess we will," I said. "Okay, I'm going back to Jess's house. But I'll come back tomorrow, at around four-thirty, after musical rehearsal. Let's see what else we can find."

I texted Jess, who wanted in. I told her she could come, but she had to follow mine and Maxi's instructions. She had agreed, but when we got to the house and started the search in the master bedroom, she was squeamish.

We moved to a less private area. I was going through a cabinet in the den off the kitchen, rifling through boxes of wires and obsolete remote controls, when I glanced over my shoulder to see Jess peering into a box in the closet without taking anything out.

"Jess, we do not have time for this," I told her for the second time.

"Well, sor-ry if I think it's weird to be going through your dad's stuff!"

"I told you that's what we were going to be doing! You were the one who insisted on helping."

"Maybe I can be moral support instead."

"What does that entail?" Maxi called from the kitchen, where she was going through a junk drawer with batteries, old mail and paper clips in it.

"Good vocab," I called back at her. "And good question."

"I'll make you guys snacks," Jess said desperately.

"Keeping us fed regardless of the circumstances. You'll make some doctor or lawyer a great Jewish wife someday," I said. It came out nastier than I meant for it to.

Jess pressed her lips into a hard slash, trying to keep her face straight, but failing to halt her mouth's determined downward tilt. I felt terrible, but I was desperate to keep searching, so I didn't stop as I threw her a meagre bone. "Some pizza bites would be great."

I heard Maxi mutter a quiet, "Thanks," to Jess as she came through to the kitchen, stepping over the detritus of Maxi's search to get to the freezer. There was a squeezing feeling in my chest. I thought about how 'thanks' could mean so many things, and how it sometimes means 'I'm sorry'.

When Jess silently put a plate of warm pizza bites on the kitchen island, I shoved the things I was searching back into the cabinet and slid onto a stool. "Thanks," I told her.

The next time, Dad was away on a business trip. None of us was entirely sure why a doctor might need to drop everything and go to Las Vegas for a weekend, but Maxi and I didn't care. It was the perfect opportunity, after weeks of being thwarted, to continue our probing of Dad's house. I thought there was a good chance we would find something we could use to get rid of Candace. Maxi was less sure but wanted to help.

I was relieved when Maxi said she would come, because that meant she hadn't given up completely yet. This time, out of kindness, Maxi suggested that we not invite Jess to the search. I agreed on the condition that Maxi take over Jess's role and provide the snacks. We had the whole weekend to ourselves to toss the house, and since Mom no longer read any of Dad's communiqués, she didn't know he wasn't home. Candace had, as far as we could tell, gone with Dad. "You don't think Candace left Candy home and hired a dogsitter, did she?" Maxi asked worriedly as we went in through the garage door.

"No way a dogsitter is good enough for that bitch," I said.

"Don't call Candace a bitch," Maxi rebuked. "Women shouldn't tear each other down using sexist language."

"I was talking about Candy, the actual female dog," I said, "but thanks for reading over my sociology essay for me."

"No, you weren't," Maxi said, kicking off her shoes in the mud room by habit. But Dad wasn't here, and I was going to wear my shoes all over his house.

"We're going to have to go through Dad's room today."

"Okay, but we're not touching Candace's stuff."

"Why not?" I asked indignantly.

"Do you want to get a disease?" Maxi asked, grinning.

"Atta girl," I said.

Candace's presence was only noticeable where I'd first seen it: in the walk-in closet, the right half of which had been given over to shades of magenta and lime green, and on the 'hers' side of the his-and-hers bathroom counter, which was covered in shiny bottles. Remembering how it had felt to see these here the first time, when I'd learned that Dad had secretly moved her in, I obeyed an impulse to open one of the bottles and pour its contents down the sink. I replaced the contents of what was apparently a sixty-five-dollar jar of cold cream with the whole contents of a tube of Preparation H from Dad's medicine cabinet. Two birds, one stone.

I moved on to Dad's night table, which had on it one of many identical black pairs of Walgreens reading glasses, a copy of the *Wall Street Journal* and a manila file. I looked at it cursorily, dismissing it as a patient chart, which would be unethical and unenlightening for me to open. But there was nothing in the place where three coloured stickers with the first letters of a patient's last name belonged, and some of the papers peeking out of the file looked like a spreadsheet. I opened it, resolving that if I saw a patient chart inside, I'd close it before I could read any of the words.

It wasn't a chart. It was a spreadsheet, logging cheque numbers, amounts and dates, and a column for notes. It showed that Dad was giving six thousand dollars a month to Mom in child support for the last year, except for a row in which he'd decreased the amount to four thousand, five hundred dollars and added a cheque for the remaining one thousand, five hundred dollars with a note that said Jess's parents' names and address.

I took photos of some of the papers. Then I replaced the file, closed the door and walked out of his room. In the hallway, a framed poster of the Hippocratic Oath caught my eye. 'First, do no harm...'

THIRTY

Maxi did not speak to Dad when he finally called to ask why she wasn't at his house, two weeks after she stopped going. She did not speak to him when he rolled down his window and shouted hello at her on his way past her bus stop one morning before school. And she did not speak to him when he went to her basketball game at the JCC and ran up and down the sidelines cheering at her.

"Maxi has gotten much better," he said as we watched her pass the ball. "Despite her height disadvantage."

"Everyone on the team is short. Anyway, people used to think Jews were good at basketball because we're short so we have better balance," I said. "Also because we're sneaky."

Dad pursed his lips. He left after Maxi brushed past him, close enough that when she tossed her long, wet hair over her shoulder, it left a mark on Dad's sport coat.

"Is Passover Dad's holiday this year, or Mom's holiday?" she asked when I caught up to her.

"Mom's," I said. We drove to Mom's house in silence. When I pulled into the driveway, Maxi put her hand on the door handle and waited for me to shut off the car. I didn't.

"Are you coming in?" she asked.

"Are Mom and Jared home?"

"Yeah."

"No."

"You're going to have to talk to him eventually."

"Why? Are you going to have to talk to Dad eventually?" I asked.

"That's different."

"Why?"

"Because Dad actually did something wrong!" she said. "All Jared did was get run off the road. And you know what? I think Dad did it."

"Dad didn't run Jared off the road," I scoffed.

"How do you know?"

"He just didn't. There are lots of bad drivers in Rockland, and it's not his style. He doesn't hurt people physically. Just leaves emotional scars is all," I joked. "Speaking of which – do you have any ideas for how to use the dirt we have on Dad?"

Maxi sighed. "I don't know. He *did* report Jared to the police."

I swallowed hard. "What if we tell him he has to get rid of Candace? Or is that too much? Maybe she just has to move back out?"

"I don't know. I'm not sure there's any point, anyway." Maxi looked through the window at Mom's house. "Just come hang out inside for a while. You don't have to talk to Mom or Jared. Gabby and Zara are home, too."

"Okay," I said, feeling a little surge of panic at Maxi's defeatist attitude. If she gave up, it would just be me on my own. "I'll come inside, but I won't talk to Mom."

"Hi, Emily!" Mom chirped when I came inside and kicked off my snowy boots in the foyer.

"She still isn't talking to you," Maxi said.

"Okay, hon," Mom said. I looked at her. She was wearing a bathrobe and holding one of those prank gift glasses, overly huge, that was three-quarters of the way filled with red wine.

"Gabby, is Mom cooking something?" I asked as she trotted into the room.

"Graciela. She's Jared's home health aide."

I made a face and followed Gabby and Maxi upstairs. I noticed as we climbed that there were no longer any haphazard piles of things on each step, waiting for their owners to take them upstairs. The carpet in the upstairs hallway, too, was clean and clear of any objects. The door to my bedroom at the end of the hall, which I had not slept in for a very long time now, was closed. I opened it, half expecting to find that it had been turned into a flower room with an impractical flagstone floor, like Myrna Loy wanted in *Mr Blandings Builds His Dream House*. Mom had always adored that movie. But instead, it looked like I had left it – but cleaner. The room smelled lemony, and the clothing that had been tossed on my bed was gone. Further inspection revealed that it had been hung up in the closet. Even my bathroom was gleaming.

"Did someone clean my room?" I asked, joining the others in the den.

"Graciela did that," Zara said. "She cleans everything."

"I thought you said she was Jared's nurse," I said to Gabby.

"She's not exactly a nurse. She just kind of does everything," Maxi said. "All the stuff Mom used to do."

"It's kinda nice," Gabby said.

"Yeah, things have been kind of okay around here," Maxi continued. "I know you think it's weird, but Jared's still really nice, even though he still can't walk yet. And I think Mom's pretty happy. She said she and Jared are going to get married this spring."

"She didn't tell me that."

"She was going to. Anyway, Mom got Graciela to come so that she could go back to the jewellery store more often. And Graciela always remembers to make us what we like for dinner, and pack us lunches."

"Plus, she lets us watch whatever we want on TV until Mom comes home," said Zara. "And Mom said we might even be able to get a dog!"

"That wouldn't be a dog for us," Maxi explained. "She was talking about an assistance dog for Jared."

"What would it do, fetch him things?" I asked.

Maxi shrugged.

"But Mom said that when the dog isn't working, we can play with him," Zara assured me.

That reminded me of something. "Where is our parrot?"

"Gone," Gabby said vaguely.

I decided to let this go and at least pretend to do my homework. When I opened my backpack, they followed my lead. Though I was distracted, thinking about what they said and what I'd seen for myself so far, my sisters worked quietly until Graciela shouted up to us that dinner was ready. "That's my cue," I said, stuffing things in my bag. "Gotta get back to Jess's."

We hurtled down the stairs in descending age order, but I stopped in the foyer to put my shoes back on as the rest of them continued into the kitchen.

"Emily, honey," Mom said, leaning against the door from the foyer to the kitchen. "Can I talk to you for a minute?"

"You can talk, but I won't listen," I said, sitting on the bottom stair and lacing up my boots.

"That's okay," Mom said. "Emily, I want you to move back home. We miss you very much. I miss you very much. And I understand that you're not a huge fan of the way things turned out, but if you just give it a chance, you'll see that things are better now. Better than they were before your father moved out, even."

I stood and crossed my arms. "Is Jared still living here?"

"Yes."

"Then I'm not."

"Your father lives with someone," Mom pointed out.

"Drat. You have me there. Wait – nope, I don't live with him either."

"Why are you punishing me?" Mom asked, her mouth open too wide, showing me Shiraz-tinted teeth. "Your father is the one who moved out."

I glared at her.

"Em, really. Just give things a chance. I'm not asking you to do it for me."

"Then who?"

Mom looked inside the kitchen, where I could see that Gabby was trying to shove a green bean into Zara's nose and Maxi was trying to stop her. Graciela was looking at them uninterestedly.

"We'll see," I said, and I closed the door behind me much more quietly than usual.

THIRTY-ONE

"Zara, I thought you were going to have Regan over this afternoon for a playdate," Gabby said.

Zara looked up from her bag of Pirate's Booty and stared at her for a moment. "Oh yeah," she said. "What time is it?"

"It's four-thirty," I said. "Maybe you should call her."

"I don't want to call her house. Graciela, can you call her for me?"

"*Lo siento*, my English no is good," Graciela said, sounding more Ecuadorian than usual.

"*Eso es una mentira, y todos lo sabemos*," Gabby said, crossing her arms primly. "Zara, would you like one of us to call for you?"

"No," Zara said. "It has to be a grownup. I told her someone would be here to watch us."

"I can pretend to be Mom," I said, and made a phone out of my left hand and imitated Mom's exasperated 'Hello?' to illustrate my point.

Gabby rolled her eyes. Zara giggled but said no, that she'd rather wait for Mom to get home. The store closed at five, so she would be back soon, with Maxi, who had been working with her that day. I'd resumed my shifts at the store since moving back in with Mom, but she'd decided only one of us could work at a time to cut back on business expenses. Maxi promised that she would work on Mom while she was there but be really subtle – just reminding her of the good times we'd had as a family. Like our trip to Miami, right up until the rental car broke down and Mom said she'd told him they should have paid more for the roadside assistance, and he yelled at her that she could just go back home early if she didn't like his vacation. Or the trip to London, right up until Dad insisted on a day trip to Stonehenge in the pouring, horizontal rain, and Mom came down with a cold and wouldn't leave the hotel for the rest of the trip. Or the time we went to the Grand Canyon, right up until Dad ordered 'chili con carne' for dinner at the ranch and Mom made fun of him because she said that was redundant, and Dad got angry because what he said was technically correct and that was what the menu had called it, anyway.

"Suit yourself," I told Zara, only slightly miffed.

Mom and Maxi were in the door by five-twenty, so the store must not have been very busy. That meant Mom would be a little edgier, so we would all have to be careful not to upset her. She threw her jacket over the end of the banister instead of hanging it up in the hall closet and didn't even kick off her shoes before stomping across to the liquor cabinet to open a bottle of cabernet.

Zara wisely said hello to Mom and told her that all her

homework was done and that she'd eaten a healthy snack and nothing else since she got home from school before asking Mom to call Regan's parents and ask where she was. Mom was surprised to hear that Regan hadn't come home with Zara on the school bus, which was what she'd thought the plan was, but Zara had thought Regan was staying for after-school club first and would be dropped off at our house after that. Regan's mom had paid in advance for the ten-week session, but 'wasn't about to waste free childcare'.

"Okay," Mom sighed, setting down her wine glass on the coffee table. "Bring me a phone."

Zara went off in search of one of the forever-misplaced portable landlines, pressing a button on the phone's base in the kitchen that caused the receiver to emit a shrill beep until we located it behind Mom's back, in the couch cushions. Mom pulled it out and asked Zara to bring the class contact list from the corkboard in the den. She dialled Regan's home number and seemed startled when someone answered right away.

I was paying close attention to what was happening but trying not to be too obvious about it. I stayed bent over the dining table as if I were still doing my Sociology readings and listened to Mom's side of the conversation. It didn't sound like it was going well, and a quick glance at her expression confirmed it. "I see," Mom was saying into the receiver. "Actually, she's my fiancé's home health aide, not a housekeeper. And I don't really know what concern it is of yours, but I've seen her Green Card."

Zara looked at me questioningly, but I gave her a tiny headshake to warn her not to ask any questions and to just be quiet. Nothing good would come of interrupting Mom right now. Mom had stood up and crossed one arm, continuing to hold the receiver to her ear but looking like she was ready to slam it down on whatever surface was closest.

"What does it matter whether or not she has a driver's licence, Elise?" Mom was saying, gesticulating with her free hand. "She's not their chauffeur; she's just an adult in the house to make sure it doesn't burn down!"

Whatever Regan's mom said in response, it made Mom angrier. She was pacing back and forth across the living room. "What fire?" she demanded, stopping and putting her hand on her hip.

Gabby, observing from behind the doorway to the kitchen, exchanged a glance with me and gestured in the direction of the backyard. Immediately, I knew what she meant. Last week, on one of the first mild nights of this year, Zara and Regan had been playing in the backyard and asked Graciela if they could make a fire in the fire pit and roast marshmallows. We didn't even have any marshmallows, but I wanted to buy some croissants for breakfast anyway, so I agreed to go to ShopRite and get them. Gabby came along, too, because she wanted a hydrating mask for her hair and corn muffins. Maxi was busy doing her homework, so she stayed home. But Mom and Jared were out at one of his physical therapy appointments, so it was only Graciela watching Zara and Regan. When Gabby and I got back, the fire was crackling nicely, and the flames were jumping to about Zara's waist height. Zara and Regan were dancing around the flames like little witches, careful not to fall into the stream, and Graciela was keeping her distance – although she did approach the fire to light a cigarette, which we all knew she wasn't supposed to do any more than we were supposed to eat marshmallows. It was all fun and games until we saw Dad's glow-in-the-dark yellow car pull into his driveway, after pausing and rolling down a window to look into our backyard, and we'd all stopped laughing and held our breath waiting for him to get out and scold us for having too much fun. He hadn't, and we'd put the incident out of our minds and hoped he'd let it go, but it was becoming increasingly clear that what had actually happened was Dad had called Regan's mom and told her that Regan and Zara were playing with fire, observed only by a smoking illegal immigrant without a driver's licence.

"Yeah, absolutely, all the best, Elise," Mom was saying in a tone that would have better matched her words if she'd said something like 'a pox on your family'. She hung up and threw the phone back onto the sofa. "Well, I hope you're all happy," Mom shouted.

Jared wheeled himself into the living room to see what all the fuss was about. "Is everything cool?" he asked Mom.

"No, it's not. My children are doing their best to get themselves taken away from me. What with Emily's stunt and whatever idiotic thing you did," she said, turning to glare at Zara, whose lower lip was looking dangerously wobbly, "your father is building a custody case against me."

I felt a strange mixture of savage glee and chagrin at this. It seemed my revenge plan was working better than I'd intended. I did want to hurt Mom, since I found out she only asked me to move back home so that Dad wouldn't reduce the monthly payments, but I certainly didn't want Zara to end up having to live with Dad. I couldn't lose sight of the ultimate goal: to get things back to the way they were.

Mom stormed off to her room, followed by Jared. Gabby, Zara and I looked at each other without saying a word. When Maxi appeared, wet hair piled on top of her head, and asked what had happened this time, we only managed to grimace at her. But she didn't need to know the details.

She'd gotten the gist of it by now.

THIRTY-TWO

Mom accused me of dragging my feet because I didn't want to help get ready for Passover, but that wasn't the issue. It's just that I thought that by now, we'd be doing it together, as a family. Plus Dad, minus Jared. Also, I didn't know what a horseradish looks like.

I pulled into the ShopRite parking lot and had to circle around for a while until I could find a spot. It was packed. Mom had been right. I should have gone earlier. I took Mom's credit card, the shopping list and my keys, and shoved them all into the pockets of my sweatshirt as I kicked the car door shut.

In the produce section, I picked up a brown blob and examined it. I lifted it to my nose to smell it and turned it around in my hands, but it kept its secrets. I looked for a label anywhere for a clue, but there wasn't one. I brought it to my nose again and licked it tentatively. I made a face at the taste and put it back, and looked up to see an old woman looking at me, disapproving. I stared her down until she scuttled away in the direction of the cooking sherry.

"Is this a horseradish?" I asked, holding the brown blob up to show a nearby stock boy.

"It's ginger root," he said.

I tried again. "Is this a horseradish?"

"Regular radish."

"Listen," I said, surreptitiously eyeing his name tag. "Sean, this will be a lot easier on both of us if you just tell me what a horseradish is."

"Third time's the charm?" Sean tried.

"Fine. What about this?"

"That's a parsnip," Sean said, making a cartoonish, apologetic face.

I threw the parsnip at it.

"Okay, okay," Sean said, holding up his hands in a combination of self-defence and surrender. "Here." He handed me a brown blob that looked identical to the first thing I tried.

"You said this was a ginger root."

"It looks a lot like ginger root. It's a very understandable mistake."

"Sean, are you by any chance a firstborn?"

"Yes, why?"

"Well, Sean, if you don't get me through the rest of this list real quick, you're going to find out." I shoved the list at him. "Hurry up. It's already almost noon."

Sean examined the list. "Parsley, lamb shank, eggs... wait, is this for Passover?"

I squint at him. "Maybe."

"I'm just asking because all the other Jews just bought that," Sean said, pointing over his shoulder at a freestanding display erroneously labelled 'Delicious for Passover'. It was covered in premade Seder plates with each of the components individually shrink-wrapped. There was even a delicate chunk of horseradish and an already-boiled egg.

"Oh." I plucked the list out of his hand. "Then your services are no longer required."

"Happy holiday," Sean said.

Is it? I wondered as I glided my cart past him and to the display. It is technically a celebration, I guess. But eating matzah for eight days feels more like a punishment to those of us who are not criminally insane. I picked up one premade Seder plate and examined it. It checked out. I balanced it in the top part of the shopping cart and crossed six things off my shopping list.

I made it to the seasonal aisle at the same time as Mrs Schwartz. We stood and surveyed the wreckage together.

"Jesus Christ," I said.

"God, I know," said Mrs Schwartz, reaching all the way to the back of the empty shelves. "I think they're all out of Passover cake mix."

"Yeah, but there's sawdust in Aisle 4. You won't even know the difference."

Mrs Schwartz laughed and patted my cheek. "Say hello to your mother for me," she said. "We miss her at shul."

"I'll pass it along," I lied, and Mrs Schwartz tossed some fruit jellies into her cart and walked away smiling.

I managed to transfer the ShopRite Seder plate to our hand-painted ceramic dish without anyone seeing that I cheated, but Mom walked in as I was dumping the little pile of parsley out of the plastic container.

"Hi, honey," she said, dropping her bags onto the kitchen armchair.

"Hey," I said, holding the evidence of my corner-cutting behind my back.

"What are you doing?" she asked.

"Nothing."

"Ohhhhhkay," said Mom. "Listen, your uncle is coming tonight."

"Which one?"

"Dan..."

"That's great!"

"...and he's bringing Richard."

"Noooooo! They'll be hours late and they'll bring something dumb. Don't you remember how last year, they brought scotch? A grain alcohol, for Passover, because they left too late and none of the places you could buy Kosher wine were still open. And then Richard did his Exorcist voice and Dan started saying, 'The power of Christ compels you!' over and over and flicking the scotch at him!"

"Well, it wasn't any worse than when your father's sister used to come."

I sidled over to the garbage can and tipped the crumpled plastic into it and considered this. "You're right," I said. "Do you remember that year you'd recently cut your hair, and Auntie Martha was the first one to get here?"

Mom snorted. "Yes, she didn't even make it over my threshold before she told me that she liked it the other way better. And then she told Maxi that she put the forks on the wrong side. Who the fuck does she think cares? God?"

"Yeah, and then Uncle Ronald claimed he had never heard of a knish. After living in New York for sixty years. What's with that?"

"That, honey, is called being a self-hating Jew."

"Well, it's dumb."

"Yeah. Did you manage okay?"

"Yep."

"Got everything?"

"Yes."

"Even the horseradish?"

"Yes, Mom. I know what a horseradish is."

"Nobody said you didn't," she said, backing out of the kitchen with her hands raised.

The phone rang as Mom headed for the dining room. Gabby's heavy footsteps clomped down the wooden stairs as she flung herself down them. "I'll get it!" she shouted, sliding into the kitchen in her sock feet. She tossed her long hair behind her shoulder and picked up the phone. "Hello? Uh-huh. Okay. Yep. Yes." Gabby put the phone back in the receiver. "Dad says Happy Passover," she said, and she stomped back up the stairs.

THIRTY-THREE

The next time we found something incriminating at Dad's, we weren't even looking. I asked Gabby to check the mail at Dad's house while she was checking Mom's mailbox, hoping that some of the college decisions I was waiting for had made their way into Dad's mailbox by mistake – no amount of wheedling or threatening notes to the mailman could persuade him there was any difference between the two Price mailboxes – and anyway, she could reach his without taking an extra step past Mom's.

Mom and Maxi were at the store. Zara was having a playdate at one of the few friends whose families still welcomed ours, despite Dad's attempts to rope them into a custody battle they wanted desperately not to be involved in, at least not in any way besides gossiping in the pickup line at the elementary school. Jared, and therefore Graciela, were out. So it was just me and Gabby staring down at the brown envelope on top of a pile of printer eight-by-eleven white envelopes addressed to me. It was addressed to a Mr and Mrs Price, and the return address was the Clark County Clerk's office in Las Vegas, Nevada.

"They could mean Mom," I said.

Gabby's baleful stare told me she didn't believe me any more than I did. She snatched the envelope and, with an alarming expression, sliced it open with Mom's dagger-shaped letter opener. She tore the letter out and slammed it down against the table with a flattened hand.

"They got married." I didn't look at the document, and I wasn't asking.

Gabby was still expressionless but had started chewing on the ends of her hair again – something I hadn't seen her do in months, and I figured she didn't know she was doing it. I didn't stop her.

"Well," I said, "you're already not talking to him, because of the Jared thing. Zara isn't talking to him because of the Regan thing. I'm not talking to him because of the child support thing. So – I guess it's Maxi's turn."

"We can't tell her in front of Mom," Gabby said, leaping to her feet but then standing still, as if she'd gotten up to do something but now couldn't remember what.

"We'll get her alone when they get home. While Mom showers." Mom was biking to and from the jewellery store with Maxi, in an apparent attempt to spite Dad, who had smugly forbidden us from bicycling after Jared's accident, which Dad said proved that it just wasn't safe. Jared was fully supportive of Mom's new-found love of biking, coaching her on the stationary bicycle in the living room with a fervour we all found disturbing. The idea of spiting Dad appealed to me, but biking did not, so when I worked, I still drove, and Gabby, too, insisted on being driven.

"I'll make sure Mom's in the shower," Gabby said.

"Fine. I'll handle Maxi."

Maxi's exercise-flushed cheeks drained faster than a bottle of wine on Passover when I handed her the marriage licence. "But how could he?" She turned over the document, but there wasn't anything there, and it wouldn't matter, anyway. "How could he?" she repeated.

"It was when he was supposedly on that business trip a few weeks ago," I said, as if that were an answer at all.

Maxi offered a nonsequitur of her own. "Mom can't know," she said, and she looked up from the licence. "She can't."

"I know," I said. *She'll find out*, I didn't say. Maxi kept looking at me, and I thought I detected a little tremor in her lower lip, so I started to say, "I was accepted to—" but Gabby came rushing back into the den.

"Graciela's room is empty," she said, panting and holding out a piece of loose-leaf paper with neat script handwriting on it. "Mom hasn't seen it. She went straight into the shower. I said 'hi' to her, but she didn't really answer me, just sort of waved me off." She proffered the paper, and I grabbed it, tearing it a little.

"Mom was in a very bad mood today," Maxi said, as I read it over. Graciela had written a sort of note of resignation, saying that Mr Jared told her that her services were no longer needed as he would be moving out of state.

"Mom must know," I said. Nobody answered me. "Right?"

"Like I said," Maxi repeated, "she was in a very bad mood. She hid in the back the whole time. She wouldn't talk to me at all, not even when this guy who came into the store asked me to try on something he said he was buying for his girlfriend, and I didn't want to, so I said I had to ask her permission so she would come out and tell him not to be such a creep."

"So she must know," I said.

"What do we do?" Gabby asked.

This was supposed to be a good thing. One step closer to fixing everything. So why didn't it feel good?

"I guess we make dinner," I said. "Since Graciela is gone." We allowed ourselves a quiet thirty seconds of mourning for Graciela, and then Gabby went into the kitchen and assembled the ingredients for a vegetarian meat sauce. It was a good idea – Zara would eat it without complaining when she got home, and not rush right into Mom's room to disturb her.

When it was done, and there had been no sign of Mom, I filled a bowl with pasta, fake meat and grated cheese, plucked a basil leaf from the pot on the windowsill, and brought the food to Mom's room. She answered my knock on the door with a grunt, and I opened it to find that she was lying down in complete darkness with the blanket up to her neck.

"Mom?"

"What, Emily?"

"I brought you dinner," I said, and I crept closer to her and put the bowl down on her bedside table.

"Thanks," she said, but she made no motion towards it. "Close the door behind you."

I stayed put, too. "Mom, what's going on?"

"Jared decided to move on. Go to a better place for someone with disabilities."

"Oh. Dignitas?" I arranged my face into a caricature of sympathy, trying for a laugh but ready to settle for tears.

Mom neither laughed nor cried. "Milwaukee," she said.

"Why Milwaukee?" I wrinkled my nose in unjustified distaste.

"His parents," she said. "They modified their downstairs into a handicapped-accessible suite for him."

"Oh," I said, when it became clear she didn't plan to say anything else. "Seems like an overreaction. He's going to recover, and I heard they put in speed bumps because of what happened."

"I'm tired, Emily," Mom said.

And she stayed in bed after that.

THIRTY-FOUR

The difference between going to synagogue by myself and going with Dad and my sisters was that alone, people weren't sure what to make of me. At Kiddush after the service, several people I recognised but couldn't name asked if I wanted to sit with them. I ended up uncomfortably sat with the family of one of Maxi's friends, mainly because I at least knew her mom's name was Judy. I picked at my pizza bagels, answering direct questions with minimal information, which was warmly received. A chorus of 'Mazel tov!'s went up when I said I'd accepted a place at Penn State – information that had not yet seemed to register with Mom or Dad, not even when I told them about the merit scholarship. I felt awkward, but it was nice. It was a surprise to everyone when, as Rabbi Gold greeted me while doing his rounds through the Simcha Room, I started crying in response to his, "How are you?"

Rabbi Gold ushered me into his office, brushing off clingy congregants in his kind way, never making anyone feel underappreciated. His empathetic tears began when he sat across from me at his desk, which stopped mine. I told him nearly everything, though I minimised how badly Mom was doing, and he went quiet for several minutes before he looked me in the eye and said, "I think you should all join us on our trip to Israel next month."

Mom didn't even ask what exactly going to Israel had to do with anything when I told her the rabbi had suggested it, but it didn't matter, because she perked up at the prospect of it. "All right," she said. "Call the rabbi and tell him yes, and if there's a deposit, pay it." She reached over to her purse, which was on her bedside table, and tossed me her wallet. She didn't get out of bed, but she did sit up straight, put on her reading glasses and fire up her laptop.

"What does going to Israel have to do with anything?" Maxi asked when I told her.

"I don't know," I admitted. "But Mom seems into it."

Gabby just shrugged when we told her to make sure her teachers gave her a list of the assignments she would miss that week. Zara asked if there would be a pool at the hotel, and I said probably yes, though I knew we would stay in at least three different hotels but didn't know for sure whether any of them had a pool. The odds, I imagined, were good. Good metropolitan elites that we were, everyone had a valid passport and their own luggage, so we threw a range of clothing into our bags – "Pack layers," Mrs Schwartz had said, "and some clothes you wouldn't mind getting paint and stuff on" – and we drove to the synagogue at four-thirty in the morning to board the bus with the rest of the group.

Mom was the first person in the car, but she didn't honk until we came out like Dad would have done. She took slow, deliberate sips from her travel coffee mug and smiled at each of us when we hopped in.

Despite a few glitches – Zara had answered, "Yep!" when the security personnel at the airport asked her if anyone had helped her pack her luggage, but the staff had deployed some rare common sense and asked the follow-up question, "Who helped you?" and had been satisfied by the answer, "My mom!" – the travel went smoothly. Movies were plentiful on the plane, the coaches and hotels all materialised as expected, and our days were full of ladling soup in homeless shelters and painting walls at schools. We made a few diversions based on terror threats, like an alert that changed our scheduled visit to Sderot, but our days were full and our evenings with the dozen members of our congregation were pleasant. Mom even talked to people we hadn't known before, and I only saw her have one glass of wine over three whole days in Tel Aviv – and even that was only white wine. When the rabbi asked if anyone wanted to volunteer to lead part of our service in front of a stretch of the Kotel that allowed co-ed congregating, Mom raised her hand, and then Gabby took inspiration from her and said the prayer for peace without even having to read from the laminated cheat sheet the rabbi offered her. On our last evening in Israel, we had a dance party with locals we had worked alongside all day, and they presented each of us with a necklace that said 'Ahava' – 'love' in Hebrew – with the letters stacked like the famous 'LOVE' statues in places like New York and Philly.

We returned to New York bronzed, fulfilled and tired

and – though we didn't know it until we got back to Mom's house – with full voicemail and email inboxes, crammed with increasingly hysterical messages from Dad.

THIRTY-FIVE

In retrospect, the death knell of my family was not Dad's marriage to Candace – after all, wedding vows are made to be broken – but the fact that Mom had, in some people's opinions, kidnapped us. Maxi had approached me in my room at Mom's house timidly while we were trying not to listen to the CPS lady and Mom's lawyer downstairs. Twirling a strand of hair around her finger, she said she thought it was best if we stopped trying to interfere with Mom and Dad's relationship.

"It's not that I blame you, Em," she said. "It's just that the whole Israel thing was kind of your idea. And that really just made everything worse."

"It wasn't my idea! It was Rabbi Gold's idea. I didn't know what else to do."

"That's what I'm saying," Maxi explained. "We don't know what else to do. And whenever we try anything, things just get worse. I don't think Mom and Dad are ever getting back together now. And I think things almost were better for a while, before we got involved."

"When?" I demanded.

"Look, Em. I know how angry you were about Jared, but when he was here, things were okay."

"That wasn't because of him. That was because of Graciela."

"Well, whatever. You know what I mean. The thing is, Dad and Candace are *married* now. I think you lost."

"Me? *I* lost?"

"Okay, *we*," Maxi corrected, with an irritated huff. "Whatever. I just mean, I don't think there's a point anymore. I think *we* should just let it go."

"And how am I supposed to do that?"

Maxi looked away. "You'll be going to college before you know it."

When I was applying to college, I was left to my own devices by Mom and Dad. They were too busy hating each other to ask me what I scored on my SATs. For the record, it was a 2130. But they each found the time to lecture me about what I should and should not do with my life.

Dad struck a single note on the few occasions it occurred to him that it was a good time to impart his Fatherly Wisdom. "You should choose your major very carefully," Dad had said one day as we drove into Manhattan to visit his famous dermatologist – him for a chemical peel I was absolutely not to mention to Mom, and me for a facial as a reward for my relatively good behaviour. "Art is all well and good, but it doesn't pay the bills, and you are a very expensive person to support. I think you should plan to go to law school."

"Why law school?" I asked. "I thought I had more

choices. Aren't upper-middle-class Jews also allowed to be doctors and sometimes even professors?"

"Do you want to be a doctor?" he asked.

"Fuck, no!" I said.

"Teachers don't get paid much," Dad said.

And that was that.

Mom had raised the subject with me precisely once, while we were on the plane to Israel, and Maxi, Gabby and Zara had fallen asleep. "Remind me where you're going to school, again?" Mom asked, absentmindedly stroking Zara's hair in her lap.

I side-eyed her across Gabby's spread-eagled form. "Penn State," I said.

"Why did you choose that one, again?"

"I don't know. They offered me money. Didn't make me take any SAT IIs."

"Oh," Mom said, and she had another sip of wine. Her teeth were the colour of an eggplant. "What are you going to do there?"

"Gain fifteen pounds and develop moderate to severe alcoholism."

Mom made a sour face that matched her breath, and waited.

"I don't know. You don't declare a major right away. Gen eds, then we'll see."

"Good," Mom said.

"Why's it good that I don't know what I want to do? Jess knows. She's going to be pre-med. So are Thalia, Julia, Raven, Mark, Jeremy and Steven. Everyone knows what they're going to do."

"They'll change their minds," Mom said. "It's better not to know yet. Or else you might make a big mistake."

I stared at her. She sighed, and continued. "Do you know why I own a jewellery store now?"

"Mid-life crisis?"

Mom snorted. "Emily, please. I'm trying to have an important conversation with you."

"Okay, fine. Keep going."

"When I was your age, I let myself get caught up in what everyone else around me was doing. All the other Jewish children of immigrants in my neighbourhood were going to be doctors and lawyers. I knew for sure I couldn't be a doctor. I don't like sick people."

"I know," I interjected, remembering all the times me and my sisters had been sick over the years, and it was our friends who dropped off the chicken soup from the deli.

"Anyway," Mom continued, "I just kind of got swept along, and I knew before I even made it to law school that I hated the profession, but it felt like it was too late already. I went to school, and I did well; I was always a good student. That wasn't the problem. And I got recruited as an associate right away. But I hated it. And then when I had you, I took a break, and that break lasted until… well. Your father could force me to work, but he couldn't force me to be a lawyer."

"Oh."

"I don't want you to make the same mistakes I did," Mom had said.

In the end, my major was the last thing on my mind.

The day I was informed that all of us would have

to testify before a judge as to which of our parents we preferred to live with was the day I packed my car and plugged University Park into my GPS. It was the same day I confirmed with Donna that Poco had been picked up by the horse shipping company, and I would meet him in Pennsylvania the following day, at Donna's sister-in-law's farm.

It was also my eighteenth birthday.

When Dad lost his bid for primary custody, he moved himself, Candace and Candy the Shih Tzu to California. I found out when a very small box of my things from Dad's house arrived at my dorm, with a Los Angeles County return address in Candace's handwriting.

There wasn't any family to say goodbye to anymore, so I just drove.

PART III

PART III

THIRTY-SIX

Jess had a very hard time understanding what I was saying to her. She seemed to think it was a joke for a while, too, which I couldn't understand, because I can't think of a less funny premise for a joke than 'imagine if your parents who ruined your life with their messy divorce got back together like nothing happened and you only found out because the world is improbable and small and has a sick sense of humour'. But once she got her head around the idea that I am neither mistaken nor kidding, her advice was sound. "Look, I've been having trouble getting a flight out there, but I think I've got one booked now. I'll be there soon. Mike described that device you found, and I have an idea what it might be. For now – lock your door, run a bath and take a beta-blocker," she advised, and when I told her that I am out of beta-blockers, she covered up a gasp of dread and said, "Gin, then."

I climb into the very small bathtub with my tiny bottles of gin I got Yossi to deliver to my door, having locked the partition door between Mike's room and mine, put the do-not-disturb sign on my front door, and locked the bathroom door for good measure. Jess's last words ring in my head, though – "It's possible that this is a good thing, Emily" – so I take a deep breath, screw my eyes shut and duck below the water for as long as I can stand it. The tub is too small for me to do this without contorting myself, and the water is scalding. The blood pumping – too fast – through my veins makes that rushing traffic sound in my ears, and it's better than the sound of my friend telling me that any of what's happening is a good thing. I come up for a gasping breath and inhale the rest of the mini bottles in between pants. It's not helping much, though, because now I'm thinking about Mom's wine-stained teeth, like rows of purple bruises in her mouth, for all those years after Dad first moved out – and that makes me more anxious.

The panting gives me an idea, though. I stand up, not caring about how much water sloshes out of the tub, and towel off. I will go find Sven, I decide. He's a little off, but he is a dog person. I will ask to borrow Prince Charles. I'll find Wilcox, go somewhere nice, find a park or something where there's shade so he doesn't have to loll his long, narrow tongue out of his smooshed face. Maybe we will share a popsicle or something. I'll ask Sven what flavour he likes. Then he can run around until he's exhausted and while he naps in my lap, I'll bury my fingers in his fur and feel his heartbeat, and try to match my breathing to his.

I listen at the partition door and look through the peephole in my front door, but there's nobody there. So I get dressed quickly, throwing on jeans – I note that they are a little tight, but they're jean-leggings, so aren't they usually tight when you first put them on and then falling off by the end of the day? – and Teva sandals, which, I realise as I fasten the Velcro, are the only thing I've bought since I arrived in Israel – and I had to order them online, because it's so hard sometimes to find anyone to escort me out. Maybe it wouldn't be a bad idea to buy some stuff after Prince Charles gets his walk. It always seems to make Jess feel better when she's stressed out – shopping is an activity in and of itself, for her. I remember the time she dragged me into a bridal shop once and roped me into pretending that she was getting married and I needed to try some maid of honour dresses so that the salesladies would fawn over us and bring us champagne. That did make me feel a little better. And it might be amusing to drag Anderson into some stores.

On the way to the door, I pause and think about leaving Mike a note to say where I've gone. I don't want to talk to anyone besides Prince Charles for a while, but I don't want to worry him anymore. It'll only make him angry if he worries for nothing. I write something to let him know I'm okay and I'll be back later and talk to him, but not give him enough information to find me. Besides, I don't even know where I'll end up yet. I slip a note that says I'll be out walking Sven's dog and see him later, with two little 'x's as an afterthought, underneath the partition door.

I sneak out the door and make a bee-line for Sven's room – equidistant between both James's room and mine, and on the same floor – speed-walking with my head ducked. So it's not an enormous surprise when I collide with someone coming around the hall corner towards the stairs. It's not even a surprise that that someone is wearing shiny, pointy men's shoes that look expensive. I sigh before I've even looked up and made eye contact with James.

"Where are you going?" James asks.

"To see Møkkalasset," I say, and I move to duck around him, but he gets in my way, and puts an arm up against the wall to block me.

"Don't corner people like that," I spit at him. "What if I had PTSD or something?"

"You aren't a veteran."

"There are other kinds of PTSD," I say. "Move!"

"If you're going to Møkkalasset, I'll come with you," James says, unbothered by my anger. "I think we both ought to speak with him about the case. It's becoming impossible to do our jobs, with neither of our clients attending—"

"No," I say. "I'm not going about the case." I duck under his arm, but he grabs my shoulder lightly. I stop dead and do not turn around. "Remove your hand from my body," I tell him in my coldest, calmest voice.

He does, and I keep walking, but he catches up with me, only needing one step for my every three. "This isn't about the case, is it?" he asks.

My shins burn, but I keep up the pace. "No," I say. "Stop following me."

"I am accompanying you," he says.

I wave a hand at him dismissively but refuse to look at him. "Semantics," I say.

"Clarity," he counters.

"Look." I stop, and glare at him. "I just need to borrow Møkkalasset's dog for a little while."

"Why?"

"It's personal."

"You can trust me."

I bark a short, bitter laugh.

"You can. I might surprise you. What's the problem?"

"I just…" I sigh, and hold my hands up in a half-shrug. "I got some bad news today. About my parents."

"Splitting up, are they?" James grins.

"Worse," I tell him. "Un-splitting up."

James looks comically surprised for a minute, but rearranges his features into his default cool, detached amusement. "Well, I saw Møkkalasset take that mutt of his to a very put-upon-looking Yossi, and I heard something about a doggy day care. He's not back."

My shoulders slump a little and my heart races even faster at the thought that there's no relief on the horizon.

"D'you know what? I have an idea. Come with me," he says, and to my surprise, I follow behind him as he strides towards the stairs.

"I can't believe you're allowed to leave alone, and I'm not," I tell him.

James ignores me and motions for a waiter. He orders for both of us and hands the menus back. "It's all quite clear now," he says, clasping his hands together over his stomach and looking at me down the smooth planes of his face, head leaned lightly back against the tall back of the leather banquette.

"What's clear?" I ask, bitter because I don't know what he means, and nothing makes a lot of sense right at this moment.

255

"You," he says, and unlaces his fingers to gesture at me. "Child of divorce. It's all personal," he says.

"And what about you? Happy family?" I sneer a little even uttering the phrase.

"Christ, no," James says, and laughs with genuine mirth, knocking his head against the wall.

I really don't know what to make of that, but I don't want to encourage him, either, so I just take the opportunity to fold my cloth napkin into a bird of paradise. James has stopped laughing and watches as I shake the napkin out and refold it into a swan. "I learned it on YouTube," I tell him, because I can sense him wondering, and I don't want him to know about all the time I spent moonlighting for caterers while I was pretending to my parents that my internships were paid.

James picks up the swan and examines it as if he's trying to work out how I did it. He hands it back with a raised-eyebrow expression that says he's a little impressed but can't quite bring himself to tell me so aloud. I shrug and unfold the swan, placing my napkin back on my lap and folding my hands on top of it, like Dad's mother taught me. Then I scowl and put my elbows on the table. "So," James says, and I look at him sceptically. "Speaking of birds."

"We weren't."

"Do you feel like talking about work for a while now? It usually helps," he says.

It does usually help me, so I give him a 'go on' gesture and pick up my martini glass.

"I'd like to propose an idea, something that actually occurred to me when I took my inspiration from you and did a little research into family court decisions regarding custody arrangements. As you know, one of the biggest compromises we have to reach is about the custody of—"

"Jerusalem, yes," I say, reaching into my glass to pull out the lemon twist and deposit it on my bread plate. James resists complaining about my table manners, even when I follow that up with wiping my finger on the edge of the tablecloth. I put my drink down and sit nicely, because it's no fun being uncouth if it's not going to get a reaction out of anyone.

"Right," James says. "And most of the proposals we were considering were variations of the idea of cutting the baby in half. Deciding where to draw a boundary line between Jerusalem and East Jerusalem. But what if – and bear with me here – there's a better way?"

"Such as?"

"Well, if a divorced couple had, shall we say, twins, no judge would suggest each parent just keeps one."

James has obviously not seen *The Parent Trap*, starring Lindsay Lohan and Lindsay Lohan. "Well—"

"They wouldn't," James says, in an And That's Final voice. "Usually what would happen is one of the parents would be awarded primary custody, and the other would get visitation."

"I know," I say. "Please arrive at a point."

"…But," James continues as if I have not interrupted him, "there's a slightly more unconventional arrangement that more separated parents are adopting. There's a caveat that it tends to be adults who are going through amicable divorces who choose to try this, but by and large, I think it

will work better for us because we're talking about a city –
and those can't be moved from place to place on alternate
weekends."

I grab my glass by the stem like a reality television star
prepared to toss its contents in someone's face and glare at
James. He gets the message.

"Instead of moving the children," he finishes, "the adults
move. It's called bird-nesting. It's quite a brilliant idea. The
children stay in the family home, and the adults take turns
living in it with them. The rest of the time, the adult who
doesn't have custody lives in an apartment or something
nearby. Sometimes, the adults even share the apartment, as
it's not as though they're ever there at the same time."

I stare at James, unsure if I should laugh because he's
so clearly having me on. This is the most ridiculous thing
I have ever heard. There is no way he can expect me to
believe even for a second that there is any divorced couple
on earth who would even consider such an arrangement.
James is looking at me expectantly, and I don't know how
to react yet, but then I raise the fist with the glass in it and
toss the remainder of the gin at his face.

James blinks and picks up his napkin and dabs at the
admittedly less dramatic tiny droplets of liquid that made it
onto his stupid cheekbones. I guess there wasn't as much left
in the glass as I thought. "What is wrong with you?" he asks.

I stand up, and my napkin falls on the floor. "You know
what?" I say, surprised at how calm I sound. "What is
wrong with you? Why would you play such a cruel joke on
me, today of all days? Did you think it would make me cry?
Quit? What?"

"What are you talking about?"

"Bird-nesting," I hiss at him. "I don't believe it for a second. What I apparently did believe is that you understood, and were trying to help. But I am already as upset as I can be, and you did *not* make it worse."

James sighs and looks up at the ceiling. I glance up at it, too, just in case, but there's nothing there. "Please sit back down," he says, and he reaches into the leather briefcase on the banquette beside him and pulls out a book. I look at it warily but see it is a book by a retired family court judge, and that it is annotated with several sticky notes. James is looking for a specific page, and doesn't seem to be trying to trick me, so I sit down – but on the very edge of the banquette. He finds the page he is looking for, and slides the book to me.

This concept, known as bird-nesting, eliminates some of the behavior that makes children feel like ping-pong balls. The stress, hassle, and inconvenience is a burden that falls to the parents, rather than the children.

"Okay," I say, processing. "Okay."

"And 'I'm sorry I threw my drink in your face like a child," James adds for me.

"Children don't drink," I say. I'm still looking at the book, but I'm no longer reading it. Instead, I'm trying to imagine what it would have been like, for me, Maxi, Gabby and Zara – especially for Gabby and Zara, who had to ping-pong across the country a few times a year long after

Maxi and I had gotten out. I try to imagine Mom changing the sheets on my parents' old bed and leaving with a small rolling suitcase, smiling at Dad as he passed by her in the hallway, to toss his sport jacket on the bed and unpack his khakis and boat shoes. Then Candace follows through the door behind him, with a Louis Vuitton weekend bag over her shoulder. I shudder violently, and James puts a hand on mine.

"Maybe this wasn't such a good idea," he says. "I really was trying to distract you. I can see now that it isn't helping. We could pick this up again tomorrow, or the following day."

"No," I say in a hoarse voice. "No, I'm fine. I have a few questions."

"Okay."

"As far as applying this to Jerusalem, I assume you aren't talking about citizens sharing homes, but government offices being shared – law enforcement, city council, that kind of thing."

"Right," says James. "A schedule could be reached so that respective major holidays are taken into consideration. It would be complicated because of the lunar calendars involved, but manageable. And there would be an office block for both governments to share that is outside the city limits for their 'off' time. They could continue to work on long-term projects, carry out meetings and do almost everything a full-time government would do. They would only not be in situ during that time, and the rules the people living in the city limits would have to follow would change."

"There would have to be as little difference as possible so that you don't have someone doing something on a Tuesday that is illegal but would have been fine on Monday," I muse.

"Yes. But things like rubbish collection, maintaining roads – the stuff of everyday governance – these are not things that are subject to much ideological or religious difference," James says, lighting up a little with his belief in the brilliance of this idea. "You and I both know that it is as much about who gets to say they are in charge as it is about anything else."

"It'll be complicated."

"But it's at least worth presenting the idea to our clients. Don't you agree?"

I think about how Liora will likely react to my proposing that Israel and Palestine share Jerusalem, and I am not excited about it. But still, I nod. "It's worth exploring."

"Then we use the time we're spending trying to get hold of people to strategise individually," he says, "and then do our damnedest to get our clients on board before our next meeting."

The waiter chooses this moment to arrive with our food – James has, of course, ordered us very sensible grilled fish and vegetables, which I only wrinkle my nose at a little – so I nod and attempt a smile. "Yep," I tell him. "Sounds good."

For a moment, I consider telling James about Farooq's farm, and the gadget I found. Instead, when the waiter leaves, I silently hand James my clean and dry napkin to replace the one he had to use to wipe his face, and he silently accepts.

THIRTY-SEVEN

Mike is in his room when I get back, I can just tell. James has walked me to the door, and I now feel it is very important that I get rid of him before Mike sees that I was with him. Not because he doesn't trust me, but… well, it would look bad if I abandoned him at the Dead Sea only to hang out with James, that's all. I hover with my key behind my back until James gets the message. He takes a step back and reaches out a hand. I shake it, and before he lets go, he tells me that he's sorry about my parents and he hopes things work out for me.

"Thanks," I say.

"I'll be in touch after I speak with my client," he says.

I take a breath before I open my door. I know Mike will hear the heavy metallic thunk of the lock releasing and be waiting for me. I listen hard to hear whether there are any voices coming from the room, but I don't hear any, so I think the coast is clear. But when I open the door, I see that there's a light on in my bathroom and the bedroom partition door is open – and more than one person's shadow is obscuring the light flooding through it.

Then my bathroom door opens and my mother steps out. "Oh, Emily," she says. "There you are."

"What are you doing here," I sigh. It isn't a question. Trust Thom to allow in the only people I don't want to see.

"Your jeans look a little tight," she answers, and I ignore her, suck in my stomach, and go over to the door. I can see Dad and Mike sitting at the little table in his room together, faces lit by their respective screens. Dad is wearing his reading glasses, even though his phone is the size of an iPad and the type is so large I can almost read it from a few yards away.

Dad tilts his chin down so that he can look at me over the rim of his glasses. "It's very childish to flee, Emily."

Mike looks at me warily. I stamp my foot. Mike shuts his eyes, puts his fingers to his temples and massages them. "I want them out of our rooms," I tell him.

"This hotel isn't very nice, is it?" Mom remarks as if she hasn't heard.

Mike opens his eyes. "Maybe we should pick this up again tomorrow," he says.

Dad folds his reading glasses and puts them in the pocket of his sport jacket. I notice the skin of his neck, around the too-open collar of his linen shirt, looks a little wrinkled, like a California raisin. His face doesn't, though, and I remember about his secret chemical peels back in New York. I wonder if it became a couple activity for him and Candace. I wonder what happened to Candace. Dad spent a very long time insisting that she was a part of his life, and therefore ours, and if all of that was for nothing, then I'm definitely going to start yelling again. "We'll see you for dinner tomorrow, Emily," he says, as he stands up and pushes his chair in.

Mom comes up from behind me and makes a big deal of sliding past me through the doorway into Mike's room, and takes Dad's hand. "We eat dinner at nine o'clock now," she says smugly.

"How very European," I say. "Fuckity-bye." I step backward and slam my partition door so hard it bounces off the door frame and back at me, but my hand is still extended from slamming it in the first place, so I shut it again and hold it closed. I stand there, heart beating so hard I can almost feel it in my palms, until I hear Mike's front door open and shut. When he knocks lightly on the partition, I move away from the door and flop onto my back on my unmade bed, arms spread like a starfish but with my feet on the ground, and stare up at the ceiling.

Mike sits on the edge of the bed, facing straight ahead, and pats my knee.

I cover my face with my hands. My skin feels hot to the touch, and a little tight, like I'm just out of a scalding shower. Or a skin peel. I wonder again what on earth happened with Dad and Candace, and I let out a big, rumbly sigh. "I'm sorry I abandoned you at the Dead Sea."

"I know," Mike says. "Overall, you could have handled it worse."

"How could I have handled it worse?"

"You didn't assault anyone or damage any property."

"Thank you for your high expectations of me," I start to grouch, but I don't really want to pick a fight with Mike right now, so I rein it in.

Mike resumes rubbing my knee. "Did hanging out with Prince Charles help?"

"Um, yes," I say, keeping my hands over my face.

"You didn't get the dog drunk, did you?"

"What? Why?" I move my hands and open my eyes. There are blurry spots from how hard I was pressing them with the heels of my hands.

"You smell of gin," he says, and he smiles.

"I didn't share it."

"Can dogs drink alcohol?" Mike asks, and even though he's clearly trying to distract me, I decide to let him.

"No, they have small livers," I explain. "Dogs can't have alcohol or chocolate, so we have to be extra nice to them to make their lives worth living." I sit up and pat the hand on my knee to say thank you.

"So, tomorrow..." Mike trails off.

"No way," I say. "I'm busy. I'm onto something, and they are not going to ruin this."

"Do you want company tonight, or not?" He takes my hand between his so I know whichever answer I give him is okay.

"I think..." I look at him. "I don't think I'll sleep much tonight. I have a lot of thinking to do about this idea James – this idea I want to discuss with the PM right away."

"Okay," Mike says. "Listen, we missed a few texts from Jess." He shows me the phone.

Ugh! Delayed! Flying sucks so much! Hope to see you guys soon.

Delayed again. No reason given.

You're not going to believe this, but my flight is now cancelled.

"That sucks."

"It's just the usual bullshit," Mike says. "She'll be rebooked by now."

He kisses me on the cheek and squeezes my hand. "You know where to find me. Do you want to go for a run in the morning?"

I really should. "I might check out the gym instead," I lie.

"Breakfast, then?"

"Sure. Nine okay?"

"Goodnight," he says, and he closes the partition door most of the way but leaves a slight gap so I can see it's unlatched. I wait until I can hear him go into his bathroom and do the same with my door.

I – of course – cannot sleep, so I wander out of my room, hoping Mike won't hear me leave. I'm wearing workout clothes that are comfortable enough to sleep in, if I could sleep, but presentable enough for me to sit in the lobby in, too.

It's not a surprise this time that Anderson is sitting in

the lobby, legs crossed, reading a Dan Brown novel. I shuffle over to him and sit down in one of the armchairs nearby. "Can't sleep?" he asks, too cheerfully for two in the morning.

"Do you ever sleep?"

"Regularly," he says.

"No, I couldn't sleep."

"It's smart to get out of bed when you can't sleep. My therapist says lying there getting stressed out about how you're supposed to be asleep will only ever make it worse, so you should try doing something else until you feel tired, and then lie down and try again."

"Mine told me the same thing," I say. "I just needed a change of scenery. I'm thinking about this idea Browning has."

Anderson dog-ears his page and puts down the book. "Want a sounding board?"

"It'll sound crazy," I demure.

"Try me." Anderson looks very interested.

"It's – well, have you heard of bird-nesting?"

"No."

I run through a very basic explanation of bird-nesting as a custody arrangement, and Anderson furrows his brow and listens attentively. "Anyway," I finish, shrugging, "we were thinking of that as a solution for the Jerusalem situation. I don't know. It could be crazy enough to work."

"Yes, it could," Anderson says, frowning.

"You think it could work?"

"I do," he says.

"Well," I sigh. "I have to get it past my client. Whom I can never seem to get ahold of, anyway. And she…"

"Won't like it."

"Will not like it," I confirm. "But if I can just get her to listen…"

"Yes," Anderson says. "It might work."

"There's something else." I tell him about the gadget I found at Farooq's farm, and how I need Jess to get here to help me figure out what it is, because I don't know who to trust yet.

Anderson's lips are pursed. "Is something wrong?" I ask him.

"No," he says, and smiles a smile that doesn't quite reach his eyes. "I think it might be my bedtime, though. You should go back to your room, too."

I feel a little strange about this abrupt end to our conversation, but I can feel my eyelids droop a little, so I nod. He stands up and offers me a hand, and I use it to pull myself upright. "I'll walk you back to your room," he says, and it doesn't really feel like an offer, so I let him.

THIRTY-EIGHT

Thom did promise me that I would get to see PM Reznik today, but I am still surprised when he pops in from God knows where at breakfast and confirms that she will arrive at eleven o'clock. He tells me she said she had to rearrange a lot of very important things in her schedule in order to be able to work with me, but that she had managed to clear most of the day.

"What, exactly, is more important than this?" I ask Thom.

Thom shifts his weight uncomfortably. I have not asked him to sit down and join me as I nurse my third espresso *hafukh* since Mike went off to do some grading in his office. I still don't ask, even though Thom is looking at the chair like he can will it to pull itself out and seat him.

I sigh. "Never mind. Room 105 again?"

"Whichever one you want," Thom says, and I remember that there isn't anyone else around to use the other rooms. "Do you need anything else from me before your meeting?

Do you want to go over anything? I wrote up a report on the water situation—"

"No, thanks," I cut him off. "I have something to talk to her about that's a little more pressing." Thom looks worried, not interested, and doesn't press me for any more information. I wonder if Anderson has briefed him already, but I don't think so – which is interesting. I have not seen Anderson at all in the hotel this morning, not even in the lobby or the breakfast room. I wonder what he does when he's not watching me, or meeting with Thom. Maybe he does sleep after all. Or maybe – I feel the hair on my arms rise at this thought – it's someone else's shift. There could be another person keeping watch over me that I don't know about, even though Thom swore up and down that there isn't.

Thom has now put his hand on the back of a chair, and I think he might be about to sit down without an invitation, so I push my coffee away and stand up. "Better get showered, then," I say.

"Good luck," Thom says.

I know what he means, but I still tell him that I haven't hurt myself in the shower yet.

There's time before Reznik arrives, but I don't need to review the research about bird-nesting that I've done. There's not very much written about it, and what there is I can already see when I close my eyes, like the words have been seared onto the inside of my eyelids. So, with a heavy heart, I put on some gym clothes and head down to the fitness centre to try and burn off some of my nervous energy.

The fitness centre is a windowless basement with a handful of old workout machines – they don't even have screens – and a few standing fans. There's a TV, though, mercifully. I find the remote for the TV and hop on the elliptical. I move my feet until they are about level on the machine, so that I can stand without holding on, and flip through the channels. There is a news channel that's in English, so I turn up the volume and start moving. But I can't focus on the ups and downs of the global markets, or the weather disasters, or the latest world leader photo-ops – even when I spot Alisha in the background of one of them, standing over the president's shoulder as he high-fives a kid in a refugee intake centre – they're somewhere in the undesirable parts of America, where they decided there's room.

Instead, I go back to thinking about what it might have been like if my parents were like 'Sally' and 'Bob' from the bird-nesting case study in the *American Journal of Psychology*, sharing our family home in Rockland County, with one small condo in one of the developments off Main Street – near the McDonald's – where all the non-Jewish people in town seemed to live back then, and probably still do. Gabby and Zara could have been sitting at the kitchen table, doing homework and eating organic cheese puffs, at the exact moment Mom rolled a suitcase past them out the front door, and Dad rolled one in. Maxi and I would have left the house that morning and said goodbye to Mom, who'd wave from the armchair by the big kitchen windows as we walked to the corner bus stop, and come home to Dad microwaving salmon burgers for dinner. In this version of events, there's no Jared, and no Candace. Mom and Dad's bedroom stays looking more or less the same, with its Pottery Barn furniture unmoved and the same neutral duvet cover and pillowcases on the bed as ever. Mom's makeup and perfume would still be on the tasteful vanity in the corner, and Dad's ties still hanging on a rack over the closet door.

My eyes are stinging a little bit, but probably just from the sweat. The machine is groaning at me, and swaying a little with my speed. I lower the resistance a little bit, but I don't slow down – inertia is on my side now.

I'm trying to redirect my thoughts a little bit when the opaque glass door swings open and – of course – James walks in. He's wearing an Oxford University T-shirt and matching blue and white shorts. I look down at myself and notice I'm wearing some worn Penn State stuff in the same colour – Mike's shirt, I realise. I tense a little as James approaches the treadmill, but he holds up a hand with a water bottle in it and nods, and I see that he has headphones in. I turn my face back to the TV, even though I'm still not listening. Ten minutes later, when I realise I've been at it for half an hour, I decide I'm done. I wave politely at James, who is running very fast, as I toss my towel in the bin by the door and head up to get showered for my meeting.

I'm staring at the conference room door absentmindedly, holding a cup of improvised iced coffee – a mug of ice that Yossi produced from thin air, to which I added hot espresso from the machine in the lobby, and some half-

and-half, resulting in a lukewarm oily mess – when it flies open. The prime minister's driver-come-bodyguard opens it, looks around, then steps aside for Liora to get past him. She is, once again, wearing shades of beige and holding a bag of Bamba snacks. Then it clicks for me – if she eats the beige-powdered peanut puffs constantly, then the outfit choice isn't about liking beige; it's about camouflage. She'll never get caught out by a candid photo of herself covered in peanut dust.

"*Nu?*" Liora says, as I sit there looking at her.

I'm confused – what is she waiting for me to do? – and then I realise, stand up and hold out a hand. She puts her stuff on the table, bats my hand away and hugs me – tersely, if it's possible to hug someone tersely.

"Where have you been?" I manage to say without sounding too much like a spouse who has been keeping dinner warm for the last two hours.

"'Where I have been'," repeats Liora sarcastically. "*Mah aht choshevet?*"

"I don't know what to think. Because you didn't show up for several meetings, and I haven't been able to reach you at all."

She gestures at herself, and then at me. "Now you have reached me," she points out, and I can't really argue with that, so I sit down and open my notes. I wait for her to get settled, which unfortunately involves opening the Bamba, whose smell begins wafting at me.

"So," I start. "I have a proposal to make, but I need you to promise to hear me out before you say anything. You're not going to like it at first, and you're going to think it's impossible. But that's what I thought at first, and now I think it might be crazy enough to work."

Liora waves a hand in a characteristically imperious fashion, and I take that as a 'go ahead'. I try to inhale through my mouth to minimise the smell of the Bamba.

"Okay," I begin. "So, you know how in a divorce, usually the parents share custody and each have their own homes, and the kids move back and forth?"

Liora stares at me.

"Of course you know. Well, it's not ideal for a lot of reasons, mostly for the kids, so there have been a few creative solutions attempted. One of them is called bird-nesting – have you heard of it?"

More icy staring.

"Bird-nesting is where the kids don't move back and forth – the parents do. So, they stay in the family home with the children, but they alternate living in it with them so that only one parent is there at a time. And when they aren't in the home, they go somewhere else – sometimes an apartment, sometimes even one they share."

Liora is looking sceptical now. "This, I would not do for my ex," she says.

Liora was married? Why didn't I come across this in my research? I'm thrown for a second, but I shake my head a little and continue. "My parents wouldn't have been able to do it, either. But it's a nice idea. And some people apparently can make it work," I say, passing her a few highlighted printouts I made in the hotel's business centre before the meeting. The psychology journal case study of 'Sally' and 'Bob' and their Upper East Side brownstone and

Midtown crash pad may not be the most representative, but it was the most amicable one I could find, so it's at the top of the short stack of papers.

"So why are you telling me about this?" Liora asks, folding her arms and not picking up the papers.

"Well, it's an alternative custody arrangement, and it's used so that kids don't have to move around – so it might work if the 'child'" – I make air quotes – "can't move. For instance…" I trail off, finding it hard to say it out loud, as Liora glares at me with steely eyes. I think she knows what I'm getting at but is going to make me say it before she explodes at me. I push my rolling chair back subtly, hoping to be out of her reach in case her explosion is literal or violent in another way. "For instance," I start again, "like Jerusalem."

THIRTY-NINE

This is how the whole project ends – not with a whimper, but with the bang that Liora's fist makes when it comes crashing down on the table in between us, sending Bamba flying out of the open bag. I flinch, and flick a wayward puff away from me.

"No," Liora says, and she's not yelling at all, but it's almost scarier that she sounds so calm while her body language is so hostile. She bangs the table again, and repeats, "No."

"Just think about it," I say. "One Jerusalem, like you wanted. No Jews need to move anywhere. It will still be the eternal capital of the State of Israel. The US Embassy could stay here, like you've always wanted. You'd share it, but without cutting it in half."

"No!" Liora says, talking over me.

"Jerusalem can't move, so it can't shuttle between countries," I continue resolutely. "You don't want to divide it. This is the only way it's fair to everybody and you still mostly get what you want. You'd treat the administrative offices like the family home in this study" – I tap on the papers she still hasn't glanced at – "and most of the employees could be hired by both governments. I doubt the garbage collectors care who's paying them, as long as they're paid. And you'd share an office block outside city limits during the 'off' time, or something like that. Not all employees would need to report to work during that time, which people would love – only the essential ongoing work would need to be done."

Liora closes her eyes and mutters something that sounds suspiciously like '*dafuk barosh*', which I'm pretty sure means something like 'fucked in the head'.

"I know," I tell her. "I know it sounds fucked. But you have to promise me you'll think about it. There's no point in doing this if it's just going to be the Camp David Accords, take infinity, or Oslo III. The only reason to even bother trying anymore is if we're going to think out of the box."

"This is your idea?" Liora asks, looking livid.

I suspect saying either yes or no is the wrong answer, but that she might at least respect me if I claim it as my idea even though she looks like she might hit me. "Yes," I say, only croaking a little. My heart is in my throat, and it's difficult to talk around it. I wish, yet again, that I had any beta-blockers left. Without them, sitting here feels physically like being on that elliptical did this morning. Like my body can't tell the difference between Liora and a cheetah, though in its defence my eyes can't either right now.

"Yes," I say, and it comes out angrier than I expected it to. "This was my idea. And you know what? It's a great idea, if you could stop being so selfish for a moment. You grownups always think about what you want the most, but do you ever even think of your children? Maybe we don't want to lug suitcases back and forth across the street for a few years until Dad decides one day to up and move across the country. Maybe flying all the way to California as an unaccompanied minor sucks, especially for Zara, who's afraid of goddamned heights! So perhaps, maybe, might it have been easier if we all got to stay the fuck put while the people responsible for the ongoing bullshit suffered the inconveniences?"

"You are—" Liora starts, while I try and catch my breath a little, but I inhale deeply as if about to dive underwater and continue.

"No!" I borderline yell. "This isn't a game, okay? It's not about trying to score points! We have to find a way of cutting this baby in half without killing it." I don't know what to say next. I'm still a little oxygen-deprived from shouting run-on sentences. I have a delirious vision of a gameshow set, with bright cobalt blue backgrounds and two contestant podiums. The host, who appears to be Steve Harvey, stands between the man and woman competing and says, "Let's..." and then a screaming studio audience of Midwestern Americans with bad haircuts and shoes scream, "Cut! That! Baby!" and cheer, and cheer.

I take another deep breath, which comes out shakily, and realise I've leapt to my feet, and Liora is sitting down and watching me with an expression I wouldn't quite call fear but which is at least apprehensive. "I'm not sorry for yelling," I say hoarsely, when I can breathe a little easier, even though my heart is still pounding. "This is it. You take it or leave it. You agree to consider this, and at least have a meeting to work out the details with the others, or I'm done. I'm out. They won't be able to force me to do this anymore."

There's a knock on the door, and it's Anderson, with one of Liora's henchmen on his heels. "Everything okay?" he asks, leaning into the room and looking it over without opening the door all the way.

Well, I certainly can't ask her about Farooq's farm now. Instead, I say, "My client was just leaving. She needs to go think over our discussion from today." I say it without even glancing at Liora for confirmation. I refuse to even appear open to the idea of backing down. Because I'm sure I meant what I just spewed from my mouth – this is the last ounce of effort I plan to expend on this project. And I suspect that after this trip, I will be done trying to deal with Mom and Dad, too. Leave Maxine and her tolerant, patient, clinical new personality to deal with the Mount Everests and Marianas Trenches of peaks and valleys that are Mom and Dad's relationship.

Fuck them. Fuck all of them.

Liora has risen and is gathering her things. Anderson seems more or less satisfied that there's no imminent danger inside this room, so he nods and withdraws his huge hairless head from the room and shuts the door lightly. I wonder if he's still standing right outside, if he has been all along, and how much he may have heard – but I don't care. Because I don't believe that Liora is going to consider anything, much less this brilliant and insane custody arrangement, so I'm already laying new bricks in the wall

I've built to protect myself from getting too invested in any of this.

Liora walks all the way to the door and puts her hand on the knob before she says anything. She turns and fixes me with a look so hard that her eyes look black. But she says, "I will consider what you said," and pushes through the door with her customary energy, like a team of football players bursting onto the field.

Anderson is not standing outside the door when I have collected myself enough to walk through the hallways, but he does come out of nowhere to match step with me right around the corner from the elevator. "Everything okay?" he asks, not giving away anything in his tone or expression.

"I think," I say, "possibly, yes." I push the elevator button.

"That proposal you mentioned – I take it that didn't go over so well."

"It did not," I begin, and Anderson nods, and interjects.

"Oh well," he says. "You tried your best."

I frown at him. "It didn't at first. But I think she might consider it." The elevator door groans open, and I step inside.

"Hmm," Anderson says.

I look at him questioningly, but he hasn't followed me into the elevator, and the doors start to close. "Wait – what is it?" I ask, but the elevator is already pulling away from the ground, and Anderson's downturned expression is just a ghost on my retinas.

Back in my room, I consider going over to knock on James's door to tell him how things went. I am blistering with curiosity to hear how things went for him, too. And a little part of me wants to tell this to someone who is in the same position as me, and has the best chance of fully comprehending what a coup it is for me to have even gotten the concession I did out of my client, that she would think about what I said. I turn my room key over in my hands, trying to decide if I want to get up out of my chair or not. I feel completely drained, yet fizzing with energy. For a moment, I consider exercising for the second time today. Outside, this time, though – I don't think anything could compel me to visit the fitness dungeon more than once in a single day.

Then, I remember that I either need to have dinner with Mike and my parents tonight or creatively get out of it. I sigh. I really wish I had some beta-blockers left. Or this is going to be the thing that finally makes me take up smoking. Mom once semi-seriously suggested taking up smoking to me as a method of weight loss, and it's entirely possible she will again, after that comment about my weight yesterday. And it's true, I may have gained a couple of pounds since I've been here – but it's hardly my fault. I'm under a lot of pressure, and I don't have a kitchen or anything. All anyone ever seems to want to do is make me go out to eat dinner with them, and that includes Mom and Dad.

I put down my key. I'll call James, I think – or pop over to give him a quick update – but later, when I'm on my way out to dinner with Mom, Dad and Mike. It's already somehow four o'clock, and I do feel like going outside for a bit, just for a walk. I don't care who follows me. And, actually, I don't think I will listen to any thinky NPR podcasts while I walk. I've had that Fall Out Boy song stuck in my head since that car ride with Anderson, and I want to see if I can get it on this ancient BlackBerry somehow to take with me instead. Then all I have to think about is walking to the beat.

FORTY

I'm in the shower when I hear Mike come in and call a greeting through the cracked bathroom door. I turn off the water for a second so he will hear me say hello, then turn it back on to finish rinsing out my hair. Anderson had materialised behind me somewhere between the King Solomon and the Jaffa Gate. Walking around the Old City made me feel very dusty today for some reason – maybe because it was so crowded with people. I noticed people were holding balloons and eating round, yellow cookies with blackish blob in the middle. Something about them rang a bell, and I was curious enough to consider asking someone, but ultimately didn't feel like removing my headphones or talking – just focused on the sights and smells, instead.

As I towel off, I think I should ask Mike if he knows whether today was some sort of festival or something – I'm at least pretty sure it's not a Jewish holiday – but the thought gets crowded out of my head when I catch sight of the clock on my bedside table. It is seven-thirty, and my parents said that they would come take us to dinner at eight. I can hear the sink running in Mike's bathroom, and I assume he's washing up and getting changed for dinner.

It seems likely that if I try to hide, I'll be found, and the only other option – running away – might well have me literally running into Mom and Dad in the lobby. And while I'm sure Yossi would enjoy the spectacle, I'm not inclined to grant him one since he deliberately stopped holding the door open when he saw me coming in earlier, then made a face at me. So I take a deep breath and open my closet, and start rummaging for something to wear that is likely to attract the fewest critical comments from Mom. This eliminates anything with any kind of stripes, anything not in earth tones and anything too tight, short or low-cut. I suspect a lot of things are too tight on me right now. I feel like an overstuffed cushion in my own skin. Too much stress-eating and too little stress-exercising. I try not to let too much guilt seep into my thoughts as I rifle through the last few hanging garments.

There's a three-quarter-sleeved faux wrap dress – one I remember Jess giving me as a gift when I'd tried it on while shopping with her in Ann Taylor but couldn't afford it. She'd said it looked too good on me to pass up, but I was still pretending to Dad that my internship was paid, so I declined it. She bought it for me while I wasn't paying attention, having sneaked it into her own pile of stuff on our way out of the fitting rooms. I protested, but she called it an early birthday present, and then went ahead and bought me another gift when my actual birthday arrived a month later. It's only a dress, but it makes me feel loved.

And it is flattering – it's the kind of cut even Mom approves of, that's almost universally flattering. And it's black, which Mom says is slimming. I put the dress on and decide to put on the aspirational heels Thom packed for me, the ones I never wear at home because they hurt too much – for some reason, having a pair of shoes with sharp heels that could also function as weapons is appealing tonight.

"Ready to go?" asks Mike, knotting a tie as he comes through the partition doors.

"No."

"You look ready," he says, kissing me on the cheek. "You look beautiful."

"Thanks." I sigh.

"I have an update from Jess," he says. "She texted that she got rebooked. But then that flight was delayed too. She said" – Mike pulls out his phone and reads Jess's text verbatim – "'Mike, the shitgibbons who run this airline are driving me insane.' Apparently, they boarded this flight but have been sitting on the tarmac for a couple of hours."

I sigh. "Great. Jess is trapped at Newark Airport, and I'm stuck having dinner with my parents."

"It'll be okay. I'll be right there with you."

I give him A Look that he correctly interprets as me asking him in what universe this dinner could possibly be okay.

"Let's get it over with, then," he says. "I saw them in the lobby on my way up. They're waiting for us down there."

He's right. Their cavernous, yawning need to suck me into their drama will only widen if I delay meeting it. They'll just escalate by coming around at a more inconvenient time or making a scene. I grab my bag and head for the door. "Into battle," I say. Mike follows me to the elevators. While we wait for one to arrive, I take his hand.

Dad has prevailed upon Yossi to call a cab for us, a request which I am sure would have had to be delivered alongside a wad of shekels, based on Yossi's general attitude towards the duties of his job. Also, it's not necessary to call cabs here. If you pause for too long on the sidewalk, a cab driver will slow down, honk at you and give you a 'Nu? Get in already.' gesture. I'm not complaining about taking a cab, because my feet hurt already, but Dad's manner of giving staff – whom he insists on calling 'service people' – showy amounts of money and watching them scurry around to do his bidding has always turned my stomach. "It's their job to serve us, Emily," I remember him telling me in front of a hotel housekeeper in Florida when I tried to take the bedding he'd had sent up for the extra cot from her and said I could make the bed myself.

We all sit in the back of the cab in uncomfortable silence. Mike compensates a little by humming tunelessly to himself and tapping the armrest on the car door. I glance back through the rear windshield at the black car following us, and then watch Jerusalem rush by through the windows, still marvelling at the simultaneous familiarity and strangeness of the city. It had been getting dark when I returned to the hotel before my shower, and is now fully dark, but the buildings are pale enough to be visible even without street lights. Finally, the cab stops, and I roll my eyes to myself at the fact that Dad has found what is surely the most American-looking steakhouse in the entire region and chosen that. Dad is an immovable object who has never found himself up against an irresistible force.

Though Mom has not spoken other than to say hello before we got in the taxi, I can see in the dim light of the steakhouse that she's wearing a placid expression – there's a slight upturn to the corners of her mouth that is both relaxed and smug. I want to say something to wipe that little smile away, but Mike has taken my hand again and squeezes it in warning, so I shut my mouth again before anything untoward comes out.

Dad's first complete sentence of the evening is, "I'd like to see a wine list," said to the hostess before we have even fully sat down at the table.

"I would like to see a cocktail menu," I counter, kicking off my shoes under the table. Mike looks worried.

I feel the urge to break this weird silence swelling in my chest, like a balloon. I'm starting to fidget a little. The moment the hostess has handed over the menus and is out of earshot, I start in. "I would just like to know what the hell is going on," I say.

"What do you mean?" Mom asks, all wide-eyed, though I notice her eyebrows don't go up. I wonder if she and Dad are getting couples Botox now.

"What do you mean, 'what do you mean?'" I ask. "You know what I mean."

"I think what Emily means—" Mike starts, trying to help, but he can't help me now. He can't help any of us. We need professional help.

"I know what I mean, and so do they!" I say, raising my voice a little.

"Don't raise your voice, Emily," Dad says, not looking up from his menu. He is holding his phone over it, using the flashlight function to illuminate his menu, even though he'd never order anything but a rib-eye, 'just a little pink in the middle', with two sides of vegetables and no potatoes – that is, when he's eating red meat.

"Then tell me what in the hell you are doing here!" I whisper-shout.

"We told you," Mom said. "We're here to get married. It was Rabbi Gold's idea."

I think I'm about to pass out from anger. "I meant," I say, "how did this happen?"

Dad clears his throat, puts down his phone and menu, and tucks his reading glasses back into his pocket. "I don't know what it is you want to hear."

"An. Explanation," I say through gritted teeth. I am unconsciously fingering my steak knife, which I only realise when Mike puts his hand on top of mine and moves them both into his lap.

"We ran into each other a few weeks ago," Mom says. "That's it. Are you happy?"

"Am I—!"

"What do you want from us?" Dad wonders again.

"So where did you two reconnect?" Mike interjects desperately.

Dad drums his fingers on the table and addresses me. "Your mother and I ran into each other near Skid Row," he says. "She was on a mission trip, volunteering with the homeless there. I was lost. I didn't see her at first – but I saw Rabbi Gold and went to say hello to him. There was a whole group from the JCC. There were several people from the synagogue. They were wearing matching shirts." He stops talking. He looks as if he thinks he's finished explaining.

"A *few* weeks ago?" I prod, teeth still clenched.

"Several weeks ago. July."

"I don't understand," I say.

"I don't understand what you don't understand," Mom says. "Your father and I ran into each other several weeks ago, and now we're getting married."

"Re! Remarried!" I say, now yelling, and a few heads turn in the restaurant, but they don't seem too disturbed. Israelis often yell, anyway.

"A normal child would be thrilled that her parents were getting back together," Dad says.

It doesn't go unnoticed by me or by Mike that Dad has just called me abnormal. And a child.

"I don't think it's strange for Emily to be a little taken aback – given the history – that you are getting remarried." Mike says it politely, but I can see that he's angry on my behalf.

"Thank you," I say to him. I try to lower my volume a little, and it works, though I sound very strained. "After more than ten years" – I struggle for a word that can contain the experience of the divorce – "apart. You just happen to run into each other and now you're getting remarried? What about… what about everything? And Candace?"

"What about Candace?" Dad asks, frowning.

"What about Candace!" I repeat, astonished, and I

look at Mike. I start laughing, just a small giggle, but I can't contain it, and soon I'm hysterical. I laugh, and laugh, and Mom, Dad and Mike stare at me – respectively embarrassed, annoyed and concerned. Eventually, my abs ache enough and I'm out of breath enough that I quiet down, but I'm still wiping away tears. Out of the corner of my eye, I see Thom half-rise in his seat, but Wilcox grabs his sleeve and pulls him back down.

Mike leans over and whispers in my ear, "Do you want to get some air?"

"No," I say at normal volume. "I don't need any air. I need – you know what? I need to leave. Will you take me?" I push my chair back and try to shove my swollen feet back into my shoes. Then I stand up and wait for him to answer.

Mike looks ambivalent. He hates to be rude, and this is almost definitely rude. My parents have invited him out for dinner, and he accepted. We've also entered into a social contract with the hostess, in his opinion, once we sat down – this has always been a quirk of his, feeling like it's too late to leave once we've been seated, even if we only then discover there's nothing on the menu we want and they haven't even brought us water yet. But unlike Thom, who had foolishly ordered food he would now have to leave behind, he also looks a little bit pleased.

I don't figure out why until I look over at him, in the back seat of the black car with Thom between us, and see him smiling in the light of the passing street lamps. He's not happy we left – he's happy we left together.

The second Mike and I make it back to our rooms, I'm kissing him. It's going great, and then not at all. I open my eyes. Mike has taken a step back and stood up straight, so I can't reach his face. He looks conflicted.

"What?" I ask, and try to get on my tiptoes so I can reach his face again, but he stops me with his gentle, but firm, grip on my waist.

"We need to talk," he says.

FORTY-ONE

I stood up to my parents, and I'm kissing Mike. Things are great. And then, they're not – because he's pushing me away.

"Emily," he repeats.

"Now? We need to talk now?"

"I think now," Mike says, letting go of me and perching on the edge of my desk. He folds his arms across his chest.

I sit down in the desk chair. "About what?"

"I really get it, you know," Mike says. "Your parents. They're…" He shakes his head.

So? I want to ask, but Mike usually arrives at his point eventually. I wait.

"What I mean is," Mike continues, giving up on finding a word for what exactly it is that my parents are, "I understand, you know, you."

My nose wrinkles a little bit, as if there's a whiff of something unpleasant I'm starting to notice. "What do you mean, you understand me?"

"Why you're the way you are so much of the time."

"The way I—"

"I'm not talking about when you ran away the other day, at the Dead Sea. You were shocked, and I understand wanting to get away from them. But out of curiosity, did you think about me at all? You left me there, and took the car."

I realise at that moment that I have not asked – and Mike has not volunteered – how he got back to Jerusalem. And, almost in the same instant, I realise how he must have returned. "Oh my God, I'm so sorry," I tell him.

"I've never had a more awkward car ride with anyone's parents," Mike says. "Not even my friend's mother who used to call me 'the Oriental kid' in the carpool."

"I'm so, so sorry. I didn't think."

"I know that. You don't think; you just run. Then you make it impossible to communicate with you, so the rest of us have nothing to do but think!" Mike isn't yelling, he never does, but he's as close to it as he gets.

I feel the warm spread of panic in my guts. I don't say anything; I just do my best to keep looking at him, and listening.

"I get why you'd need to run from your parents. I do. But I do not understand why you keep having to run from me."

"I didn't," I protest. "I wasn't, I was running away from them."

"I said I'm not talking about that day," Mike says. "I'm not holding that against you. I don't know how I'd react if my long-separated parents showed up out of nowhere, floating in the Dead Sea, where I least expected."

"Then what—"

"Emily, I proposed to you, and you ran away and hid from me, then didn't answer any of my calls or emails, nor did you show up when I got on a plane to move here to teach semi-permanently, and then all of a sudden when it suited you, you had an apparatchik fetch me from my office and haul me to live in a terrible hotel with you while you work on a secret mission" – Mike takes a deep breath – "and then you alternately push me away and pull me back in until I'm dizzy, all while declining to talk to me – I mean really, really talk to me – about anything. And then this evening, I find out from Yossi that after your most recent episode of fleeing from me, you ended up going out with that Browning guy, after going on about how much of an asshole he is. God knows what you two talked about, although Yossi said you were gone for hours, so presumably you managed to say something to him, at least – though not to me!" Mike has uncrossed his arms and is gripping the edge of the desk on either side of his legs.

Something is starting to bubble up inside me, and it's going to come out soon. Until it does, I don't know what it will be. I keep my mouth pressed shut and try to breathe through my nose.

"Are you still not going to talk to me?" Mike says, a little bitterly.

It comes out. "I told you years ago that I don't know how to do this." It comes out like a little bit like a sob. I wrap my own arms around me tightly to try and hold myself together. "When we met," I continue, breathing very fast and shallow, "I told you that I don't know how to do any of this, and that you should run away from me right then because it was only a matter of time before you wanted to. I warned you, but you didn't listen. You said you weren't going anywhere."

"I never have," Mike says. "I never wanted to. I still don't. It's you who keeps running."

I'm crying now, quietly, not making a show of it or for any reason but that I can't seem to not cry. Something in Mike's face softens a little.

"I don't want to do it," I admit. "I can't help it."

Mike exhales, then gets up, pries my arms loose from my own torso, then hugs me. "I know you can't," Mike says. "I just wanted to hear you acknowledge that. And maybe that you'll consider trying to do something about it."

"Like what?" I sniffle into his shirt.

"Like therapy," he says, "not instead of the beta-blockers or Poco or any of it. In addition to those things you already do to cope."

I stiffen but don't say anything.

"I know you've had bad experiences of therapy before. But it wouldn't have to be like it was when you were a kid. Nobody's going to force it on you, and nobody's going to make a court case of what you say in there. It's not a trick. And I know there are some bad therapists – but there are also some very, very good ones. The kind who can turn a depressed, adopted teenager into the well-adjusted adult you know and love."

I pull back a little to look at him. "I didn't know you went to therapy."

Mike shrugs. "Maybe we were both too okay with you being the messed-up one of the two of us for too long."

I smile and rest my cheek on his chest again. I'm not ready to agree to anything like therapy yet, but I am willing to think about it. We stay there for a few minutes, until my neck hurts, so I break free and cross my arms mock-sternly. "Gossiping with Yossi?" I ask Mike. "That's a new low."

"I felt stupid as soon as I'd said it," Mike says, covering his face with one hand.

"I was looking for Sven. Well, Prince Charles. I just ran into him and we ended up working. It was helpful, but only because work is a good distraction. He had a very interesting idea."

Mike grins, relieved both that I do have an explanation and that I'm letting his small lapse into jealousy go. "Tell me about it?" Mike asks.

"Tomorrow," I tell him, and reach up to kiss him again.

The BlackBerry's shrill ringing on my nightstand is what wakes me up. I accidentally slap Mike in the face blindly reaching for it.

"What? What's wrong?" Mike says as I flail around above him trying to silence it.

"Shh. Nothing," I tell him, grabbing it. It's not an alarm – it's James. I think it's the first time he's called me since we've been here. I answer. "Hello?"

"Good morning. Did I wake you?"

I look at the phone. It's almost ten, so I lie. "No, of course not," I say, covering the speaker while I clear my throat and sit up straighter. "What's up?"

"I'm afraid it's not good news. Can we meet to discuss? Soon – half ten?"

"Is that nine-thirty, or ten-thirty?" I ask, feeling my heart start to race already. Bad news? Urgent? What does he know?

"Ten-thirty," he says, like I'm the idiot.

"Why not just say ten-thirty, then?" I mutter.

"Ten-thirty, then – downstairs? Yossi said none of the meeting rooms are booked, so we can use any one that's empty."

"Of course none of the meeting rooms are booked, James," I say, hopping on one foot towards the shower and trying to kick off my pyjamas. "I'll be down there at ten-thirty." I toss the phone at the desk and throw open my closet.

Mike has gotten up and opened the thick curtains. The light is blinding, and we're both squinting. "Everything okay?" he asks.

I shake my head. "Don't know. He says it's bad news, and I have to go discuss it in half an hour."

Mike stretches. "I better get moving, too. I have class this afternoon. Will you let me know how you're doing after?"

I grab a pair of black jeans and a comfortable blouse and throw them on my bed. Then I give Mike a quick kiss on the cheek, tell him I'll text him so he can check it when he's not busy, and get into the shower before it warms up.

I learned long ago that the most respectable thing to do with my hair when I haven't left enough time to dry it correctly is to dry the roots and sling the rest of it up into a messy bun, so I do that while slipping on a pair of flat shoes, then dash out the door for the elevators. I can only take a full breath in when it starts moving, empty except for me, and I use the mirrored surface to double-check that I'm presentable. I am, loosely speaking, so I focus on taking a few deep breaths in and out, four counts each way and holding for two in between each inhalation and exhalation. I wish, for the millionth time in the last few days, that I had some beta-blockers left. But this time, something occurs to me – Mom's serene expression, her relaxed posture. And I didn't even see her drink any wine.

She's on something. Something good, something better than beta-blockers.

Mom's got benzos. And I'm going to get some. I just have to get through whatever this is first.

Thom is in the elevator when I get in it, which is a surprise. I squeeze in beside him. "What are you doing?" I ask him, talking over the creaking and clanging.

"Nothing," he says, clutching a folder to his chest.

That sounds about right.

"Have you seen Anderson around recently?" Thom adds.

"Yes, around. You know, keeping an eye on me."

"Hm," Thom says.

"Your shoes are dusty," I tell him.

"No, they aren't," he says.

"Okay," I reply. The elevator stops. I look at Thom strangely, but he's lost in thought, and I have somewhere to be, so I let it go.

When I exit the elevator on the first floor, I see James

right away. He's in the first conference room, making tea. Pointedly not from the hot water dispenser that's been in this room every time we have, but from a pocket-sized electric kettle he appears to have brought with him, along with his own personal stash of loose tea. It's from a pretty teal canister labelled 'Fortnum & Mason – Royal Blend'.

"Would you like some tea?" James asks as I plonk down into a chair opposite him.

"No, thanks," I say. "I don't like it."

"What do you mean, you don't like 'it'? You don't like what? Royal Blend?"

"No, tea. I don't like tea."

"But that's ridiculous. It's like saying you don't like" – James casts around for something that's as stupid as me not liking tea – "I don't know, fruit. You can't dislike the entire category. They all taste different."

"Would you please," I say very calmly, "get to the goddamned bad news."

James sets down his many tea-making instruments and clears his throat. "Ah," he says. "Yes. Not to worry, it's nothing dire. It was always unlikely."

I press my hands together and hold them tightly against my mouth to stop any trembling, now from frustration as much as anxiety.

James continues. "I'm afraid my client was quite clear. He will not consider the bird-nesting model of custody of Jerusalem. He did reiterate that it would have to be the capital of the Palestinian state as defined by us – though, frankly, he stormed out so abruptly that I didn't even get to clarify whether he meant East Jerusalem or the whole of it."

I am completely crushed. And stunned. "But my client is on board," I say. "And this was your idea. You have no idea what it was like, bringing this proposal to Liora. I assumed that you wouldn't have even suggested it if you didn't have at least an inkling that you could get your client on board."

"I didn't say I had the chairman's support."

"It was implied! Why would you put me through that if—"

"It's not a punishment, Emily. It's just how these things go. Of course, you know that, being a lawyer yourself."

I feel my cheeks redden a little, part embarrassment, part rage. "Did you even try?" I ask. "Did you really, truly try? I did. I dug deep. I gave it a hundred per cent. And she said she would consider it. And now what – I go back to her and say, 'Never mind, the chairman isn't interested after all, forget I said anything?'"

James takes a sip of his tea and puts the mug down soundlessly before answers. "That may not quite be necessary."

"Then what?"

He tents his hands together on the table and looks up at me through his dark eyelashes. "I think it's possible I could get him to reconsider, but I'll need a major concession from the PM."

"This *is* a major concession from us!" I say, clenching my fingers around my armrests. "Shared custody of Jerusalem is a major concession from the PM!"

"I'm afraid my client doesn't see it that way."

"How does he see it?"

"I think he might be willing to see it your way if" –
James sits back a little – "PM Reznik concedes that the
State of Palestine will be allowed to develop a nuclear
programme."

My jaw drops.

"I do understand that this will be rather a hard sell for
you," James says.

"You—!"

"I know," he says. "But it is what it is. I spoke with him
on the phone again yesterday evening, after our disastrous
meeting in the morning, and he said he would reconsider
if Israel does not object – or ask the United States to object
– to its development of a nuclear programme."

My thoughts are whizzing through me as fast as my
blood is pulsing in my eardrums. But then they slow
down, and I'm able to hold one in my brain long enough to
examine it. "Hold on just a minute," I say. "You say you met
with Barghouti yesterday?"

FORTY-TWO

I'm on the verge of a big realisation, but it keeps getting away. I don't think James is telling the truth about meeting with Barghouti yesterday – there's something in the back of my mind telling me he can't have. And if he didn't, then there's no way I'm mentioning a nuclear programme to Liora.

"Yes," James says. "I met with Barghouti yesterday."

I hold up a finger to stop him talking so I can think a little more. "No," I say slowly, as the understanding starts to coalesce. "You didn't."

"What are you talking about? Of course I—"

"You didn't," I say, firmly. The little round cookies, the flurry of activity around the mosques, the people all dressed up – it all clicks. Something I learned back in Religious Studies, years ago. Something I learned from Mike. "Yesterday," I say, looking James in the eye, "Mahmoud Barghouti will have been, alongside millions of other Muslims around the world, celebrating Eid al-Adha. One of the most important festivals in the Muslim calendar. And you, James Browning, were no more in touch with your client on that day than I would have been in touch with mine on Yom Kippur."

James looks momentarily startled but manages to rearrange his face into his usual impassive but amused expression. "I didn't know you were familiar with the holiday," he says.

"Clearly."

"But how can you be certain I didn't speak with him?"

"You basically just admitted it," I say. "And I was a Religious Studies minor."

James frowns a little at that, and I panic. For a moment, I managed to forget that I'm not the Emily A. Price I'm supposed to be. Was the real one a Religious Studies minor? Does James know the details of her CV?

"I can't believe you," I continue, partially to distract him if he was thinking that Emily Price does not have a minor in Religious Studies. But now that the confusion is wearing off a little, and the situation is crystallising, I feel a powerful surge of rage travelling through my body. I stand, my movements feeling a little jerky and out of control because of the sheer force of the anger. I'm trembling a little again, but right this moment, I don't wish for beta-blockers to wall me off from the intensity of the feeling. This time, I need it. I'm drawing strength from it.

James stands, too, a little afraid. Good – he should be scared. I think I might hit him this time. And I suddenly know for sure he's never taken a punch at all, or thrown one – just laughed snottily on the side-lines of the playground while he directed some other snotty little boys to bully the target he'd chosen.

"You," I say, leaning forward and jabbing my index finger into his lapel, "are going to be very, very sorry."

I'm about to tell him what he's going to be very sorry for, and why, when James interrupts me, by saying, "You know, you're adorable when you're angry," and then, before I can intake enough breath to shout at him or finish winding my arm, his thin-lipped mouth is on mine, and he's grabbed the bicep of my throwing arm to stop me from preparing to hit him.

I always think, in moments between unwanted touches by men, of how I'll respond the next time. Cat-called at by an NYC sanitation worker hanging off the back of a garbage truck to yell at me? Throw whatever's in my hand at his head. Leered at by a man on a bench while I'm jogging past him in Central Park? Double back and ask him what the fuck he's looking at. Dentist plants a wet, lingering kiss on my forehead? Stab him with whatever sharp implements he keeps nearby. And yet... almost every time this kind of thing happens, my reaction is the same. I freeze, full of disbelief that anyone would be so bold, so predatory, so *rude* as to violate my bodily integrity and personal security in that way. Signing up for Krav Maga after the most egregious instance of being groped in public and anything else I ever tried to do to be ready the next time was nothing but a very specific brand of esprit de l'escalier. Too late, and too hypothetical.

Unfortunately, this time is no different.

I remain immobile for what feels like at least half an hour while my head floods with exclamation marks. But then, this time, something kicks in – fight or flight, maybe, but whatever it is tells me I need to do something about what's happening. First, I yank my arm out of James's grip, which has softened because of the false sense of security I unintentionally cultivated by not immediately resisting.

Then, I bite him.

He makes an indignant sound and pulls away from me. "Ouch! Why did you do that?"

"Why did I—! Why did *you*?"

"Oh, please," he says.

"Excuse me?"

"I wanted to," he says. "You wanted me to. What's the problem?"

The first thing I want to say is Mike, Mike is the problem. Only he's not a problem – of course he isn't! – and the problem is not that I belong to someone else; the problem is that a co-worker of mine, to whom I never gave any kind of indication that I would welcome it, responded to me telling him that he has crossed a professional line by lying to me and failing to fulfil his obligation to his own client, by putting his stupid mouth on my mouth. It's only the flourish on top of the fancy stationery that is James Browning that he decided to do it in a meeting room, in the hotel where my boyfriend – whom he has met – is also staying.

"You are truly a garbage person," I hiss at him, wiping my mouth with the back of my hand. James tasted like tea, which I hate, and now I have to taste it without even drinking it. I smooth down my blouse, trying to stop my hands from shaking, pick up my notebook and walk around the table towards the door, but James is standing in front of it. "You're in my way. Again."

"Where are you going?" James asks. "We weren't done discussing the nuclear programme issue."

"I'm going straight to Thom, so he can tell Alisha what happened here."

"Really, Emily," James says, crossing his arms. "Just because you can't admit that you wanted me to kiss you, that doesn't mean you need to go running to teacher to tattle."

"Not that," I say, using all my energy not to stamp my foot in frustration. "The part where you lied to me about the Jerusalem custody deal, didn't present the deal to your client – as you have a duty to do – and then tried to deceive me into a suggestion to the Prime Minister of Israel that could alone be responsible for World War III."

I push past him and out the door, where I nearly collide with Yossi. "Oh," I say, "It's you."

"*Nachon*," he says, a little too sarcastically even for my taste. "It's me."

"What do you want?"

"'What do you want?'" Yossi repeats, mocking my tone. "Only to tell you that Michael" – Yossi always Hebraises the pronunciation of Mike's name – "was looking for you, and I brought him here. About five minutes ago," he adds meaningfully. I think about five minutes ago, and the glass window in the door of that conference room, and it adds up to what Mom always called a catastro-fuck.

"*Ben zonah!*" I say, and rush off. Behind me, I hear Yossi cackling and calling after me that I know just enough Hebrew to get by around here, after all.

I do a quick mental triage assessment and decide that making my report to Thom can happen later. First, I must find Mike as quickly as possible. I only hope that he hasn't left the hotel, but that's not really his style; it's mine. And Yossi would have pointed me at the door for the sheer amusement of seeing me try to track him down in a still-unfamiliar city that Mike knows better than I do. I realise with some sadness that I wouldn't even know where to begin to look for him here, even though I would have been absolutely guaranteed to find him back in State College, in the early days, and even in New York. I know so little of his life now, and I have nobody to blame for that but myself. Stupid, I tell myself, but then I add petulantly: stupid *James.* I didn't do anything wrong, not this time.

There isn't time for a shitty elevator, so I run up the narrow stairs, slipping a little on the threadbare carpet down the centre. But I hear a voice calling after me, so I don't slow down. No, I think to myself. Not now. I don't hear you.

"Emily!" Mom's voice cries out louder, and then she's caught up with me.

I don't look at her. I jam my key into the door.

"I couldn't remember what room was yours, just the floor," Mom says, as oblivious to my cold shoulder as she always was when it suited her better not to notice.

"I can't talk to you right now, Mom," I say, trying to get inside the room without her following, but she's so close on my heels that she slips in. "Mom!" I say, but she's looking over my shoulder.

"Oh, hello, Mike," she says, then turns back to me. "Emily, your father—"

"Don't care, please leave!" I turn and give Mike a desperate look. He is wearing a grim expression and has his arms crossed.

"Your father," Mom presses on, "is still married to Candace."

"*Mom*, I – what?"

Mike clears his throat. "You know what, I'll go," he says, moving to go through the partition door into his room and then on to – where?

"No!" I say. "You, stay. Mom, you go! I can't do this right now. I have enough going on—"

"For God's sake, Emily. What can you have going on that's important?"

I close my mouth and reach around her to open the door to my room. I am going to simply push her out.

But the moment the door opens, Dad is filling the doorway, and then he's inside, too.

"No, no!" I say, and this time, I do stamp my foot. "I will not let you do this. Not this time. You have no idea what I'm dealing with, with work—"

"'Work,'" Mike repeats sardonically, at the same time as I see Dad roll his eyes up to the ceiling and clench his jaw muscles.

I know that Mike isn't saying the same thing as Dad, but it's a blow to have them both express their doubt in me in synchrony like this. But Dad is a lost cause, as far as I'm concerned, and Mike isn't. So I hold up a hand to silence Dad, and turn away from him and face Mike. "I know what you saw, but please know that I had no idea that he was going to do that, and I didn't want him to, and I am going to go straight to Thom and tell him what happened so they can find someone else to represent his client."

Mom, sensing that the attention is off her now, starts to cry. "Your father," she says again, as if he were not in the room now, "is planning to be a bigamist."

"I am not!" Dad says. "I'm divorcing Candace."

"I thought you already did!" I shout, then immediately hate myself for giving in and getting involved.

"Your mother killed Barbra Streisand," Dad adds, after a moment of silence.

"No, I didn't! I set her free!"

"Well, African greys aren't really adapted to Rockland County weather," Dad snapped.

Mike sits down hard on the desk chair, which buckles slightly under him, and presses his fingers to his temples.

"And your mother," Dad continued, "conveniently forgot to mention that she's in bankruptcy proceedings. They would have started right around the time when – hmm, let's see – we just happened to run into each other in LA."

"You would have used that bird against me."

"What?" I interjected.

"Your father told the judge that I was teaching Babs to disparage him to you girls," Mom said.

"Well, you were," Dad countered.

"What is it you want from Emily, here?" Mike says.

My hero. "Yes, what the fuck do you want me to do about it? Babs is dead, and so's your marriage. Congratulations. You're divorced. Go be that."

"That's it?" Mom says, lip trembling theatrically. "That's all you have to say?"

I look at Mike, and he nods. "Yes," I say. "That's all I have to say."

Mom and Dad both look at each other, horrified, then look back at me.

"You should go," I add, in case it wasn't clear. "Because I'm busy. I have very important work to do."

Dad scoffs.

"Well, when can I talk to you?" Mom asks.

"I don't know. I'll be in important meetings tomorrow. Tonight, I should prepare for them. You can call me and ask first before you come over."

"You don't have to invent fake meetings, Emily," Dad says. "It's really very childish."

I want more than anything to tell him just how important my meetings are. I know I can't, but I do believe it would be worth it to see the look on their faces when they see me sitting with Liora Reznik, and her listening to me, like I'm a real person. I struggle to think of anything I can say to shut them down, but again, Mike comes to my rescue.

He gets up from the chair and stands next to me. "She's not inventing meetings," Mike says. "I'm involved with the case she's working on. It's extremely important. I barely get to see her. She's exhausted, and the last thing she needs is you adding to her burden. She asked you to leave her to it for the day, and call her before either of you visits again, and that's completely reasonable."

Dad looks surprised to be talked back to by anyone other than me. But when he's caught off guard, he usually reacts by doing what he's told. Fortunately, that means heading for the door. Mom doesn't know what to do with herself, either, so she follows him. I hold my breath as Dad opens the door and steps through it, hardly daring to believe that this whole 'boundaries' thing all those therapists were constantly going on about could work.

But of course, before the door shuts behind them, Mom has one more thing to add: "By the way, Emily, your sisters start to arrive tomorrow. Maxine is going to be my matron of honour."

FORTY-THREE

I look at the door for a while after it closes, too emotionally wrung out to react to this news.

"Should I..." Mike trails off. "Hit him?"

"Who?"

"James," Mike says, like that was obvious.

I laugh. "No. It's okay. I bit him," I say. "And I'm going to report him."

"Good," Mike says.

"You don't even know the half of it," I tell him, and then I explain about Eid, and how James had lied to me about everything to try to get me to agree to incite World War III.

"What are you going to tell Liora?"

"Nothing, yet." I don't tell Mike that I've started to form something resembling a plan, because what I'm going to do, I know for sure he is not going to approve of. So instead, I ask if he wants me to get Thom to bring us food from that American restaurant again.

"Whatever you want," Mike says. Then he reaches in his

pocket, pulls out his phone and frowns. "That's weird. Did you hear my phone?"

"No, why?"

"More texts from Jess. I was just thinking we should have gotten some update by now, but I didn't hear the alert, even though I thought I turned on the volume so we wouldn't miss it." He passes me the phone:

> Oh my god! Yes! The pilot says we are going to take off in ten minutes, going into airplane mode now, see you guys soon!

> Guess where I am? France. I'm in fucking France. We had an emergency landing. There was smoke in the galley. They're saying we will be able to get back on the plane as soon as they can be sure it's safe. But I don't buy it. They told us to take our luggage with us, and the flight crew will be out of hours soon.

"Well, I have to get moving. Will you promise to let me know if she says anything else?"

"Of course," Mike says. "She's having a hell of a flight." Here is my plan: first, I'm going to call Farooq and tell him I haven't forgotten about him. Then, I'm going to have lunch with Mom and Maxi. I am going to do this, not because I want to have lunch with either of them but because I know Mom is always on her best behaviour with Maxi. That means we will not be discussing the fact that my father is still married to his second wife, whom I feel I now finally know for sure Dad was seeing while still with his first wife – Mom. She will also not be discussing her apparent bankruptcy, which I can only imagine Maxi doesn't know about, especially if Mom managed to keep it from Dad until now. We will exchange pleasantries and maybe talk about the wedding on a surface level. And, of course, we'll exchange another thing: Mom's secret weapon in her battle to make a good impression: her benzos. That one will be a one-way exchange from her to me.

If I can get through a lunch with them, I can get some of Mom's pills. Then I can hold on to them in case I do need to call Liora in for a meeting to tell her that James tricked me. Just knowing I have them as a backup plan should help. And of course, I could take one for when I go see Thom about the other thing James did, if I get enough.

And – this is the best part of my idea yet – Anderson or Wilcox will have to drive me. I'll show up late, at least twenty minutes late so it's later than Maxi usually is on purpose so she can come rushing in and talk about how busy she is with patients and have the whole table's attention. They'll see I'm being driven around by someone who is clearly a bodyguard, and they'll know, without me having to say anything indiscreet, that my client is as A-list as they come.

The specific part of this plan that I think Mike will object to is all of it. But Mike is teaching again today, so by the time he finds out – if he finds out – I'll already have the pills. Besides, however much he complains about my plans, I think he likes that I think outside the box.

"Hey, Thom?" I say into the BlackBerry as I force my feet back into the evil pointy shoes. "Do you know where Anderson is?"

"No, I don't." Thom sounds tense. I remember that he was acting a little strange when I ran into him in the elevator on the way to see James yesterday, too.

"Um, okay. Do you know when he'll be here?"

"No, I don't."

"Okay, then do you know where Wilcox is?"

"Him, at least, yes. Why?"

"I need to borrow him, for a ride."

"Fine, fine," Thom says, and I hear the phone moving away from his face already, as if he's about to hang up.

"Wait!"

"What?" Thom says, muffled, before putting the phone back to his ear. "Do you need something?"

"There's something I need to discuss with you, but it's not urgent. Can I come find you in the hotel this afternoon?"

"Fine," Thom says, and he's hung up.

It's strange, but then, Thom is strange.

I call Mom. It's the same number she's always had, and one of only a handful of phone numbers I know by heart.

"What is it, Emily?" Mom asks, in a serene voice that tells me I'm definitely right about the Xanax.

"Lunch?" I chirp. "When do the others get here?"

"Maxine gets in first. I guess you and I can have lunch with her."

"Okay," I say, like it's a concession, and not my exact plans. "Dad coming?"

"No," she says.

"Okay, then." I suppress my glee and give her directions to a fancy organic delicatessen-type place I saw on my walk to the Old City. It's not far enough for me to justify being driven there, but it's all part of the plan. It'll appease Maxi, and it'll be the kind of place Mom hates but knows she has to pretend to like, and which both of them are quietly impressed by. "I'll see you there at one-thirty."

Mom sighs.

I ignore her. "Bye," I say, and hang up.

I half expect James to be waiting to accost me in the lobby or something, but he's nowhere to be seen – that's good, I guess, since it must mean he's hiding in shame. Neither is Thom anywhere to be seen, and Anderson still hasn't resurfaced. But Wilcox is waiting on one of the overstuffed armchairs, and I'm happy enough that everything is going to plan that I don't even think to ask him where he disappeared to the other day – the day at the Dead Sea, which feels like a hundred years ago – when I ended up getting in Anderson's car without realising it. I just ask him how he is, and when he says, "Good, thanks," I tell him I'm the same.

It's a beautiful day. The sun is shining, a temperate breeze is blowing and I'm about to get my hands on some Xanax. I roll down the window of the car a little, so I can enjoy the breeze without messing up my hair right before I see Mom.

"I'm just going to need to clear it again with Mr Newhouse before I take you anywhere," Wilcox says, lips turned down a little.

"Sorry about that, again," I tell him.

He shrugs it off. "Big meeting?"

"You could say that," I tell him. I catch a sweet smell on the air wafting into the backseat and wonder if it's the bougainvillaea I see climbing the stone buildings all around that smells like that, or maybe something else. Jasmine? It's calming, and even though I don't believe in aromatherapy or essential oils – there's just nothing so effective as Xanax in the natural world – I think I'd like to track that smell down and get a spray of it for my pillow.

"Okay, let's go," Wilcox says, hanging up the phone.

He opens the door for me when we get to the restaurant. He's pulled up right in front of the glass window, like I'd hoped. I can see Mom and Maxi at one of the rustic wooden tables, looking at me. Wilcox notices, and asks if they're who I'm here to meet. When I tell him yes, he smiles and offers to walk me in, as if I could say no. But today, I want him to. "Thanks," I tell him. He holds the door for me and stands outside the restaurant, facing the street.

Maxi is burning with obvious desire to ask me about Agent Wilcox, but she's fighting the urge. I smile sweetly at her, and she reluctantly pushes back the bench so she can stand up. Since she married Orson, she's done this cold air-kiss and hand-grazing-bicep thing instead of our usual family style of either hugging warmly or giving the cold shoulder entirely. It is very Protestant of her. I notice that her hair has even more highlights in it than last time I saw her, and she's now achieved an approximation of a colour one might call honey blonde – and it's been straightened.

"So," I ask her, sitting down. "How's Boston?"

"Fine, Emily," she says.

"Wicked," I jab.

"Are you going to tell us who that is?" Maxi inclines her head at the window, where the back of Wilcox is visible, his black suit flapping in the breeze.

"Oh, him?"

Mom puts her wine glass down passive-aggressively. I didn't notice the wine when I sat down. I wonder where it came from.

"He's just my driver," I say hastily. "It's a precaution. My client insists."

Maxi chews on the insides of her cheeks, resenting that she'd had to ask the question and unwilling to ask me any more of them.

"Where are the children?" I ask her. "Did Ellie like the Breyer horse I sent for her birthday?"

"She's three, Emily," Maxi says. "Orson had to put it away on a high shelf where it wouldn't get broken."

"She can break it if she wants," I mutter. "What about Scott?"

"He's fine," she answers.

"They're with the nanny," Mom supplies, knowing what I was getting at. "And Orson."

"They're not coming, then?"

"Coming? Where – here?" Maxi wrinkles her nose.

"Orson didn't even want me to come. He says it's not safe."

I scoff. "Their grandparents are getting married. Again."

"Yes, Emily. I know. That's what it said on the invitation."

"What invitation?" I glare at Mom.

"We didn't send you one because you're already here."

Mercifully, a server chooses that moment to arrive. She's beautiful, like an offensive proportion of Israeli women are. She addresses us in English, having heard us talking.

Maxi orders a couscous salad bowl and a glass of chardonnay. Mom orders the same. I roll my eyes at the both of them and order Tzfat cheese bourekas – making a point to do it in my much-improved Hebrew.

"You speak Hebrew now?"

"We both do," I remind her. "*Aval hitamanti.*"

"When would I have time to practise speaking Hebrew, and why would I?"

"Um, I don't know, maybe because you're actually Jewish," I remind her. "Although, I like your *shiksa* costume," I add, gesturing at her hair, sweater set and string of pearls. "Twenty-seven going on forty."

Mom takes a very drawn-out sip of wine like someone else might take a deep breath before speaking. "That's enough, Emily," she says. "What did you want to talk about?"

"Your wedding. Can I have a Xanax first?"

Maxi asks pointedly whether I have a prescription, and I tell her to go ahead and write me one if she wants, or otherwise it's none of her business. Mom tosses her purse at me, and I rifle through it. She's got a whole bottle in here, not just a few in a discreet pill case. Jackpot. I open the bottle with my hands under the table, so I can slip out several tablets at once and drop them into my purse, which is open on the floor between my feet. I take the opportunity to check my phone, but there's no update on Jess from Mike. "Thanks," I say, passing the purse back to Mom. "Where and when is the wedding?"

"The soonest Rabbi Gold could get here is Sunday," Maxi says. "So probably early next week."

Despite myself, I'm a little bit looking forward to seeing Rabbi Gold. I realise I haven't seen him in years – although his synagogue is only forty-five minutes from the city, without traffic, I haven't wanted to go back. I have preferred instead to imagine it is the same as it always was, with the same people there every Saturday at nine, and the same ones lingering until well after Kiddush. Instead, over the last couple of years, I would occasionally slip into the back rows of various Conservative synagogues one or two neighbourhoods away, trying to time it right to join the congregation right before the Torah service, and leave before lunch. Then I'd buy a bagel with tuna from some hole in the wall and eat it while walking home – a good fifty blocks, sometimes more, but I never took the subway. The subway is very un-Shabbat.

"Maxine has been very helpful with making arrangements," Mom says.

"I didn't know there were arrangements."

Maxi gives me a look that says it's so typical for me not to know about there being any arrangements. It gives me a strong flashback to the kinds of looks we used to exchange while Mom took sips of wine back when we were both teenagers, and Maxi was Maxi, not this Maxine creature I don't know. Her look should have said, 'Can you believe our parents?' but now it says, 'What's wrong with you?'

"Anyway, I have to get back to work soon. I was just wondering what the plans are. And I thought it would be nice to see you." I let the implication that it has not turned out to be nice to see either of them hang in the air, and at that moment, our food appears. Maxi eats her couscous and salad with flared nostrils, and for a second I see her fourteen-year-old self underneath all those layers of WASPy Bostonian disguise, and I almost laugh. She hates the couscous. It's probably the dill. We've both always detested it. But however Can-I-Speak-To-Your-Manager-White-Lady she looks now, she's still the Maxi I know, who would never risk hurting a chef's feelings by failing to eat a dish in a restaurant.

"Your father and I have decided to have a small ceremony at the Dead Sea," Mom says. "Rabbi Gold said it was very symbolic."

"What, of a salt content hostile to life?"

Maxi slams down her fork. "No, Emily, of it being the lowest point on dry land. There's nowhere to go but up."

I laugh. Nobody else does, but that's okay. And when Mom needs to pee after her second glass of wine and Maxi goes with her, I slip some more Xanax from Mom's purse, leave enough shekels to cover the whole meal and a generous tip on the table – finally, a use for my new salary – and head back to the hotel to speak with Thom about James.

FORTY-FOUR

"I'm sorry, did you not hear what I said?" At the edges of the benzodiazepine bubble I'm in, I can feel something frantic pressing in.

"I just don't know what you want me to do," says Thom.

"I would like you to get James fired," I explain, as if to a child, "for sexually harassing me."

"That's not up to me," Thom says.

"Well, Alisha and Helen aren't here, and I can't really talk to Sven about this, can I?"

"No."

"I'm telling you that I've been harassed by James Browning, and that he's making a hostile work environment. How am I supposed to work with him?"

"I'm sympathetic, I really am," Thom says. "I just don't have the authority to replace James. But we can talk to Alisha soon."

"What if I tell Liora, how about that?"

Thom blanches. "Don't do that. She'll have him bumped off."

I raise an eyebrow. Would it be so terrible if the Shabak or Mossad or someone just got rid of James? Would it be so terrible if all the Jameses of the world just went away?

But Thom is reading my mind. "You'll just have to deal with it," he says. "For a little while, until Alisha gets back."

"That's not fair," I say.

Thom shrugs.

At my desk, I roll the BlackBerry around in my hands and think about who I could call. Or maybe I should let this whole thing go. But how can I? Won't I be betraying all women if I let James go unpunished?

Would I be betraying all of Israel and Palestine by getting side-tracked?

I nervously eat my way through another minibar bag of Bissli. These ones are onion-flavoured, and I hate them.

But then, I have an idea. Maybe I can get revenge on James. He wronged me, both by lying and then by kissing me against my will. But revenge doesn't have to be specific for it to work – that's the beauty of it. They say living well is the best revenge. Well, in this case, the best revenge is getting the best deal for my client, isn't it? I open my notebook and flip to the notes I made for the bird-nesting proposal to Liora, and turn on my computer.

The way I've framed this has been designed to appeal to Liora, so they will need to be edited a little bit. As I type, I edit each line to say the opposite thing. "Good for Israel because…" becomes "Good for Palestine because…" and anything minimising how much is to be lost is instead maximising how much Palestine stands to gain. It gets dark around me in the room again, but I keep working by the light of the laptop screen. I finish as Mike comes back from work.

"I'll be ready to go in a few minutes," I tell him when he pops his head out the door. "I just have to go downstairs to the business centre to print something out."

"No rush," Mike says. "There's something playing in English every hour on the hour, so we can wing it."

"Great," I say, and I give him a genuine smile. "I'll be right back."

Yossi agrees to see to it that my letter to Mahmoud is hand-messengered to him. I slip one of the King Solomon's cards, on which I scribble my BlackBerry's number, into the envelope before I seal it and hand it to him. I feel a little hesitant, because Yossi doesn't seem like the most trustworthy person I've ever met, and he's prone to gossip. But he tells me sternly that he is a professional, and what do I think, that he will read my letters? He doesn't care what's in my letters.

"Of course you don't. You don't care about what happens between me and my boyfriend, either."

"I do not," Yossi confirms.

"Have you seen Anderson?"

"*Mi zeh*, Anderson?"

"Suit. Earpiece. Bald."

"I don't know," Yossi says, sounding bored with me already.

"Fine." I march back to the elevators.

I keep compulsively checking my BlackBerry screen. Mike seems to notice, but doesn't say anything about it, over takeout in the dining room. "Did you speak with

Thom?" he asks instead.

"I did."

"How'd it go?"

"It was very frustrating. He doesn't seem to think there's anything he can do."

Mike looks shocked. I'm shocked that he's shocked, but then, I remember how often over the years it had turned out that even good, liberal men I was friendly with had never thought about what it might be like to be a woman in any real detail. There was Jon, a co-worker of Jess's who was shocked when Jess casually mentioned how she would hold her keys in her fist while walking through dark alleys. There was Alex, my friend from Religious Studies 110: Hebrew Bible, who was blown away when our classmate told a story about an internship advisor propositioning her, then giving her low scores in the report to the university for her grade. And now Mike, just assuming that injustices like sexual harassment by a fellow member of an elite government legal team would be swiftly dealt with.

"It's okay," I tell Mike, patting his hand, which has stopped delivering food to his mouth. "I'm handling it."

"But you shouldn't have to," he says.

"But I do," I say. "So I am."

"How?"

"A taste of his own medicine."

Mike looks confused and concerned.

"No, I mean, he lied to me about presenting a deal to his client. So I'm doing it myself. Cutting out the middleman."

"Is that allowed?"

"Absolutely not," I say.

"Well," Mike says, resuming eating his salad. "Neither is sexual harassment."

I check my phone again discreetly. Nothing from Mahmoud yet, but there will be. I know it.

The reply from Mahmoud does not come in the form of a text message. Instead, it comes in the form of two bearded bodyguards who are waiting for me inside my room when we get back upstairs. Yossi is there, too – he has his hands on his hips and an exasperated expression on his face.

"What's up?" I ask him.

"I told them to wait outside. They would not," Yossi says.

"Who are you?" I glance at my desk, with my work laptop and some papers on it – but I had put away all my papers and shut down the laptop before I left. An old habit from having sisters, then roommates.

"They work for Mr Barghouti," Yossi answers for them. "They have touched nothing. I made sure."

"Oh, good," I say, and turn to Mike. "I'll see you tomorrow?"

Mike hesitates a little but squeezes my hand and makes a point of going to his room through the partition door, rather than going back out to the hallway.

"Yossi, would you please let Thom know that I've gone to meet with Mr Barghouti?"

Yossi hesitates, too, which surprises me. I wouldn't have thought he cared about me either way. I wonder if he has his own orders from Thom, or someone more important. But he shrugs, and leaves.

I turn to the two men, who have stood silently in front of the chest of drawers since I got back. "Okay, we go," one says, now that it's just us.

"Go where?"

"Ramallah," says the taller of the two.

"Oh, I'm not supposed…" I trail off.

The shorter man raises an eyebrow and pauses with his hand on the door handle.

What is it I'm afraid of? Upsetting Thom, who has pretty much abandoned me since we got here to do everything on my own? Upsetting Alisha, or Helen, who have been even less available? Or, if I'm honest, am I a little afraid of Ramallah – the West Bank, a place I only ever hear about on the news, and only then when something violent happens? Have I internalised some of that fear and mistrust of Palestinians that seeped through back in Hebrew school, when we learned about modern Israel?

Well, none of those is a good enough reason not see this thing through as best I can. I shake my head and tell them it's nothing – and follow them out the door.

FORTY-FIVE

The Mukataa, or headquarters, of the Palestinian National Authority in Ramallah looks just about like any other building in the region – made of pale, yellowish stone with some anachronistic glass, and walls in front of it. It's late when we arrive – it took about an hour to drive here. I looked out for the infamous Qalandia Crossing, but either I missed it or there's another, better way for important people to get between Jerusalem and Ramallah.

Neither of the guards talks much on the drive, and I wonder if it's because they maybe don't speak much English or Hebrew. But when we pull into the complex of ordinary, pale buildings with square windows, the shorter one gets out and opens my door for me, and says, "We will take you to President Barghouti," it is in barely accented English.

Inside, it looks like any other nation's governmental buildings. There are shiny, tiled floors, gold-framed photographs and some wood panelling. I look around with interest, but make sure to keep up with my escorts, who admittedly don't seem too concerned about me accidentally learning some Palestinian state secrets and bringing them back to Liora. When we stop outside a plain door, the shorter bodyguard waves a key card in front of it and holds it open for me but doesn't step inside. I take a deep breath and go through the door.

Up close, Mahmoud Barghouti looks kind of like any of the Sephardic grandfathers at my old synagogue. He's dressed casually, which surprises me, because in every photograph of him – and the time we met – he's been wearing a pinstriped suit and sometimes a keffiyeh, either around his neck like a scarf or on his head. But now, maybe because of the hour, he's wearing khaki pants and a short-sleeved polo shirt.

Barghouti holds up a piece of paper I recognise as my note to him in his right hand by way of greeting. He waves it at a chair at a small wooden table in the middle of the room, so I sit down obediently.

"*As-salamu 'alaykum*," I say.

"*Wa 'alaykumu s-salam*," he says. "This is a very unusual position I am in. Very unusual."

"I know, and I'm sorry, but—"

"Yes, yes," he says. "It is not your doing."

"Well – yes," I agree, startled. "Nor my client's. She doesn't know I'm here."

Barghouti sits down opposite me, heavily. I notice that he's in his socks, too, like he kicked his shoes off behind his desk and grew accustomed to the comfort. He puts the note down and taps it. "Thank you for telling me this," he says.

"I just thought – I don't know. I know it isn't appropriate.

But I think James – Mr Browning – may have gotten in the way of something good. I know I shouldn't be telling you this, but my client is open to compromise, here. I just think that if we could only give this a real shot, the rest would fall into place. Cutting the baby in half, so to speak. You know, like King—"

"King Solomon, the wise," Barghouti said.

"Exactly," I say, trying to mask my surprise.

"I know who King Solomon is," he mutters.

"Course you do," I say.

Barghouti stands back up, slowly, and it strikes me again that he's an old man. There's nothing scary about him at all, like this. He pads over to his desk and picks up the rest of the proposal I'd rewritten into his point-of-view, and shuffles them.

"It would need some fine-tuning, of course," I say anxiously, unable to read his expression.

He waves the pages at me. "You are interested in an answer in principle, yes?"

"Yes."

"In principle, I am open to this," he starts, and I open my mouth to speak, but he silences me with a look. "If," he adds, pausing for emphasis, "if it is really true that Prime Minister Reznik has agreed to consider sharing custody of Jerusalem with Palestine."

"She has!" I burst out, and then almost immediately wonder if I've oversold her commitment to the idea, but I don't have time to walk it back, because the door flies open at that moment, and in come the two guards – and this time, they're not alone.

James is between the two men, looking ruffled and angry. And that's before he sees me. When he does, his nostrils flare like an angry horse's, and he looks like he's about to snort and start pawing at the ground, too.

"Excuse me," he says loudly, "what is the meaning of this?"

Barghouti gestures at the table, and the two guards frog-march James over to it and push him down, hard, into a chair. I almost get concerned at the rough treatment, but decide he deserves it, and cross my arms.

"Emily, get out," James says. "Clearly I need to speak with my client."

I open my mouth at the same moment as Barghouti slams his fist on the table, crumpling my notes. "You do not give the orders here," Barghouti says, voicing my exact thoughts.

James looks furious but says nothing in response. The two men are still standing on either side of him, and he seems to realise he's miscalculated. But he's still somehow got some bravado left in him, and he looks at me and says, "What have you done?"

"*Me?*" I say.

"She has done what you should have done," Barghouti says. "She has presented an offer to me that I needed to consider. And I have considered it."

"Emily," James repeats. "What *have* you done?"

I square up my shoulders and unfold my arms, resting my elbows nonchalantly on the armrests. "It's like your client says," I tell him. "I was just doing your job, as well as mine."

"Mahmoud," James starts, addressing him for the first time. "Mr President," he amends, seeing Barghouti's expression. "You told me that I should use whatever tactics I saw fit. And this is what I saw fit. I was going to bring this idea to you, but not yet. It was a strategic move. I could have got you—" He cuts himself off, as if sure that mentioning nuclear weapons is not the best idea right now.

"Enough," Barghouti says. "You are dismissed. Take him away."

The two men force James back to his feet.

"Wait," I say. "Where are you taking him?"

"Back to the hotel," Barghouti says, looking at me with furrowed brows.

"Oh, okay," I say. "Carry on, then."

James is awash with rage as he's marched off, and this manifests in making the tip of his pale, aquiline nose very red. I pull out my BlackBerry and snap a photo. Barghouti looks exasperated but says nothing. I put it back in my pocket – I can send it to Mike later.

"So, now what?" I ask.

"We will meet with your client," Barghouti says.

"Okay. But – don't you want counsel?"

"Do I need it?"

"I don't know," I say truthfully. "I think we're on the same page here. But maybe Ali— maybe the Deputy Assistant Secretary will feel otherwise."

"Do we need your government?" Barghouti asks.

I think about this, too. "Don't we?" I ask, unsure.

Barghouti turns his palms up in that gesture of not knowing.

"I guess we can just – play it by ear?"

Barghouti nods. "Arrange a meeting with Reznik," he says. "As soon as possible."

"Okay," I agree. "That makes sense. At the hotel, as usual? With Møkkalasset?"

"Fine," Barghouti says. "It is late. I will send you home."

"Fine," I agree. Then, I smile, and reach out a hand. He shakes it. "President Barghouti," I say. "This is good. This is really good."

FORTY-SIX

The ride home is as quiet as the way there, and I can't see much in the darkness, anyway. So I let myself doze off a bit. The men who drive me back are the same ones who brought me, so I relax into the usual highway sounds.

When I get in, I find Mike asleep in the chair at my desk, which means he was trying to stay up. But Mike has always been the early to bed, early to rise type, and I'm not surprised he didn't manage it. I rouse him enough to make him lie down, and we both fall asleep instantly.

"So, what happened?" Mike asks, the moment my alarm goes off in the morning.

I lurch into a sitting position. "Everything!" I tell him. "It's all happening. Barghouti fired James, and he likes the proposal, and I have to set up a meeting right away!" I start to dial Thom's number and then backspace and type in Liora's instead. No more middlemen.

"James got fired?" Mike asks, pleased.

I hold up a finger to shush him when Liora picks up the phone. "Shalom, Liora? It's Emily. I know it's Shabbat.

But we need to meet right away, this morning. Barghouti is ready to work with us. And it's all because of the birdnesting."

"Ten o'clock," Liora says.

"Great!" I hang up. Mike is looking at me expectantly, but it's time to get moving. "I'll talk to you more about it later," I assure him. "But it's on, it's all back on. Oh my God, Mike, I think this really might be it. I think we've got a Jerusalem deal. And if we can solve this…"

"…The rest falls into place," Mike finishes for me. "I agree. It's always been the biggest hurdle. Land can be traded to accommodate settlements. Deals can be struck with water and power supply. But there is only ever going to be one Jerusalem."

"Exactly," I tell him, throwing clothes around, looking for something to put on. "Anyway, I need to get dressed, and I need to get a conference room – oh, and I need to let Barghouti know to be here at ten. But I don't have his number. Could you go down and get Yossi to deliver the message for me?"

"Sure," Mike says, grabbing my shoulders for a second to stop my rushing around. "Listen, Jess says not to worry, by the way. They're rebooking her, and they said they'll upgrade her to business class as an apology. It won't be long now. What can I bring you for breakfast?"

"Good. Text me, even if I'm in my meeting. And I'm not hungry," I tell him.

"You need something."

"Coffee?"

"Coffee and something," Mike amends.

"Fine. A croissant, please."

"I'll be right back," he says, and he kisses me and then releases me back into my flurry of preparations.

I promised Mike that I would eat the croissant once he assured me that Barghouti had received the message, and he said Yossi had sent it and would get me the reply when it came. I looked at the clock – it was already eight forty-five. "You have to go teach your Skype class, don't you?" I ask Mike.

He looks like he is thinking about telling me he doesn't. "I could stay," he says.

"Go, go! I'll call," I promise.

"And you'll eat the croissant?" He looks at the untouched pastry on my desk.

"Yes, yes, I said I would," I tell him, but I have no desire to eat. Coffee, on the other hand, is going down great, and I'm buzzing. "Go to work!"

Mike leaves so slowly I can feel him giving me a chance to change my mind, but I can't have him in the room with me, anyway – and I'm not nervous. I'm excited. It looks similar on me, but it's a completely different feeling as far as I'm concerned. I take out one of my purloined Xanax in the bathroom and consider it, but toss it down the sink drain instead. There's a role for medicine in my life, but this isn't it. I don't need to be insulated from today.

The phone rings – the landline in my room – and I launch myself over the bed to answer it, somehow keeping my coffee cup level enough not to spill what's left all over me. Yossi tells me that he has confirmation for me, and that he went ahead and booked all the conference rooms so that nobody else would be up there all morning. He sounds as excited as I am.

"Thank you," I tell him, and decide not to remind him that he has no other guests. "By the way, have you seen Thom?"

"No," Yossi says, and I can almost hear his raised eyebrow.

"Where is he all the time, when you need him?" I ask rhetorically.

"*Aht tzricha mashehu?*" Yossi asks.

"No, I don't need anything. I think I have this under control. In fact, if you see Thom, just tell him I'm busy working but I think I've made a breakthrough and he should just leave me to it."

Yossi agrees and hangs up, and I finish getting dressed. I still don't feel like eating the croissant, but I take a giant bite of it before I toss it into the mini trashcan under my desk and gather up an armful of my notes. Who knows? If we can get them both to officially sign off on Jerusalem, what else could we figure out today?

But for now, there's time for another coffee, so I open the door with one hand before catching my armful of stuff and using my foot to kick it open wide enough to go through. I rush down to the lobby to the coffee machine, looking over at Yossi to smile a thank-you at him, but he's busy with a couple of girls with wheelie suitcases, so I start off again for the breakfast area. But Yossi looks over at the same moment, catches my eye and points at me – and the two girls with suitcases turn.

For a second, I'm not sure it's them. I haven't seen either one of them in almost a year. And Gabby tends to change her appearance often. But it's definitely Gabby, though the violet streaks in her hair are new. And God, that's Zara next to her, but she looks so much older. Nineteen – it's shocking. Zara is in head-to-toe athleisure, like most undergrads, but she still looks shockingly mature to me – like the difference between her at barely eighteen at her high school graduation, the last time I saw her, and her now was a decade, and not a little over a year.

Gabby and Zara roll their suitcases towards me, and I look around for an empty chair to dump my things in so my hands are free.

"Hi," Gabby says, running a hand through her hair so the deep blue shimmers in the sunlight before the top layer of her hair – still mahogany brown – falls over it like a closing curtain. Zara lifts a hand in a little wave, which I ignore to hug her.

"How's Portland?" I ask.

"Weird." Zara grins.

"Good weird?" I check.

"Yeah," she says.

"Zara had a connection in Chicago, so I moved my flight so we could come together," Gabby says.

"Right, how's Chicago? How's the gallery?"

Gabby shrugs. "They're putting one of my pieces in the exhibition next month. It's just a short one, but it's kind of cool."

"That's amazing," I say, and I hug her too. Gabby smiles a little. "Did you tell Mom and Dad?"

Gabby gives me A Look.

"Right, well – are you staying here?"

"Mom and Dad told us you were staying here, so they got us a room," Gabby says. "I think Maxi is staying somewhere else, though."

I'm surprised they were allowed to book rooms, but maybe Yossi just assumed there was a family exception to Alisha and Helen's rules. Or my assumption that they booked up the whole hotel was wrong, and it's just that nobody else wants to stay here. Either way, I'm glad they're here. "Yeah," I say, rolling my eyes a little. "Orson booked Maxi into the Waldorf. It's not too far, though."

Zara yawns.

"Oh, you guys must be tired – and anyway, I don't know what Maxi or Mom told you, but I'm actually here working—"

"They said!" Gabby interrupts.

"Well, I can't say too much about it, but I've got a very important meeting soon, and I don't know how long it will be. But maybe we can have a drink or dinner later?"

"Can I drink here?" Zara asks.

"Yes," Gabby says. "But don't we have the rehearsal dinner tonight?"

"Mom didn't tell me anything about a rehearsal dinner. Wasn't their first wedding enough of a rehearsal for them?"

Zara grins. "All the more reason to have drinks first."

"I'll come to your rooms when I'm done – will you be around or are you exploring?"

"I've more or less seen it, on Birthright," Gabby says.

"I might go out. But I'll be back by, what, five?" Zara asks.

"Sounds good," I tell them, and gather all my stuff up in my arms again, shifting it all as my laptop starts to slide off the slippery binder. "Room number?"

"Two-ten," Gabby says.

"It's so good to see you," I tell them both, surprised by how much I mean it. "At least there's one good thing to come out of this wedding."

The floor is quiet. I can hear an obnoxiously loud clock ticking somewhere in one of the rooms, but the only clock in the room I chose – the one farthest away from overlooking the lobby – only has a digital display on the TV screensaver. Liora and Barghouti don't use the front entrance to the hotel anyway, as far as I can figure out, but I thought the most privacy I could manage would be helpful. We are so close to a breakthrough – the breakthrough – and we don't want any interruptions.

Liora is the first to arrive. She is wearing beige – again – but today she's wearing Tevas and a shift dress. "I have not agreed yet," she tells me before she has even sat down and opened her Bamba.

"I know," I tell her. "But you will."

"Maybe," she says stubbornly.

"You haven't thought of a good reason not to, have you?" I'm not really asking. "Because if you had, I would have heard about it, and you wouldn't even be here."

Liora narrows her eyes at me and opens the bag of peanut puffs. We sit in tense near-silence – except for the crunching sound – and wait. With one moment to spare, the door swings open and the two men from last night follow Mahmoud Barghouti inside. He is wearing a suit again, but his shirt is unbuttoned at the collar, and his keffiyeh is draped around his shoulders. It's like Casual Friday for peace talks in here.

Mahmoud's bodyguards go back outside, though I can see their shadows through the frosted glass, so I know they don't go far. To stop anyone else from bursting in dramatically, I slide my chair back and turn the lock on the door. Mahmoud takes a seat opposite Liora and then seems to realise he's forgotten something, and stands up, leans across the table and reaches out a hand. Liora looks startled and offers him the bag of Bamba reflexively, but he shakes his head a little, and she understands. Cautiously, as if reaching out to pet a lion, she reaches out her own hand and grasps his. They hold on for a moment and let each other go.

I clear my throat. "Well, you both know why we're here—" I begin, but then there's noise in the hallway.

"They're in here," I can hear a familiar voice saying, getting closer. We all freeze and watch the door. It rattles, but the latch holds. Liora and Mahmoud look at me, and I go to the door then hesitate. Anderson bangs on the door. "Open up!" he orders.

"No!" I yell.

"Then back up!" Anderson shouts, and I leap backward as he smashes the little window, reaches an arm through and unlatches the door. He pushes through, followed by Alisha and Helen.

Thom is miles behind.

"Just what the hell," Helen says, her voice even more clipped than usual, "is going on here?"

FORTY-SEVEN

"All of this," Alisha adds, waving her hand in a circle that encompasses me, Liora, Mahmoud and the Bamba snacks on the table, "stops right now."

Thom, having apparently run behind the others, is having trouble catching his breath.

"Do you need a paper bag or something?" Helen says, forcing the words through her teeth.

Thom shakes his head 'no' frantically, and doubles over to place his hands on his upper thighs, breathing hard. "Let me," he pants, "explain."

"Explain?" Alisha asks. "I paid you to be my eyes and ears. Do you even know what's going on here? You said you could handle her."

"Hey!" I interject.

Liora stands up and crosses her arms, after doing some light peanut dust removal. "We are in the middle of something," she says.

Mahmoud stands up, too, and nods once. "She is right," he says. "We are getting somewhere."

Alisha, Helen and Thom's heads all swivel around like owls, and they fix a stare on Mahmoud. But we all heard it – he said Liora was right. Liora definitely heard it, because one corner of her mouth is smirking a little bit, but her eyebrows don't move at all. Nobody else knows quite how to react, and in the moment of frozen time during which we are all thinking about whether to acknowledge what he said aloud, Møkkalasset comes rushing in, carrying Prince Charles, whose tongue is lolling out of his mouth sideways even though Sven was doing the running for the both of them.

"*Ja*, what's goin' on?" he demands. This doesn't come out sounding Scandinavian at all. It comes out sounding Staten-Islandy.

"Sven," I start, but I really don't know what to say that won't sound crazy. I reach out to take Prince Charles from him, but he twists his spaniel-laden torso away from me.

"No," he says, his accent a little more indeterminate again. "No dog for you. Why is there a meeting without the mediator – that's me – present?"

Thom has caught his breath, and I look at him for help, but he just sweats and glowers. Clearly, he feels he, too, has been left out of the loop. Well, what did he expect? I can feel an angry heat rise into my cheeks the more he glares at me. He promised help. I'm here as a favour to him – it was his mistake that turned my nice, normal life upside down. I'm here being glared at by Helen Mirren, the US Secretary of State, the Palestinian Authority President, the Israeli Prime Minister, Anderson, someone who is calling himself Sven Møkkalasset, whom I'm not at all sure is Norwegian, and a spaniel – all because of Thom's mistake. And he has the nerve to be upset? Why, because when he abandoned me, I turned out not to need him at all? "If you'll all excuse us," I say, "we were in the middle of something."

"Well, whatever this is, it's over," Alisha says. "Project Kramer is cancelled." Liora makes an indignant sound at that, and Alisha shoots her a shrivelling glare. "Don't worry," she says facetiously. "This won't affect our deal."

"Your deal?" Mahmoud says, and my stomach drops to my feet.

Helen glances at Alisha as if to confirm something, then says, "Nor your deal, Mr Barghouti."

"Your deal?" Liora mocks his earlier question.

"Okay," I say, trying to get control back. I stick my arm out and steal a pat of Prince Charles's head before Sven glares at me and moves out of my reach. "Stop. You don't know what you've just walked into. We are about to reach a deal over the custody of Jerusalem. Please, please get out of here and let us finish. If we can get this one huge thing ironed out, the rest will follow, and you'll both get to claim credit for the most significant peace deal in a millennium."

"Dreadfully sorry," Helen says, sounding anything but sorry, "but I'm afraid you've gone rather off-piste. The United Kingdom does not—"

Alisha clears her throat.

"The United States and the United Kingdom," Helen amends, "do not support this ridiculous bird-nesting idea."

"How did you—" I start, but then, the door opens one more time, and this time James walks through.

"Mummy," says James curtly, looking only at me.

"James," Helen answers coldly, also looking at me.

My jaw drops. I wish that my fit of false confidence earlier hadn't caused me to throw away my Xanax. I could use it right about now. I do a quick mental replay of my interactions with James and try to see them through this new lens, of knowing that Helen Mirren is his mother. But I can't tell if it makes any sense or not. "What are you doing?" I manage to get out.

"Well, when you told me about this absurd and dangerous idea, I simply had to let the higher-ups know," James says, folding his arms across his chest and leaning against the door frame.

"No. No," I say. "This was your idea. You presented it to me. You told me your client was already on board."

"You told me that this was your idea," Liora says angrily.

"No, it was his," Mahmoud says definitively. "She told me, in her note."

"You sent him a note?" Sven asks, aghast.

"It wasn't like that," I say, starting to feel desperate now. It's not like they say, panic attacks – the walls don't look like they're closing in, but my throat is as dry as the Negev to our south, and I can see little spots in my vision. "He—"

"It's as I said," James interrupts, directing this at Helen. "She's completely unstable."

"Wait—" Liora frowns.

Alisha cuts her off. "Enough," she says, in her booming Secretary of State voice. Thom jumps a little bit at the sound of it. "I'd fire you, but like I just said, this project has gone completely off the rails. And it is cancelled, right now.

Thom will book your flights back to the States tomorrow morning."

Shocked, all I'm able to say is, "But my parents are getting married tomorrow."

Alisha's expression makes it very clear that she does not care at all about anyone getting married, ever, least of all my parents. But she says I can fly out Monday, then. "Have an extra night, on us," she says, "for your hard work." She pats my arm as she says it, and I can't tell if she's being sarcastic or not.

Everyone files out of the room in the order in which they arrived, and though James gives me a challenging look, I don't say anything. When it's just me, Liora and Mahmoud standing around the conference table, I fall into a chair. Both of them come to my side.

"I'm so sorry," I tell them, and my voice breaks a little, and I am terrified that I'm about to cry. Liora pats my back like she's only ever seen other people comfort each other and never done it herself.

"Why are you sorry? Browning should be sorry," Mahmoud says. "I never liked him."

Liora nods. "I knew he was dishonest."

"But I ruined it," I say. "They cancelled the project."

"So?" says Liora.

"But what about the deal Alisha mentioned?" I ask her. "Or yours?"

Mahmoud makes a dismissive gesture. "I don't need their deal," he says.

Liora hesitates. Mahmoud looks at her searchingly. "*B'seder*," she says. "Israel also does not need their deal. We will do this together, no United States or United Kingdom."

I look at them both, and – seeing a real openness of spirit and goodwill that I know to be rare and fleeting – blurt out, "Do you want to come to a wedding?"

FORTY-EIGHT

I'm worn out from the hope-disappointment-hope rollercoaster of this morning. This whole trip has been like being on a rollercoaster, like one of the really loopy ones at Six Flags – first, the slow ascent of the journey to my 'job interview', then the plummeting down of finding out I was trapped in an alternate reality and being ushered onto a plane to Jerusalem, then up again, seeing Mike after so many months, then a backwards loop of James kissing me… and on, and on, and on.

I want to get off.

I'm so exhausted that I don't even yell at Thom when I find him waiting outside my room. I ignore him and open the door, and when he follows me inside, I continue to ignore him.

"Emily," he says, "look, I'm sorry, but what were you thinking? Bird-nesting? Communicating directly with Mahmoud? Going to the West Bank? You weren't supposed to do any of that."

I continue to ignore him, but I start to peel off my

clothes. I've sweated through them and I want to get in the shower right now. I can't think about anything right now except how much I want to be standing under some scalding water, hearing nothing except the sound of the droplets bouncing off my skin.

"Um," he says, growing alarmed at how little clothing I have left to remove. "I just wanted to know when you want to go home."

Home? That apartment in Harlem? I shake my head without saying anything. I can't go there. That doesn't even feel like a real place right now. I can't visualise it in any detail. I really can't think about anything beyond the wedding tomorrow. And Farooq, and Jess – I can't even really think about them, or whoever else I'm in danger of letting down. "I don't care," I tell Thom. "Monday. Whatever."

"JFK, LaGuardia or Newark?"

"I don't care. But not JFK."

"Morning, afternoon, or evening—"

"Thom? Get the fuck out," and maybe it's because I'm now reaching behind my back to unclasp my bra, but he does.

Yossi delivers two notes to me while I'm in the shower that I find tucked under a cappuccino. It's nice of him. I sit on my bed, with towels wrapped around my body and my head, to read them. They are from Liora and Mahmoud, of course, telling me where their car will pick me up.

I'm to tell Anderson or Wilcox, whomever is assigned to drive me to the wedding tomorrow, that it's being held at the Waldorf. I'll go inside, wait until they drive away, then come back out the lobby entrance to meet them.

We'll drive together to the Dead Sea, which will give us a small chunk of time to talk. Then hopefully the wedding will be brief and painless, and we can stay there while my parents and sisters do whatever it is they're going to do. If they insist on a dinner, I will sit at a table with Liora and Mahmoud and we can carry on working. Mom and Dad will never notice, and Maxi would die before she asked me what I was doing. Gabby and Zara would be having a good time, Gabby because she seems to be able to separate herself from the things that happen around her, and Zara because sanctioned public drinking is still novel for her.

Mike, of course, will help me. I'll tell him what the plan is at the rehearsal dinner tonight, but I know he'll trust my judgement on this. I'm so glad to have Mike – he's annoying sometimes, with his therapy-pushing and his always making me eat meals, but he means well and he shows up – even if sometimes I have to send in the US government to make him.

I shred Liora and Mahmoud's notes and toss them into the bottom of the trash can in the bathroom. Then, I look at myself in the foggy mirror – the towel turban on my head makes my face look a little round, or it's just gotten a bit round. I'm fairly tan, but there are even darker shadows under my eyes. My eyebrows need work. I think about the armour I'm planning to wear to dinner tonight and decide I could use some flourishes to go along with the pointy shoes. "Yossi?" I say into the phone on my bedside table. "Do you know where I could get, like... a haircut, or whatever?"

Thrilled, Yossi directs me to his brother's salon. I am

unsurprised to find a bossy, inebriated, older version of Yossi inside, and I surrender to the process. I only draw the line at letting him tattoo my face, which is a realistic way to describe the 'semi-permanent makeup' he wants to do to me, which would include tattooing lip-liner onto my mouth. "*Lo, va'lo,*" I tell him firmly. "Definitely not." Then, he puts cucumbers over my eyes somewhat forcefully, I think to keep my eyes shut while he does some more stuff to my hair. I'm not allowed to direct my own haircut in Yonah's salon. When he takes them off, he makes me bend over and hang my head upside down while he blow-dries it vigorously between taking breaks to lie down on the sofa by the window.

When I'm allowed to see, I'm not exactly Gal Gadot – but I've lost many years' worth of hair and some of the tiredness from my skin, and my shoulders feel a little straighter.

In the car to the dinner, Mike asks me if I like my new haircut before he volunteers his own opinion. "You look very sophisticated," he says, which is positive. His opinion of my plan is less positive, but he says he's on board. I run my fingers through my silky-straight, short hair a few times. Whatever Yonah had done to it had smelled foul and made my eyes water, but now it was like touching the velvety muzzle of a horse – a kind of softness that was so profound it could barely be perceived by your fingertips.

"I know it's silly," I tell him, still touching my hair, "but I feel like an entirely different person. People with this hair can laugh off rehearsal dinners for parents who were married for seventeen years and then divorced for ten."

"I don't think it's silly," Mike says, then he catches my

wrist and slips a bracelet around it. I didn't even see where it came from. It's a thick silver cuff, with a hammered surface. It reminds me of something I would have made at my mom's jewellery store – one of the bright spots in those last years before I left home. "Thank you."

"It's engraved," he says, so I slip it off and look on the inside.

גם זה יעבור

"This, too, shall pass," Mike says. "Like—"

"Like King Solomon's magic ring," I finish for him. "My favourite story. He wanted to teach his advisor Benaiah an object lesson in humility, so he sent him off on what he thought was a wild goose chase – to find a ring that can make a happy man sad, and a sad man happy. Only Benaiah did find such a ring, which was engraved with *gimmel, zayin, yud* as an acronym for this, too, shall pass. Solomon realised that his wealth and wisdom were all fleeting, and then he was the one who got humbled after all."

"And on top of all that, the ring commands djinn and lets him speak to animals," Mike added. "I thought about getting you a ring, but…" He trails off, and I start to feel bad, remembering that I ran away from him the last time he tried to give me one of those, but then he finishes: "But rings aren't practical around horses," he says. And it's true – rings are a good way to get blisters from holding the reins.

Mom and Dad are both very quiet at dinner, and if it's a rehearsal for something, I don't know what – unless it's for

Zara's future career as a stand-up comedian. She fills the silence between Mom and Dad, and me and Maxi, with funny stories about Portland and her friends and teachers. Gabby catches my eye and smiles knowingly, taking a demure sip from her champagne to signal to me that Zara is a little buzzed, but neither of us mind. Maxi is a different story, her champagne glass beside her barely touched, and her lips pressed together to resemble a cat's butt, or Dad. Mom's lips are tight, like the rest of her body, but she's at least turned up the corners a little to pretend to respond to Zara's entertainment.

"It sounds like you're loving it, Zara," I say, and down my own champagne glass in solidarity. Mike puts one arm around me and uses the other to top off mine, Gabby's and Zara's glasses.

"Oh, by the way," I say casually as Mike helps me get my jacket on to go home, "I've invited some VIP clients to the ceremony tomorrow. I hope you don't mind."

"What VIP clients?" Maxi snaps at me. "This is just supposed to be family. Mom and Dad said they wanted a small ceremony."

Dad's jaw muscles are jumping in his cheeks again and Mom looks nauseated.

"Just two people," I say. "You might recognise them, but please don't say anything."

Maxi rolls her eyes. "Okay, Emily," she says. "Sure, we won't say anything to your very important clients, if we recognise them."

It's fine with me if they don't believe me. I air-kiss in Maxi's general direction, and hug Gabby and Zara before giving my stone-faced parents a little wave. I can see Mom looking at my new bracelet as I do, but she still says nothing. I can't interpret her silence, and nor do I care to. I trot off with Mike, the right level of drunk and feeling pretty happy despite the various things I'll have to face tomorrow. Tomorrow is tomorrow, and it, too, shall pass.

FORTY-NINE

On the morning of the wedding, it occurs to me to wonder if there was a certain colour I'm supposed to be wearing or something like that. But I figure Maxi would have instructed me what to wear if that were the case, so I opt for my favourite red wrap dress – it's comfortable, I feel good in it and it's not going to be oppressive in the warm sunshine at the Dead Sea. Mike holds up two ties for my opinion, and I take them both, scrutinise them and throw them on the floor. Instead, I reach up and unbutton his top two buttons. "I wish Jess was here," I tell Mike.

"I know. But they misplaced her bags in France, and they said she couldn't travel without them for security reasons. I'm sure they'll find them and get her on her way soon," he says. "Ready?"

"Nope. Let's go."

It's Anderson I find in the lobby. He nods at us both. "Good morning," he says. "Thom says I'm taking you to the Waldorf?"

"Yes," I say, and Mike squeezes my hand.

"It's a shame the project was cancelled," Anderson says as he drives.

"Such a shame," I agree.

"But then again," Anderson says, "I guess nobody ever expected you to really be able to solve the Israeli-Palestinian problem."

"If anyone could do it, Emily could," Mike says.

"I just meant that it's probably never going to be resolved, by anyone," Anderson says, glancing at us in his rear-view mirror.

"We'll see," I say.

Anderson pulls up in front of the hotel and opens the door closest to the sidewalk for us. "You kids have a good time," he says.

"We won't," I assure him.

Mike and I go straight into the lobby, as planned. I turn to Mike as soon as we're through the doors to ask if he wants a coffee or anything before we settle in for the real drive, but before I can say anything to him, I hear someone calling my name. It's a familiar voice, but I can't quite place it. I turn around, looking for the source, and then I see him. Rabbi Gold, looking the same as the last time I saw him – when? Seven years ago, probably, at Zara's Bat Mitzvah. The last of the Price girls to become a Price woman. Rabbi Gold comes towards us, rather quickly, throwing his arms open wide for a hug as he walks. I can see a tell-tale glistening in his eyes, even from several paces away, and by the time he reaches my side, there are actual tears streaming down his cheeks. "Emily," he says, "how truly happy I am to see you!"

"I'm so happy to see you too," I say, and I'm taken aback

when my own eyes well up a little, but I will them not to come out, because I put on makeup today – a little concealer under my eyes like Yonah suggested, and I don't have the energy to do it again. I step back out of the hug, and Rabbi Gold keeps hold of my upper arms to look at me.

"Such a lovely young woman," he says.

"Not that young anymore," I say.

"So, you're getting older. It's better than the alternative."

"Very wise, as usual, Rabbi," I say. "Um, this is Mike."

Rabbi Gold greets Mike like he's a long-lost son, with some fresh tears.

"Do you want a tissue?" Mike asks him, when he's released. Rabbi Gold waves away the offer cheerfully and takes his blue silk kippah off his head, dabs at his eyes with it and puts it back on. A man like him should really carry around a handkerchief. I make a mental note to get him one, maybe in the same shade of blue silk, which matches his eyes. A belated thank-you gift, not for anything specific, but for everything.

"How are you?" Rabbi Gold asks me, when Mike goes off to get him a tissue anyway.

"I'm very well," I tell him, and break into a smile.

"And are you and Mike..." He raises his eyebrows at me.

"Rabbi, you know you're the Price family go-to if any of us needs an officiant," I tell him. "You'll be the first to know."

"I would like to get to know this Mike," he says, as Mike returns with some tissues. "Perhaps I could ride to the ceremony with you?"

I feel a surge of panic at the suggestion, and it must have flashed across my face because as he hands Rabbi Gold four tissues, Mike asks me if everything is okay. "Um, Rabbi Gold was asking if he could ride with us," I say, making a Help Me face at Mike while the rabbi dabs at his cheeks.

"Oh—" Mike starts.

"Not to worry, Mike," Rabbi Gold says, winking. "I have no ulterior motives. Remember, Jews don't proselytise."

"Of course, I'm not worried about that, I just... Emily, is there, uh, room in the car?"

"I haven't gotten that fat, have I?" Rabbi Gold jokes, patting his stomach.

There's nothing for it. I can't tell him he can't come with us. We're going to have to take him. He may not appear to have aged at all, possibly miraculously, but he has – his face is more lined than when I last saw him. I'm worried that Rabbi Gold will open the town car's door, see Mahmoud Barghouti and Liora Reznik sitting inside it, and have a heart attack.

"Rabbi, of course there's always room for you," I tell him, while Mike looks on in horror. "But I think I have to warn you of something."

This is the quietest car I've ever sat in. Rabbi Gold is staring at Liora and Mahmoud, who are staring back at him, and nobody is saying a word. Rabbi Gold has not even put on his seatbelt yet; his hand is frozen over his shoulder, grasping on the buckle like it's a buoy and he's adrift in the middle of the Sea of Galilee.

"That's," Rabbi Gold says, "she's—"

"They're my clients," I say, in a strained voice.

Mahmoud knocks on the glass between him and the driver, and a small window opens. "Some water, for the rabbi," he says, and a water bottle is passed through it. He hands it to Rabbi Gold, who takes it and says, "Thank you," but seems too dazed to know what to do with it.

"Drink," Liora orders him in Hebrew.

He does.

"Actually," I say, "maybe you can help us, Rabbi."

"Of course," squeaks Rabbi Gold, and I start to explain. Then Mike pats him on the back when he's seized by a spluttering cough at my description of what we're trying to do.

By the time we've arrived, I think we've worked out a custody schedule, and Rabbi Gold may have gained two new devotees. Mahmoud winks at me and tells him that he's much like 'your King Solomon' several times, which makes him cry, and Liora has offered him several jobs. If either of our religions allowed idol worship, I think they'd both be commissioning statues right now. As we're pulling off the highway and heading to the beach, Liora and Mahmoud lean across their seats, and clasp hands. Rabbi Gold says a spontaneous prayer. *Barukh ata Adonai, Eloheinu melech ha'olam, shehecheyanu, v'kiyimanu, v'higiyanu la'z'man ha'zeh.* Blessed are You, Lord our God, king of the universe, who has given us life, sustained us, and enabled us to reach this moment. It's the blessing for new and unusual occasions, and there was never a time that called for it more than this one.

Maxi is standing near the entrance to the parking lot to direct us to where she's set up a few chairs and, somehow, a *chuppah* for the ceremony. Rabbi Gold's hug distracts her as the rest of us climb out of the car and blink in the sunlight, which is almost violent after an hour inside a car with tinted windows, so for a moment, she doesn't see. Liora and Mahmoud have both put on giant sunglasses, and Liora is wearing a wide-brimmed hat, which are Inspector Clouseau-level disguises – but then again, nobody is likely to be expecting to see them here. And while they hide in plain sight, most attention will be on the bride and groom – though neither of them is currently visible.

"Where are Mom and Dad?" I ask Maxi, who's still being hugged by Rabbi Gold.

"Changing," she says breathlessly, because there's not a lot of room for inhaling in his hugs.

"Let's do this," I say.

"I'll escort your clients to some seats," Mike says, and Maxi pulls away from Rabbi Gold and looks around at them, but only in time to see their backs, unremarkable in their suits, except for the fact that theirs are of the business variety, while most of the people around are in the bathing kind.

"You look nice," I say to Maxi, mostly to distract her, but it's true. She's wearing an old dress of hers that I've seen before, cerulean and flowy. "I always liked that dress on you."

"Yes, well, no sense in getting something new for this," she says drily, and that plus the dress make her seem more like herself than she has in years.

"No," I agree, and I smile at her.

"Are you ready?" Maxi's nostrils are slightly flared, just one small outward sign, but it's enough.

"Are you?" I ask. "It's okay not to be. Even if it won't change anything."

Gabby and Zara come out of the changing rooms, also wearing blue, and I open my mouth to ask why I didn't get the memo, but Gabby cuts me off. "It's a coincidence, Em," she says gently. "Your red dress is beautiful, too."

Mom and Dad don't look happy. Rabbi Gold does, though. He's in his element, and while I'm not sure the rest of us are, we're all managing in our own way. Maxi has arranged and rearranged all of us in our seats a few times, while Gabby complied silently and Zara and I kept catching each other's eyes, and trying not to laugh. Mike is sitting between me, Liora and Mahmoud, who have yet to be clocked by anyone around and seem mildly interested in the ceremony – though I guess they both have experience sitting through formal ceremonies that have little to do with them while maintaining the appearance of paying attention.

I haven't been to many weddings, and I'm thinking about tapping Maxi on the shoulder to ask her how much more ceremony she thinks there will be when I become aware of a rumbling sound that gets louder, and louder. A few strands of hair blow into my face and get stuck on the Chapstick on my lips, and I swipe at them, but it's futile, because the wind is really picking up. The *chuppah*'s fabric shakes and goes taut, like a sail, and threatens to topple. Liora's hat blows off. The wind is violent, and now along with it and the noise there's a dark shadow. Other people on the beach, though there aren't that many – this one is clearly private, as opposed to the public stretch I visited with Mike the last time – are standing up and looking at us.

I look up, and I see it – a big, black, military-looking helicopter is hovering over us, and descending noisily and very close to us. Rabbi Gold has one hand on his head to keep his kippah on, and the other clutching his *tallit* around his neck. Mom and Dad are shading their eyes with their hands, and watching the helicopter lower itself down. The rest of us jump out of our seats.

The propellers slow down but haven't stopped before a door is flung open and a man in a suit comes leaping out. It's Anderson – and on his heels are Alisha, Helen and eventually Thom. I can see them yelling at us but can't hear a word over the sound of the propellers. I squeeze through the tightly placed chairs and rush over to them.

"What are you doing here?" I shout, but my voice is lost in the wind.

Alisha soundlessly yells something at me, and Helen joins in, gesticulating, but I can't hear any of it. Thom is silent. We wait, arms crossed or on our hips, glaring at each other as the propellers gradually quiet down and come to a halt.

"Why are you here?" I repeat.

"You know why we're here," snaps Helen, and points at Liora and Mahmoud. "You kidnapped two world leaders!"

"I *did not*!" I insist. "They came with me willingly."

Alisha snaps her fingers and waves the two of them over. They look at each other and walk towards her like children who have been called to the principal's office.

"Anderson, secure that building over there," Helen orders. He jogs towards the small building with the changing facilities that Gabby and Zara had been in when we arrived. "All of you, let's go."

Mom and Dad now have their mouths open in confusion and surprise, but this is the state in which people like them are most susceptible to direct orders, so they come. Alisha and Helen stalk across the gravel parking lot very gracefully in their heels, me less so, and I don't turn around to look at anyone behind us to see how they're doing. Mike catches up to me and offers his arm for support, physical and emotional, which I take. When we get inside, Anderson is ushering the last person – an elderly man in a Speedo and a bathing cap – out of the building. It's empty now, a small lounge area with a few seats, a reception desk for the hotel that owns this stretch with nobody currently behind it, and a muted TV screen playing a news channel that looked like it might be the BBC World News. I glance at it and then away as everyone files into the little building and removes hats and sunglasses, blinking as their eyes adjust.

It is at this moment that Dad realises who all these people are. "Emily," he says angrily. "What are you doing?"

"That's a very good question," says Alisha, in her Deputy Assistant Secretary of State voice, drawing herself up to her full height to add to the effect. "Because we told you this project was cancelled."

"And you've broken your nondisclosure agreement," Helen adds, for good measure. "You created a spectacle of a top-secret plan – one that was terminated!"

"You're the one drawing attention to yourselves," I argue. "A big, black military helicopter? Near the border? You frightened people."

"Silence," Helen snaps.

Thom quivers.

Mom and Dad are not stupid people. I can see that the full weight of what is happening is beginning to dawn on them as they connect the dots between the presence of the black helicopter, the Palestinian Authority President and the Prime Minister of Israel, combined with what I said – and did not say – about an important case.

Meanwhile, Rabbi Gold steps forward to try to calm things down. Alisha holds up a hand and he stops in his tracks and doesn't say anything.

But Zara does. "Look," she says, pointing at the large TV behind the empty desk. Photos of Liora and Mahmoud are both displayed on the screen next to the anchor's face, while a large bold chyron says 'MISSING' above a ticker tape that says that both governments have accused each other of kidnapping after leaving for a top-secret meeting and becoming unreachable.

Mike moves to the TV to turn on the volume, and I turn to Liora and Mahmoud. "Didn't you tell your people not to worry?" I ask them.

They both reach into their pockets and pull out their phones. "No service," says Liora.

And I guess I realise what happened. Both sides were nervous to begin with. There was just the one guard, the guy who drove the car. Eventually, they try to check in. Maybe they call three of four times, send an email or two.

They're going straight to voicemail. They both assume the worst.

It's not good, or bad; it's just unfortunate.

Then, the volume starts to go up, as Mike reaches up to press the button on the side of the TV, and a female voice is audible. The image takes a moment to catch up. When it does, it's a pretty brunette woman, talking via satellite against the backdrop of an image of Manhattan from inside some studio. And then, the lower third graphic updates: 'EMILY PRICE: MIDEAST EXPERT'.

Everyone's heads turn to me.

"I can explain?" I say. They wait. "Actually, I can't," I tell them. "It's just that usually when I say that, someone tells me 'don't bother' or 'there's no need' or something."

Helen sighs. "You thought we didn't know?"

I'm shocked. "But Thom—"

Helen barks out a laugh. "Yes, Thom. He's frightfully bad at this job, isn't he? But he does have a gift for inadvertently being useful. Far easier for us to fool you than the real Emily Price."

Alisha puts a hand to the bridge of her nose. "Well, I guess I can finally fire the moron," she says. "Now that this is all over."

Thom's mouth moves like a fish, but it doesn't make any noise. Mike and I look at him, but Mom, Dad and the others don't even know who he is. He's turned pink and it looks like he might cry.

"It's not over," I say. "Listen, we reached an agreement about Jerusalem—"

"No," Helen says. "It is over."

"But I thought if I could get a deal—"

"We are no longer interested in there being a deal," Alisha says.

I'm so surprised by that that I recoil. "No. No, I don't believe it. Why? Why put us through this if you were just going to go back to the way things were?"

"We're not here to create peace in the Middle East," Alisha says. "We're here for the same reason as always."

"Oh," Mike says softly.

"What, 'oh'?" I ask him.

"Oil. This is the only land in the region without any oil. Until now."

"Bingo, Dr Patel," Helen says.

And I'm not stupid, either. "Farooq's farm," I say, and it isn't a question.

"Yes," says Alisha. "Farooq's fucking farm. An enormous oil deposit, right smack in the middle of the goddamned desert, halfway between Gaza and the West Bank, in the most contentious bit of territory in the world."

"That's where Thom kept disappearing to," I realise as I talk. "And Anderson – he was here to make sure I didn't make any more unauthorised site visits."

Thom lets out a low moan, as if he's having a particularly painful dental procedure.

"Thom left behind a sniffer, that idiot, and when we went back to get it, it was gone. We realised you'd found it, and then when you tried to get that environmentalist friend of yours over here, we had to intervene," Alisha says, still not appearing to care that Thom is in the room.

I understand now what I'd found – not a walkie-talkie,

but something used to find oil. It would have taken Jess just one minute to confirm what it was – were they behind all the trouble she had getting here?

This was all just a cover story – and everyone except me was in on the charade. "So James knew, too. And Møkkalasset?"

Zara snorts. "Unfortunate name," she says. "Means 'pile of shit' in Norwegian."

Everyone's heads swivel around to look at her, like a flock of hypnotised owls.

"What?" she says. "I made friends with some punks in the Portland music scene. They were really into Norse gods and shit. They had this calendar of funny names of places in Norway – that was one of them. It's a lighthouse. Turned out they were Nazis, so we're not friends anymore."

Everyone gapes at her – except me. "Him, too?" I ask Alisha.

"He did go to school in Norway, when his late father, the ambassador, was stationed there. Changed his name from Frank Viscido to Sven Møkkalasset and pretended to be Norwegian when he came back, and at first, he just used it to get girls. Since then, he's been joking to potential clients for years about how if you can trust Norwegians with Israel/Palestine, you can trust them with your divorce. My ex-husband heard him drop this line at the Blue Duck Tavern and emailed me about it." She laughs. "Ironically, he and I are on great terms."

I'd worried that Sven was an imposter – a threat – and all he'd been was just another private joke between Alisha and her conscience.

Something else hits me, though. "You never thought I could succeed," I say, feeling a profound sadness fill my chest and settle on my ribcage. "You didn't even want me to. You just wanted a cover story in case someone found out why you were here – nobody would be all that surprised by yet another peace process, and they wouldn't expect too much or pay too much attention. Liora and Mahmoud were just afraid of how much worse things could get. But you don't care if nothing here changes at all, so long as you get your oil."

And now Thom is actually crying, his face in his palms and rivulets of snot coming through his skinny, chewed-on fingers.

"What can we say?" Alisha says, with a nasty sort of smirk on her face. "If it ain't broke, don't fix it."

"But it is broken," Rabbi Gold says. "It's all broken."

Everyone looks at him.

"With all due respect, Rabbi," says Helen, sounding like she feels a lot of things about his contribution that don't include respect, "the status quo is better than potentially worse unknowns."

"You can't do this to us," Liora says, stepping forward.

"Not to us, either!" Mahmoud says.

"Or to me!" cries Thom from behind her.

"Oh, don't worry. You'll both be receiving some… let's call it 'compensatory aid'," Alisha says contemptuously to Liora and Mahmoud, ignoring Thom completely.

I am surprised only by my capacity to be surprised by a cynical turn of events. Everyone is silent in the aftermath of Alisha's statement, as the profundity of the confirmation that the upper levels of government are exactly as corrupt, cynical and broken as we'd all been saying all along sinks in.

Thom, though, seems to be feeling this on a whole other level – it's like he's Julius Caesar turning around to look Brutus in the face as the last of his blood drains. He's now crumpled on the floor clutching his beloved secure phone and badge to his heart, and breathing fast, shallow breaths. I almost feel bad for him, but I don't have time to worry about him right now – I have to figure out something fast, and it's clear he's not going to be any use.

Mom is the one who breaks the silence. "Well, thanks a lot, Emily," she says. "You've *ruined* my wedding."

Mike starts to move like he's going to intervene, and I appreciate it, but I don't need him to. "That's it," I say. "That's *it*. You will either learn to stop dumping on me or you will never see me again," I say to both Mom and Dad. "And *you*," I say to Alisha and Helen, "you don't call the shots anymore. We have a deal. We made it without you – no, despite you. And just because you're cynical and corrupt and *fucked up* doesn't mean you can undo that. Right?" I look at Liora and Mahmoud, but they don't meet my eyes. Dread starts clawing its way up my trachea, with cold, sticky frog hands. "Right?" I ask again, knowing it isn't. The winds have changed. The moment has passed. Now is not the time to expect either of them to stand up to Alisha, or Helen, or their own governments, representatives of whom are currently cursing each other on international television.

Maxi makes a sound, like a shriek. "Ugh!" she says,

and stamps her foot. It's the first time I've seen her do it in about fifteen years. "Can we *please* just finish this fucking wedding already, so I can go back to my life, where people are *normal!*" she screams.

"I second that," says Gabby. "I'm ready to go home."

"Let's get this show on the road," Zara says, and starts to follow everyone, including a meek Mom and Dad, as Maxi blazes an angry path out the door.

"Hold up," I say, catching Zara's elbow as she passes by. "Maybe we could catch up for real sometime soon?"

"I'd like that," she says. "But where will you be?"

I look around. Alisha and Helen are talking to Anderson in low voices, and Liora and Mahmoud are sitting, apart, with stony expressions as they wait to be dealt with. I am officially fired. "I don't know where I will be," I say. "But wherever I go – we go," I correct, looking at Mike, "there's Skype."

"I'd like that," Zara says, and hugs me. "You did a good thing, and I'm proud of you," she says into my shoulder.

I sniffle a little bit. I never expected to hear that from anyone – not anyone in my family, at least. And now that I have, I realise that I no longer need to. But it's still nice. "Love you," I tell her.

"I love your work, Ms Mirren," Zara calls out over her shoulder as she waves and trots off after the rest of our family.

I think hard about my options. I think it's safe to say that I'll have to give up on the idea of solving the Israeli-Palestinian conflict. But I think I can at least prevent things from getting any worse. Fucking oil? That's the last thing in this world that needs to be introduced right now. I'll need some help from Liora and Mahmoud, but I think they owe me. I motion to them, and we huddle in a corner.

"Listen, you both have a chance to redeem yourselves here, but you have to go along with what I say."

"I do not—" Liora starts, but Mahmoud puts a finger to his lips in a shushing gesture, and she quiets down. He motions for me to go ahead.

"Hey!" I shout, and Alisha, Helen and Anderson look up at me. "You, Anderson – you're with the oil company, right?"

"PetroCorp," he says.

"Seriously? The president's son-in-law's company?" Mike looks disgusted.

It is disgusting, but it won't matter. "Wow. The president and the British prime minister really are as bad as each other," I said. "Well, you're going to go back to them and tell them that you were wrong – there's no oil here."

"Why would I do that?" Anderson asks. "It's huge – I'm going to be so fucking rich I won't even begrudge Thom his pay cheque, even though fuck knows he doesn't deserve it."

Thom, who has been catatonic for a while, looks up at this.

"Because if you don't, I'm going to the media."

Anderson, Alisha, and Helen start to laugh, but I cut them off.

"I wouldn't laugh. I have proof. I have the sniffer I found at the farm. There's Farooq's testimony, too. And Liora and Mahmoud are going to back me up. Right?"

They nod solemnly.

"Nobody would listen to Mahmoud, and plenty of people are happy to write off anything an Israeli prime minister says. But both of them, releasing identical statements, and making a joint appearance on *Good Morning* fucking *America*, now *that* people will pay attention to!"

"I'll help," Thom says quietly, pushing himself to his feet – but leaving his badge and work phone on the floor. "I have a contact at the *Times*."

Alisha and Helen look at me, and then each other, and race for the door, but Mike is faster. "I don't think so," he says. "You're going to going to wait here while those two" – he juts his chin at Liora and Mahmoud – "write and sign statements. Then you're going to tell the helicopter pilot to take us out of here. And if you let even a hint about the oil, or the fake talks, or anything get out, they'll be uploaded to WikiLeaks and sent to every major news outlet faster than you can say 'PetroCorp.'"

Liora and Mahmoud accept the pens and paper Thom hands them from the reception desk, and start writing their statements. Rabbi Gold tells me that he will write one, too, since he is a man of God, and surely nobody would doubt his word. I give him a hug and thank him for everything, then I go lean against the door with Mike.

"What do you think?" Mike says. "What do you want to do now?"

"Let's go," I tell him.

"You want to go to the rest of the wedding?"

"No. Go, go. Away." I can't even look at Alisha, Helen or Anderson anymore. They disgust me. And I don't want to be around my mom and dad for a while, either.

"Okay," Mike says. "We can go anywhere you want."

"It's your turn."

"My turn?"

"Your turn to pick," I tell him.

"How do you figure?"

"Ask me again," I say. "Ask me again to go with you."

Mike takes both of my hands. "How did you know?"

"I saw the paper on your desk," I tell him. "A few days ago. I wasn't snooping; it was just there. It's a good university, isn't it? And a good job?"

"It is," Mike says. "But are you sure you want to live in Luxembourg?"

"Why not?" I ask him. "I speak a little French."

"We can bring Poco," Mike adds. "I checked. He only needs a passport and a short quarantine. And we could even get a two-bedroom apartment so Jess could visit all the time, and—"

I grab his sleeve and tug him towards the door. I climb in the helicopter and pop my head in. There's a pilot.

"Does this mean—" Mike clambers in behind me.

"It doesn't have to mean anything, yet, does it?" I ask. "Except that I want to go with you, and I am. Besides," I say, holding up my arm with the hammered silver bracelet on it, "you already gave me this."

"I'm not sure 'this, too, shall pass' is the right sentiment in this case, though, is it?" Mike asks.

"I disagree," I tell him, and then to the pilot, I say, "Ben Gurion, please."

Mike takes my hand. As the helicopter rises, I look out the window at my family – Maxi is on her feet, standing with Mom, apparently yelling at her, while Rabbi Gold looks like he's trying to calm Dad down. Gabby and Zara are watching them from the seats as if they were watching a play. They shrink as we ascend, and Mike asks me what I think is going on.

"What's going on," I tell Mike happily, "is that we're going to Luxembourg!"

EPILOGUE

I throw back the yellow curtains in the guest-room to reveal an even yellower sun reflecting off the pointy church spires of Luxembourg. It is just beginning to feel warm in that hopeful early spring way. I crack the window open to let some fresh air in while I make the bed.

"I'm off," Mike says popping his head into the doorway. "What time does Jess arrive, again?"

I beam at him as I wrestle with a fitted sheet. "After lunch," I tell him. "I have a couple of lessons this morning, then I'll pick her up from the airport."

Mike sets down his briefcase by the door and comes to help me with the sheet, which is acting like a game of whack-a-mole instead of a piece of fabric. He holds the top corner in place while I nearly lose a finger slotting the bottom into place. "I'll see you for dinner, then," he says, and kisses me on the cheek.

"What are you making?" I shout after him.

"I thought it was your turn to cook," he calls back, opening the front door.

"We'll go out!" I yell, as he leaves.

"*Qu'est-ce que tu fais? Calmes tes mains!*" I say sternly to the young boy who is balancing by pulling on the reins he seems to have forgotten are attached to a very irate Poco's mouth.

"*Désolé, Madame,*" he breathes as he bounces past me. Poco swishes his tail with each thud of Jules's butt on his back. Jules is hopeless at riding, but he loves Poco. The feeling is not mutual, but I can't bear to tell him. I might ask if the school can arrange for him to ride on weekends, too, and give him some lunge lessons on another horse, to improve his seat a little. The parents of kids at this school salivate whenever more tuition of any kind is offered to their kids – maybe they think it makes up for shipping them off to boarding school for most of the year. Not that I think these kids are necessarily worse off than they'd be at home.

"Okay, Jules, *c'est assez pour aujourd'hui,*" I tell him, and Jules and Poco both collapse gratefully into a walk. I glare at Poco, who knows how to make better transitions than that, and he glares right back and drops his head to the ground so abruptly that poor Jules almost gets yanked overboard. I tell Jules he can get off and hand-walk Poco to cool down before untacking, which he does with relief.

On the ground, they'll be all right, so I head into my office off the tack room to change for the drive to pick up Jess. I check my phone – she hasn't landed yet, and there's only a text from Mike saying to have fun with Jess – and I head back out to the stable courtyard. Jules, as expected, is hand-feeding Poco his favourite Granny Smith apples with a besotted expression on his face. Poco has been brushed down, dressed in a monogrammed fleece cooler and spoiled. Nothing left for me to do here.

My phone buzzes as I wave to Jules and I'm heading to my little car. Jess has sent me three rapid-fire texts.

Aaaaaah!

I'm here!

I mean, j'arrive!

I smile and text back, 'On my way!' as I swap my tall boots for sneakers.

She's made it.

ACKNOWLEDGEMENTS

I'd like to start by thanking my mom. When I was younger, I coveted a book of hers called *Tales of Elijah the Prophet*, by Peninnah Schram. She used to read the stories aloud to me, and I loved it.

My mom even went to the trouble of writing a book just for me (and my sisters, fine) called *A Year of Jewish Stories: 52 Tales for Young Children and Their Families* in 1999. This, and forbidding me to watch television, all but ensured that I would want to be a writer when I grew up.

I suppose she could have warned me that the original stories are the Jewish equivalent of Grimm's Fairy Tales, and most end with people dying horribly (always in service of learning a lesson – but then again, they're dead, so it's a short-lived lesson). I had a bit of a shock when I picked up the Schram book a few years later. That's why she read it aloud – so she could make up new endings on the fly.

That said, my mother helped me to understand the beauty and power of stories, and the storytelling traditions of Judaism. My first published piece of fiction was a short story featuring none other than the prophet Elijah, published by Nora Gold in the Jewish literary journal *Jewish Fiction.net*, and I don't imagine that's an enormous coincidence. As another of my favourite characters would say, the universe is rarely so lazy.

My dad also deserves special thanks – he may have had his doubts along the way, but his support was unwavering, even though I never did entertain the idea of medical school, or law school. And yes, I was completely lying when I agreed that we'd only keep the horse until college. Thank you for mailing him to England for me!

Most writers know that producing a novel is a years-long process that requires the love and support of many people, and I'm pleased to say that in addition to the crucial foundation I had growing up in a house full of books and sisters who mocked me just enough, I had many professionals and friends to help me put this novel in your hands.

First, to the editors who helped me develop what I thought was an amusing idea into a full-length work with all the elements of a real story – thank you. Jon Barton and Debi Alper, you are amazing editors and mentors, without whom this would still just be a file in my cloud.

Sophia McClennen was the first person to get me published, as my nonfiction co-author and dear friend – I'm sure I would never have gone on to pursue writing without her. Thank you for believing in me.

Just as important are the many friends who read many drafts of this story, and shared their honest feedback with me. This includes my wonderful MA classmates like Tina

Baker, who deserves a special mention for giving feedback on multiple manuscripts while her own debut was being released. Zehra Jemal was not only an incredible classmate, but she also had to live with me for two years (and we still speak). To all my classmates: you are the most valuable thing about doing a Creative Writing postgraduate degree.

Thanks to all my many other friends who read drafts and held my hand in so many ways throughout this years-long process, which I'm sure felt even longer to them: Gena Radcliffe, Jennifer Stoloff, Bill O'Donnell, Erin Ayers, Jess Cody, Meghan, Ana Hancock and my beloved sisters by choice, Sarah Price, Rebecca Giglio and Monica Osher.

I am grateful to the Israeli teachers and rabbis who gave me enough of a Jewish education to be able to read, write, and swear in Hebrew – especially Mrs Cipok and Rabbis Scheff and Mitchell.

I would thank my therapist here, but actually, you're welcome – this ought to clear a lot of things up.

If I omitted to thank you, I lost sleep over it in the form of a protracted dream about being unable to find my departure gate at a vast airport while knowing I was about to miss my flight, which was particularly galling considering this took place during March 2021, when I had not stepped foot in an airport in over a year and had no concrete plans to do so. Unless I left you out on purpose. You know who you are.

Remy Maisel is an award-winning writer who has been writing professionally since Arianna Huffington personally invited her to blog for *The Huffington Post* as a teenager.

The co-author of *Is Satire Saving Our Nation? Mockery and American Politics* and *Bears & Balls: The Colbert Report A-Z*, her fiction is influenced by her love of satire and American politics.

Her debut novel was longlisted for the 2018 Cinnamon Press Debut Fiction Prize, and she won the 2020 A Woman's Write prize for unpublished novels.

She now lives in London with an ill-behaved dog and horse (he doesn't live in the flat), and enjoys running marathons slowly and getting eliminated from equestrian competitions that small children go on to win.